BETRAYAL OF A REPUBLIC

MEMOIRS OF A ROMAN MATRONA

Joost Douma

BETRAYAL OF A REPUBLIC

MEMOIRS OF A ROMAN MATRONA

Addison & Highsmith

Addison & Highsmith Publishers

Las Vegas ◊ Chicago ◊ Palm Beach

Published in the United States of America by
Histria Books
7181 N. Hualapai Way, Ste.130-86
Las Vegas, NV 89166 USA
HistriaBooks.com

Addison & Highsmith Publishers is an imprint of Histria Books. Titles published under the imprints of Histria Books are distributed worldwide.

Library of Congress Control Number: 2020938485

ISBN 978-1-59211-062-9 (hardcover)
ISBN 978-1-59211-111-4 (softbound)
ISBN 978-1-59211-158-9 (eBook)

CONTENTS

For

Jasper, Luite, Deirdre & Alexandra

— Cornelia Africani F(ilia) Gracchorum
(Cornelia, daughter of Africanus, of the Gracchi)
Capitoline Museum, Rome

PROLOGUE

haec ornamenta mea (sunt)
"There are my jewels."

MISENO, ? BCE.

A thin wisp of ash escapes from the embers and dances upward. I follow it with my eyes until the wind gets hold of it and carries it away in the open sky. The remainder of my personal archive burns in front of me as I warm myself in the chill of the morning before the fire on my terrace.

I would not be surprised if the ash came from a letter to one of my Greek friends in which I had described an intimate incident in Rome. Several years after the death of my husband, I returned late in the evening from a dinner. It was still sweltering hot, and I left the curtain of my litter slightly open. A touch of wind blew the drape aside, revealing more than appropriate. I looked straight into the face of a man in a passing litter. Our eyes met, and, in the light of the torches, I beheld the beautiful face of a young Etruscan prince. A refined, white face with sparkling dark eyes, gracefully framed with red, curly hair; his eyebrows, mustache, and pointed beard as thin as brushstrokes. He was as surprised as I was, and, with a slight smile, he made a light bow, courteous but not without a hint of mischief. The incident stirred up a physical sensation in my hips that I had not had for years, and the sweet tremble inspired a nightly dream that I described in the letter to my friend.

On the pile before me burn more dreams and secret thoughts than even my most intimate friends could have imagined. Doubts about my husband and our forthcoming wedding. Heart cries to the lovers I have known since the death of my husband. Testimonies of my love for my mother and anger over her restrictive rules. Epistles full of rage and admonitions to my sons. Pleas for mercy to my nephew Serapio and my son-in-law Aemilianus. Consoling words for my daughter and frolicsome trivialities to my granddaughter.

These embers signify a true bonfire. I commenced clearing my personal archive after I received a message two days ago. I made the preselection myself, and in the pages below, you will find the remainder of my diaries deemed worthy of preservation.

They are from my hand. Many have commented on my writings, often telling me that they preferred something written by the daughter of Cornelius Scipio Africanus, or the wife of Tiberius Sempronius Gracchus, or the mother of the Gracchi brothers. But although I have played all these roles with love, these musings are mine, Cornelia Africana!

A courier brought me the news that the Roman people had secretly commissioned two statues of my sons and installed them in the Forum a couple of days earlier. He also told me, breathless and with shining eyes, that they had proclaimed the site sacred where my son Tiberius was murdered and offered fresh fruits during a massive ceremony as if it were a holy shrine. It did not bother me that I visibly embarrassed the messenger by embracing him and letting the tears run freely down my cheeks.

I welcome his message in the liberating thought that I can finally join my husband and my children. In advance of my final departure, I have cast my bulla and crystal jewelry into the sea. The rainbows captured in the gems now belong to Neptune. I will not need a crystal in the twilight of Hades, and none of the Fates can harm me there. All the damage is done, and I already know the image I will carry in my mind's eye when I descend into the underworld.

Years ago, a friend visited me at home. In line with the spirit of our times and prompted by stories about my father's wealth, she was eager to view my jewelry. I recall I laughed aloud, and later in the day, after they had returned from an excursion, I showed her my two sons, exclaiming, "There are my jewels!" The expression on her face told me that she did not believe me, and she left my house convinced my wealth was so enormous that I must have been ashamed and unwilling to show it. I remember this incident so well because I had, much to my annoyance, a hard time finding my sons. I finally located them in the second atrium. As two young, mad dogs, snarling and biting, they were romping around and the look in their eyes instantly softened me, the ebullient glance of two young people loving to be alive.

PART 1
SENATUS CONSULTUM ULTIMUM
(FINAL DECREE OF THE SENATE)

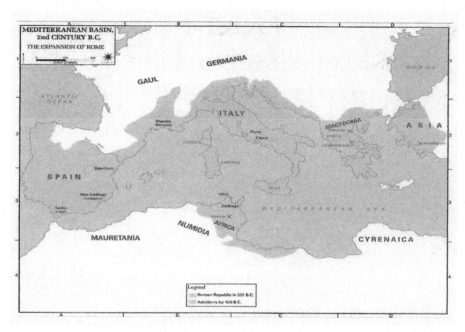

Territory controlled by the Roman Republic in the second century BCE

1.

The attack is receding. My prayers have been answered. When I hold my hands out in front of me, I can almost keep my fingers still. The cramps in my belly are subsiding. The beating of my heart is slowing. My breathing is growing more regular.

After the messenger from Rome was taken away to be fed and tended to, I retired to my private apartments and ordered a bath. I need to make my world as small as possible, and I find it comforting to examine my body. I listen to the echo of my voice as I speak the name of my husband, the father of my children. I am eternally grateful to the gods he did not live to see this moment.

What I need at this time, more than ever, is the illusion of composure and self-control. Tonight is the funeral banquet, with guests from all corners of the world, and I must make certain no rumors travel to Rome. The very thought of their probing gazes frightens me. I dearly hope they will all control themselves. I do understand that others have been gravely affected by this loss; I respect their grief, and I pledge that in good time I will devote all of my attention to them. But for now, I am silently imploring everyone to spare me, just for tonight, and not to come to me with heartfelt words of consolation. Any sincere expression of emotion would shatter me. I want diversion and commotion, guests interrupting each other and asking for more food; song, flute playing, and dance.

There are moments when I manage to step outside myself – when looking into the mirror, I confront the contrast between my inner turmoil and the calm in my face. I know if I can suppress the panic that causes this imbalance, I will make it through the evening unscathed. I am grateful that the effort required, which is visible in my reflection, will look to my guests like an expression of restrained sorrow. I find it reassuring to think this misunderstanding will sometimes even bring a smile to my face with the appropriate, befuddled undertone. All my life, people have accused me of deception. In the name of the gods, just this once, let that accusation be more than just!

Dewdrops flow together as I run my hand along the damp mural next to me. The water spills over my sons, diving from a rock into the sea. Dolphins with roguish looks await them on either side. The painter deftly captured the differences in their build. Tiberius, with the physique of a heavyweight boxer, is bending his legs. Gaius, the wiry runner, is straight as a spear. The painting is so skillful and true to life that in my mind's eye, I can easily trace their paths until the waves swallow them up.

In times of war, parents outlive their children; in times of peace, children outlive their parents. But it is my fate to have lost my children in peacetime. My mother always said I had the task of raising my children to honor their parents and to serve their homeland. She never taught me how to outlive my homeland, let alone my children. To do so would have been to tempt the gods.

For a long time after my first-born died, I found it hard to look my husband in the eyes. His features would always remind me of the boy. Midwives assured me that once a child reached the age of ten, I no longer had to be so afraid. But of the twelve children I bore, only three survived their childhood: my daughter Sempronia and my two sons, Tiberius and Gaius. Now only my daughter remains.

My sons met death, resembling the way they used their bodies in life. Tiberius used his body as a political weapon when he stood in the temple doors and blocked the entrance to our state treasury. On the day he was re-elected, he and his followers formed a human wall to protect the baskets that held the votes. When the mob of Senators and Tribunes descended on the Capitol, armed with table legs and clubs, he was waiting for them. Gaius, understanding what would happen, made his stand on the Aventine Hill, and when that failed, he ran for his life as the legislator he had been, swift and ahead of his fellow-countrymen.

As my sons grew up, I consulted Aristotle to see if his classifications of humans could shed light on their future lives, but his descriptions were not always clear, and I often arrived at combinations. Tiberius had a heavy, thick voice, often broken in the morning as if it made a slow start. Gaius' voice was high-pitched. Tiberius had coarse hair; Gaius' hair was silky. His skin was softer and more elastic than that of Tiberius. Gaius resembled the closest what Aristotle called a passionate and sensitive man: an upright stance, his arms long and powerful, his chest and hips smooth. Tiberius showed a combination of the courageous and gentle man with his burly, beefy body, broad in the shoulders, yet sensual lips. One reads the character best around the eyes, forehead, and face. I have seen Tiberius blush many times, Gaius scarcely. Gaius' glance was quick, Tiberius' slower and thoughtful with his heavy eyelids. Soul and body affect each other, and I saw in the course of time how their fates changed their looks. On the face of Tiberius appeared a mixture of bitterness and disappointment. On Gaius' face, scorn and arrogance. It makes me very sad to recall the moments I first noticed these changes.

In the warm water, my skin is like old parchment, crumpled and covered with words. Over the years, many of my lifelines have grown dear to me. My skin is my memory, and in the furrows rests its archive. Unseen by others, whenever I please, I can summon comforting images and moments by touching my fingertips to the places that once were loved. Many have embraced my shoulders and arms; thousands of hands have held mine. The delicate hands of patricians and philosophers, the knobby, calloused hands of veterans, Bona Dea! None of them held out their hands when my sons and I needed them. They often expressed their words of support merely in the heat of the moment. Yet, I still feel the afterglow of their condolences and sympathies.

When I was a child, the sight of old people's skin scared me. I remember how cautiously I sometimes caressed the cheek of my beloved wet nurse Sila. Her many wrinkles made her skin seem so loose and fragile that the corners of her mouth might tear at any moment. Now I see this pliability – however unflattering – like strength, a talent for stretching my thread of life.

Age knows no mercy. It lays our bodies' failings bare, the flaws we carry with us from childhood onward, and although we all share in this fate as we grow older, we judge one another by our weaknesses and not by our age. In Rome, the only thing that counts is the fleeting present.

Since the day I entered this world, more than seventy summers and winters have passed, but my body is still strong, still worthy of the house of the Cornelii. It has withstood the rigors of my pregnancies. It has fended off diseases that laid many others low. It is free of marsh fever, and the pain in my joints is mild. Unlike my sons' bodies, mine has never been wracked by violence. It is untainted. My mind is clear. My sight is not what it was, but my two eyes still work together, bearing witness to myself. Even my jaw has largely survived the ravages of time.

My breasts and vagina have withered, and it has been a long time since I dreamed of new pregnancies. The skin is stretched and tender like the fallen petals of a flower, swaying in the water. I mix up the births of my children sometimes, but I can still recall the sight of Gaius' wet, black crown. When I look down at the channel to my womb, the image returns of the first time my hands touched his face and ears. The delivery was like that of Artemis: quick and painless.

Gaius loved my hands. He often took them in his, spoke of their elegance, and praised the letters and epigrams I wrote with them. His devotion sometimes left me speechless.

In my long life, I have known no greater happiness than to feel the body of a nursing infant falling asleep on my bosom and to brush my lips over the soft spot on its forehead. I spent hours in the bath, holding Gaius like that. After I had given birth to him, my monthly bleeding diminished; a sign that my womb had closed once and for all, and I knew Gaius would be the last person with whom I would ever share my body.

One of my Greek slaves knocks softly at the door. I tell her to bring me more warm water. I also order her to fetch more oil to drive the taste of brine from my lips. I can tell by the hesitation in her voice, she had expected me to order her to massage me and help me dress, but I am not ready yet. My lips tell me my face is not wet with vapor but with tears, whose soundless presence overwhelms me, and I wonder, with a start, whether I wept in front of the courier and my daughter.

The courier was unfamiliar, hired by friends. A coarse, unpolished lout, who spared me no detail, despite the warning looks my daughter Sempronia shot at him. The insolent gleam in his eye betrayed a barely concealed pleasure in picking out the details that would shock me most. His language was utterly disrespectful. No sooner had I entered the room than the man asked me for more money, and he kept interrupting his account of the events in Roma with stories about his hardships. The whole time, his greedy eyes were wandering the room. His body gave off the odor of horses, sweat, strong drink, and something else I could not place. "Carrion," my daughter said. I put him up for the night outside my villa, with one of my freed slaves.

The courier almost got the better of me when he described how my son Gaius – in tears and without speaking a word – had stopped in front of the statue of his father in the Forum and gazed at it for a long time on the eve of the day all the violence burst loose. As I listened, outwardly unmoved, I had to restrain myself from cutting him off and threaten him with a lashing. My heart was crying out for it. I knew exactly how my son must have felt. Of all my children, Gaius was the most critical of his own actions, and I have no doubt he was begging his father and me for forgiveness. Forgiveness for his failure as a Tribune, as the father of his child, and above all as our son. I could not imagine any greater loneliness than Gaius felt at that moment, and the image of him standing there was almost intolerable. All the letters I had sent him this past year and all the harsh judgments I had made in them turned on me then and I felt their sting. Several times, my head grew light, and I had to hold on to my seat with both hands to stop myself from slumping forward and collapsing to the ground.

2.

Last night I received a letter from Gaius, which he must have written a few days before he died. It is not clear why it did not arrive until now. The messenger left before it even occurred to me to make him explain himself.

When the letter was handed to me, I opened it with an unthinking sense of normality, of which I did not become conscious until I saw the astonished looks on my slaves' faces. Then I realized what was happening and broke into a strange, uncontrollable bout of laughter. Fortunately, the letter gave me an excuse for swiftly retiring to my apartments. The incident left me deeply shaken. Am I losing my mind?

The letter is written in a lively, caustic style that is characteristic of our correspondence in recent years. Gaius mentions the rumor that I have sent supporters from Greece, Spain, Africa, and Italy disguised as seasonal workers to assist him, thanking me with his usual dose of sarcasm for the offer of protection and asking me to show more discretion in the future. In a sudden shift of tone, he mentions Consul Opimius' proposal to the Tribal Assembly to overturn his legislation for his colony in North Africa. He grimly suggests there is a serious chance this submission will win majority support.

As if the whole outside world were scheming to throw my life into disarray, Gaius' letter arrived at the same time as the first letters of condolence from the tight-knit circle of Roman citizens in the region. It strikes me as tactless to have sent them so soon. Why such haste? I read the predictable eulogies with bitterness; they do not deserve because it takes real courage to honor Gaius' memory.

Letters keep pouring in. Since it is difficult to find reliable messengers these days, whether hired men or slaves, some merely send wax tablets, telling the courier not to leave my villa without a reply. The sickly-sweet odor of melted beeswax fills my study as if I were conducting a secret correspondence with a lover.

The letters continue seamlessly, where the letter from my son left off. They report the death of Herennius, one of Gaius' best friends. When they took him to prison, he swung his head into the doorpost with such force that he died at once. In its final decree, the Senate gave Consul Opimius a mandate to break every law, and he has instituted a reign of terror. Some remark that he is doing the very same thing of which the Senators and Tribunes falsely accused my son Tiberius, gradually assuming the status of a King. Three thousand followers of Gaius, all Roman residents, were executed without trial and thrown into the Tiber. For days, the dull brown of the river was tinged with red. Since the fall of the Kings, Rome has never seen this much violence among its citizens.

Gaius' house was razed to the ground, and they have banned any construction on the site. It is expected that, in the weeks ahead, his followers' houses will be auctioned off at shamefully low prices. To prevent Opimius' supporters from profiting, this morning, I dictated letters to my clerks for my agents in Rome, giving them instructions to buy up as much as possible through intermediaries. Later, when the moment is right, I hope to compensate some families. Even at this stage, I know I will have to move heaven and earth to convince my agents to help me. If the news leaks, I will be accused of exploiting the situation for personal gain, and if I compensate the families, it will be seen as an admission of guilt. What is more, in these delicate circumstances, not all the intermediaries will live up to their promises. So be it. At the end of the letters, I told my agents that I accept all of the consequences, including payment of any outstanding debts on the properties. Now that I have sent the letters, I realize it would have been better to let them make these objections for themselves. It would have given me the opportunity to thank them for their words of caution. Now, I will be forced to think up a series of new counterarguments. Patience has never been my strong suit.

Opimius has also ordered the rebuilding of the Temple of Concordia at the Forum. This infamous act speaks volumes about the man's character. He will build the temple on the site that two hundred and fifty years ago was chosen to celebrate the restoration of unity between the patricians and the plebeians. I cannot explain why this proposal has dismayed me so profoundly. More, almost, than the murder of my son. Although I always rejected their arguments, in my debates with Tiberius' enemies, I at least had the sense we spoke the same language. Over and over again, I tried to understand why my son's actions inspired so much hate. The construction plans and their freight of symbolism make me feel as if I were publicly raped. The news fills me with deep despondency, alternated with blind rage, bringing on a new wave of nausea. For the first time in my life, I feel like a foreigner in my country.

3.

There is no horizon today. The blue sea, like the ocean at the edge of the world, washes unimpeded into the blue air. The white of my marble terrace is so blinding that I must be careful not to lose my balance. A sharp, icy wind from the north whips past my ears and swipes at everything on my balcony, large or small. My cypresses are like green torches, burning with a strange, cold fire. The whole world around me rattles. I have to clutch my amictus[1] to my body with both arms.

Amid all this turmoil, I look back with a degree of awe at the show of strength I put on yesterday as if it had been someone else's performance. Yet I also see, to my relief, my actions have restored order to the household. In times of catastrophe, the head of the family must always look out for signs of hostility among his people. If the position of the house is in question, the freedmen will be the first to go in search of a new place to live. The rumormongering – 'they are massacring citizens as if they are slaves' – the abrupt silences whenever I enter the room, and the secret meetings with freedmen from other households, undermine every form of domestic authority, even over the slaves, especially if a woman is in charge. The danger is that my enemies will bribe my slaves, promising liberation. I have been through this before, after the deaths of my husband and Tiberius. All eyes are now on me in search for moments of weakness. It is crucial for me to adhere to my daily routine in the weeks ahead. However, I cannot deny it is hard for me. The years have begun to take their toll.

I usually spend the morning alone on my private terrace. I can abandon myself to my thoughts here, sheltered from the wind and scrutinized only by the watchful eyes of peacocks, which Hera once sprinkled on their wings. My slave, Sila, regarded the nervous rustle that regularly runs through their fan of feathers as living proof that those with suspicious minds blink their eyes incessantly. The peacocks' presence makes it impossible for anyone to approach without drawing my attention.

Last night, I made the final preparations for the arrival of Licinia and Gaius' daughter. By decree of the Senate, Licinia has been robbed of her dowry and forbidden to wear mourning. A barbaric and humiliating deed. What do they have to fear from her now? Her husband has lost his

---

[1] A type of Roman overgarment.

life and, even in death, he is denied to her. I have instructed my people to bring her here as soon as possible. I will go to any length to prevent Licinia from searching the banks of the Tiber for Gaius' body, as Claudia once searched in vain for Tiberius.

The funeral banquet, I held the night before last, went just as I had hoped. It was a gathering worthy of my sons without a single false note. I commemorated the achievements of both Tiberius and Gaius in the company of my family and my Roman and Greek guests, managing to accept their condolences with proper ceremony. I called for nine days of mourning, made sacrifices to the dead, and had cypress branches laid by my front gate. This morning, in consultation with the magistrates, I proclaimed that the next three days would be a festival of mourning for the people of Miseno. There will be gladiatorial games. Friends will address the people, several plays will be performed, and meat and flour will be distributed. My generous financial offering overcame the last of their hesitations. If money is our new supreme deity, let friends and enemies alike take note that – in that respect – I am immortal.

It is said that old age passes us by like a waking dream because the older we become, the less sleep we get. I have come to cherish sleep as a precious commodity, more precious than food or water, but I fear the images it brings. As soon as I take to my bed at night, my mind is inundated with snatches of conversation and imaginary encounters, as if I had just awoken. Sometimes I wish that when Zeus mixed his sleeping potion for restless humans, he had added a few more drops of dew from Hades.

It seems that last night I was so exhausted, I managed to fall into a dreamless sleep, but I am sure I have a long, wakeful night ahead of me. Experience has taught me what rhythm my nights will follow in the months ahead: two of little rest, followed by one of sound sleep. I sleep best in the afternoon and frequently doze off here on my couch.

Despite my advanced age, my body's response keeps taking me by surprise. I have so much more control over my mental faculties. When bad news reaches me, as soon as I have recovered from the initial shock, my thoughts seem to order themselves of their accord, guiding me towards a broader perspective, a new line of march. These signs of mental resilience form the source of further recovery and solutions I had dismissed or overlooked start to gradually come within reach. Yet the mental exertion required takes its toll, and it is my body that lets me down.

I am losing more hair now than ever, and not only when I comb it. I am seized by cramps in my chest and arms. I am sensitive to loud or shrill noises. They have an amplified effect on my body, immediately throwing me off balance, as do even the slightest arguments between my slaves. I rely heavily on the help and support of Simo, the head of my household – too heavily, in the eyes of my Roman women friends, who say he no longer knows his place. But isn't his loyalty sufficient proof of my authority? I have always had a great need for order and regularity, but now I cannot bear even the slightest hint of sloppiness. My daily inspection of the house must be a sore trial for everyone, and I know my slaves curse me when my back is turned.

Fear is my worst enemy. After Tiberius had been killed, half my soul had died, while the other half was caught in the stranglehold of fear about the fate that awaited Gaius. From the very first morning after the murder of Tiberius, I knew deep in my heart how Gaius would come to his end, and against my better judgment, I searched for signs that might refute this certainty. Strangely enough, the very implausibility of these illusions strengthened my vain hope. Over the past twelve years, I have lived – day in, day out – between false hope and well-founded fear. With deep sorrow and remorse, I must confess I have always known the arrival of the messenger would bring not only grief but also a sense of relief.

I can live with anger and sorrow. Anger energizes me; it makes me defiant. Sorrow is like a lingering illness, an inconvenient but surmountable physical flaw. The training I received at the Asclepieum[2] enables me to tell myself that the wave of sorrow will pass in a few moments. I have learned to disarm pain and grief. It is possible to reduce them to purely physical sensations that come and go, like any other sensory experience.

However, fear is different. I have no control over it. Fear is insidious; it skulks, poisons, tarnishes, undermines, paralyzes, and destroys. Aristotle calls fear a cold wave, driving the blood and heat out of the body, turning the face pale and emptying the bowels. I am convinced you can smell fear from far away. If you smell its odor on someone else, you too will contract it, as an infectious disease. Fear is a gaping void that can only be filled with cruelty, fear's shadow.

Below me, the frothing maw of the living sea. To show me it is unmoved by my fate, it dashes its children to pieces on the polished stone of my front steps, as casually as only a God can. Their fate is mockingly lamented by the seagulls now massed above my villa, defying the wind as they try to gather their breakfast. I shudder to think Gaius' body may have been carried out into the open sea, but I take comfort in the thought there is little chance of that. The distance between Roma and Ostia is too great, and the Tiber too capricious.

In an attempt to suppress the nocturnal images of swaying reeds and mutilated shoulder blades, I stop my staring and turn my gaze to Cape Miseno. To the right of it, in the distance, I can make out the contours of my beloved island of Ischia. My last visit seemed an eternity ago. I spent many happy days there with Tiberius and Gaius. Experienced boatmen, supervised by Simo, taught them to swim and to dive for green sea urchins and squid. Many times, I saw the older men at pains to protect the

---

[2]A temple and center of learning dedicated to Asclepius, son of the god Apollo and a mortal princess Coronis. Asclepius is the ancient Greek god of medicine and healing, worshiped by the Romans as Aesculapius.

lives of my sons. The memory of the unguarded expressions with which the two boys looked up at these men, the speed with which they carried out their orders, brings a sharp pang of emotion. From the boat, they explored the steep coastline with its yellow-ochre caves and burning sands. I will never forget the image of my two sons underwater as they swam out ahead of me towards the entrance to a cave, scissoring their legs in the green sunlight of the sea. My Dioscuri.

My Greek friends contend if my sons had been twin brothers, they could have pooled their strength, and their fate would have been different. They could have worked together, like feet or eyes. 'Do not forget that even after Tiberius lost his support among the lawmakers, the people remained faithful to him, and the people may have turned against Gaius, but his reputation as a lawmaker is intact.'

Sheets of blue lightning flicker along the flanks of the mountains, accompanied by great peals of thunder and gusts of wind. All at once, the first fat raindrops strike my terrace. Above me, the clouds arch into a dark vault, and I seem to be in the depths of some vast cavern. The drenched backs of my scurrying, cursing, shouting slaves call up the images I had as a child of a battle against the Gauls from the north, with lightning, hail, felled trees, glistening rocks, and naked forms besmirched with blood and earth. My peacocks ran for cover some time ago, and Simo is urging me to follow their example. I reluctantly give in and retire to my library, where he has built a fire and drawn the heaviest curtains over the windows. I am now encircled by candlelight and darkness. Outside, the rain is pelting down, but already the thunder is not as loud as it was earlier.

In times of storm, seek signs of calm, and in times of calm, seek signs of storm. I have taken this line of verse as my guide for many years, in the false belief that people around me could foresee much quicker than I the moment disaster might strike their lives.

The rain is dying down and I long to go outside again and inhale the odor of iron left behind by every storm. People say it fortifies the constitution. When I lift the curtain covering the southern window, gray light strikes the sharp, probing features of Aristotle. What thoughts would this phenomenon have stirred in him? I often speak to him; he knows my most intimate musings better than anyone else does.

Passing slaves cast their shadows on the curtains covering the windows as if in a Greek shadow play. Some have the same build as Gaius, and I can imagine that this very moment he is walking by my window on his way to my library.

As a child, I always thought that when I died, my shadow would detach itself and descend into the underworld. My shadow, I thought, follows wherever I go to remind me that I am mortal. I took comfort in the thought that I would recognize a god immediately because he would have no shadow at his side.

I have learned from Aristotle that even forms of government are mortal and trailed by their dark sides. Every King conceals a tyrant; aristocracy decays into oligarchy; democracy descends into terror.

Gaius once told his followers that any leader who addressed himself to them had a motive for doing so, a price in the back of his mind. To no avail, my son urged his audience to listen carefully and always to ponder whether they were willing to pay the price for his services, whether or not he named it openly.

People whose price is a pure personal gain now lead our country. To pander to the populace, they act as shepherds. While they are the masters of their flocks, they are also their slaves. Although their sheep are dumb, they must listen to them every moment of the day. To conceal the emptiness of their leadership, they acquiesce to the people and their passing fits of madness, counting their sesterces every time they misled them.

Unlike many others, I consider it a privilege to have lived in a time of façades, whether made out of marble or wax. Now that the Senators have thrown off their masks, hate and malice are on the ascendant, and now that electoral bribery is coming to light, there are some who claim our society is less riddled with hypocrisy. Yet, in the concealment of disreputable practices, I saw the last remnant of shame and remorse. How can one lay bare this degeneration of the criticism of our degeneration? Who is left to talk to when one has the feeling that one's interlocutors are at the core of this decline?

4.

Before my eyes is the last hope of my lineage, in the midst of a clutch of slaves, playing with the armies Simo once made for his father and his uncle Gaius. The most impressive of all are the chariots, rigged with little sails so they can be propelled by blowing or by the wind. Even a person like me, who knows nothing about toys, can see they are little gems. Tiberius never wanted to share them with Gaius, and so Simo had to make him a set of his own. No task could have brought him greater pleasure.

Claudia and Licinia had forbidden their children to come onto my terrace in the morning, but I have granted them permission to accompany me at fixed times. There is a limit; I cannot have them here half the day. But it is good for me to see life go on around me and important for my grandchildren to regain a sense of continuity. My grandson is the eldest of the three sons of Tiberius, but he barely knew his father.

After her father's murder, Gaius' daughter behaved like a cornered animal, with pale features and dark eyes full of fear. She stared out ahead of her for hours, banging her head from side to side and seemed almost cut off from human contact. At night, nightmares entered her sleep and her screaming woke us all. I attributed these dreams of terror to the fact that her father's murderers have gone unpunished, that we have not put his soul to rest, despite the curses Licinia and I addressed to his killers. Provoked by the girl's fears, her cousin treated her with the deepest hostility in the first days after Gaius' murder, forcing Licinia to take her daughter with her wherever she went.

As I watch my grandson and hear the sounds of his lonely battles, a peculiar sensation takes hold of me, as if I were looking into a large mirror full of images from thirty years ago. Memories of our families often encompass just a small number of scenes, and for me, this sight is one of them. Gaius, with his head cocked to one side and his tongue sticking out, is reclining on the floor, surveying the battlefield. Tiberius is sitting up straight, peering tensely at his troops. Because of the difference in their ages, Gaius was often defeated, but even then, it was clear that Gaius was the better strategist of the two. Their differences of temperament were also apparent. When Gaius' army was massacred in a frontal attack, he frequently lost his temper and flew at his laughing brother, flailing his arms wildly. Tiberius would hold Gaius at a distance with one arm, until his younger brother gave up, exhausted and sobbing. His elder brother, whom he idolized, sometimes had the nasty habit of laughing when confronted with someone else's sorrow. I saw in this reaction a clumsy attempt to rein in his pity, but to those who did not know him so well, he sometimes appeared to take pleasure in other people's suffering.

I have never wanted to know how mirrors work. However, it may be correct what a mirror maker once told me: the world we see is as illusory as the images I see in his products. Because of mirrors and watery surfaces, we know – so he instructed – that all bodies and objects continuously produce a stream of images just as cicadas shed their coned wrappings in the summer and snakes their skins. Does his view imply that if I sped to Rome now, I could still catch something of my son's image? How long do these images last?

The fact is Gaius grew up almost fatherless – like many his age, but his father was more visible in Rome after death than when he was alive. Tiberius and Gaius could gaze on his statue at the Forum. His portraits were in all the public places throughout Rome. In the temple of the Goddess of the Dawn, they could find his battle scenes in the bronze plaque shaped like Sardinia. On the streets, people stopped them to recount stories. Sometimes they were veterans who told them about their father's strategies in the campaigns in Sardinia and Spain. For my sons, their deceased father was omnipresent.

I am afraid that my grandson will truly grow up fatherless. The Sempronii are not like my family. They do not belong to the select group of patricians. They cannot be honored with any public works of art or displays until they have held the highest functions of State.

My grandson is more likely to share my fate. Out of anger, my father removed all the public displays honoring him in Rome. He begrudged the Roman people even his remains! Even so, his name was still on everyone's lips when I was growing up, and his fame rose to divine heights by the time I was older.

It will need a spontaneous act of the Roman people themselves – as it was with me. They erected a bronze statue of me out of gratitude after I pled with Gaius to spare the Tribune Octavius from further humiliation. My enemies have left it intact so far. It carries at the bottom the inscription: "Cornelia, mother of the Gracchi." I was deeply touched when I first saw it. Now the inscription has a bitter aftertaste. No mother wishes to survive her sons – certainly not publicly! My enemies have succeeded in poisoning a gesture that was once noble.

It went wrong this morning. In hindsight, I can see there were enough warning signals to tell me a crisis was looming. Perhaps my daughter-in-law Licinia's arrival undid the last restraints. I suspect a certain glance from my granddaughter suddenly reminded me of Gaius' face. Whatever it was, I had to flee immediately to my bedroom, where I lost all semblance of dignity. The attack was so fierce that I crawled like a wild beast on my knees, grasping the walls and moaning from pain. I lost my grip on my bowels. The face of Gaius swayed before my eyes, mingled with images of his mutilation. The attack came in waves, growing stronger and stronger and receding only slowly, painfully.

I cannot remember how long it lasted, but it seemed an eternity before I dared to leave my room and look at Gaius' daughter, praying I would never recognize my most beloved son in her again.

PART 2
LEX SEMPRONIA AGRARIA
(THE AGRARIAN LAW SEMPRONIA)

Tiberius Sempronius Gracchus
Guillaume Rouillé (c.1518–1589)

1.

In recent weeks, I have become obsessed with the troubling thought the balance in my humors is disturbed and my body is poisoned by an abundance of bile. I seem to be surrounded by a haze and days slide by of which I cannot recall a single moment or event. Simo tries his best to conceal my amnesia from me, but he is sometimes less vigilant and by his face, I can tell I have repeated myself.

I have now called myself to order by following a strict regime. Every night, sitting on my heels in front of the bed, I whip my memory by going over every act and encounter in the smallest details. I start the morning with a stiff hike, followed by some light exercise. I take a small breakfast and until noon, I devote myself one day to dictating and writing letters to my overseers, friends and clients. The next day I force myself to sort out the legislation, speeches, pamphlets and numerous letters from my husband and my son Tiberius. I still shun my disorganized files of Gaius and to avoid clouding my mind with too much grief, I brighten my archive days with selecting copies of translations of Greek comedies and poems for my guests and friends. Six literate slaves are working on this and I enjoy watching their progress.

After my noon meal, I take a short break, undress and walk back and forth on my private terrace in the sunlight. Next, I have my oil massage and before I bathe, I play a ball game alone or with a friend. I only allow my personal female slaves to be present. I always wonder what these young girls think when they watch these two old naked, wrinkled ladies play their ball game and accuse one another of cheating like small children. In the beginning, I was barely able to play longer than the short time span of my smallest sand clock, but now I can run out the sand in the tallest one. With spring in the air and longer hours, I make use of the daylight as much as possible. Yet, I continue to feel I am not doing enough. It is not enough to receive guests and occasionally travel to Miseno or Puteoli. I consider paying a visit to my family holdings in Praeneste, and perhaps even to Rome to inspect my newly acquired properties.

2.

'The villa of the four widows.' Thus, my home seems to be known miles around here. My daughter and I are living in an outpost of Hades. Who could have foreseen that this place, which symbolizes warmth, life and joy, would attain such an epithet?

This afternoon one of my lush Greek friends remarked – everything is heavy and round about this woman: chin, breasts and thighs, and as always, she had covered herself with clusters of gold, silver and amber – that my villa merely seemed to be anchored, ready to sail away. She meant it as a compliment, 'such a svelte structure, built of marble sails', but her comments were misinterpreted and led to an abrupt silence among my Roman guests. They exchanged glances and the gathering suddenly grew tense. They know that despite my criticisms, I am very fond of my Greek neighbors. However, it takes just a few words to raise their mistrust in my Greek friends and the turmoil in Rome breathes new life in the old conflicts. In the eyes of Romans, all Greeks from the South remain suspicious, especially if their villas are located in desirable places and they are in possession of profitable vineyards and olive groves. After the departure of Hannibal, many wealthy Greek families were accused of anti-Roman sympathies, their possessions confiscated and auctioned for absurdly low prices.

I knew beforehand that numerous acquaintances would portray my departure from Rome as a flight, or worse, as a statement of support for the ideas of Greek democrats. Nothing could have been further from the truth, but from the onset, appearances were against me and Gaius' policies seemed to confirm people's judgment. With a sly smile and a skeptical look, they stared at me when I told them that I wanted to escape the summer heat, stench, and noise of Rome, and to protect my beloved library against the eternal threat of fire.

I knew this region well and I carefully prepared my choice for the location of my villa. I spent many summers here with friends and my children while my husband was away. A few miles north is Liternum, where I grew up as a child after my father had left Rome to establish himself as an exile in the new colony. His migration was deemed voluntarily.

I bought this narrow neck of land two years after the death of my son Tiberius for just a few Athenian talents. It is near swamps and nobody wanted to live here. When I came here, the wild animals had the land to themselves, but many have followed my example in the last twelve years and now the entire Cape Miseno looks like a vast garden, packed with luxurious villas. 'As if the country is hit by a white fungus,' my Greek friends and the latest Roman newcomers complain.

My little peninsula extends as a spearhead into the sea and on the narrow shaft, which connects it to the mainland, I had a fortified gate built. At the advice of Gaius, I also acquired a stretch of land on the shore side, initially to keep it free of the buildings of others. Somewhat later, I had my little theater built there, combined with a playground for ball games and surrounded by vegetable gardens, freshwater ponds, rose gardens, small farms as well as the living quarters of my slaves and freedmen. All in all some two hundred families dwell here, maintaining the grounds and living from the produce. My personal slaves and staff live in separate quarters on my island. I now get almost daily requests to sell my mainland property in exchange for offers, which greatly exceed what I paid for it. It was a wise purchase.

After my master builders had cleared the grounds, they built my villa in the shape of a fish bone with descending terraces on both sides. When they are here for the first time, my guests often lose their way, but after a few days, everyone understands the layout. It provides with its four guest lodgings enough space for a large number of visitors and I have received many travelers over the years, young and old and from all corners of our Republic.

Due to the elevated position of the peninsula, the wind blows all the quarters dry and they remain spared of the vermin from the marshes. It is so well protected I have yet to encounter the first rat or snake. Thanks to the inclines on both sides, my servants are able to collect in most months a sufficient amount of drinking water from the rain, dew and morning mist, supplemented by fresh water from the ponds during the height of summer. On the west side of my island, lies the port of Miseno. The inlet is home to naval vessels. My private terraces are situated on the east side, overlooking the wide bay of Baiae and the port of Puteoli.

The hall offers a direct view into the atrium and by extension into the summer dining hall. The dining hall gives access to the oval herb garden with a free view of the sea. It is adorned with marble benches, grape and wisteria vines and climbing roses. The entire setting offers a graceful and fragrant scene in pink, green, yellow-golden and blue tones. The four guest lodgings surround the atrium. My private rooms are located in the lee, so I can shield myself from the noise even during the most boisterous of festivities. Around my library are my sleeping quarters, my workplace, my private dining room and my bathrooms. In the winter, my baths can be heated.

I have paid much attention to the library. It is semi-detached and constructed in the shape of a hexagon. It has high windows to capture sunlight any time of the day. I have stored the oldest book scrolls in raised boxes and shelved the newer works in niches. Portraits of my husband, my children and my parents decorate the walls. In the niches, next to famous quotes and articles they have written, the busts of my favorite poets, playwrights, and philosophers. In the corners, the statuettes of the seven sages of Greece: Thales, Bias, Cleobulus, Pittacus, Solon, Chilon, and Periander.[3]

The master builders have constructed on their initiative, in line with my second terrace, half above, half under water, barriers in the shape of arrowheads, so that I, when I take a sunbath, may from time to time enjoy the fine spray of the breaking waves. They presented it as a gift and refused to charge the extra costs, but I have heard they have received numerous orders to copy it in other villas. The terrace on the port side has a spacious landing for guests and for my visits to Puteoli, Naples, and Pompeii, row boats are moored alongside my private terraces, ready for departure, day and night.

My island leaks. Two tunnels run underneath, connecting the port to the sea. According to my master builders, the tunnels also undermine the narrow link with the mainland and they predicted that, in the distant future, it would collapse. So it is true my peninsula is anchored only for the time being and one day will sail on its own.

My father has shown me how easy it is to turn your back on Rome and bury yourself alive in the past, which also prompted me to select this place. When the light of life dims, it is good to live near a port. The eternal breath of the sea provides sustenance for many creatures. As soon as I move inland, I begin to miss its voice. Whenever the wind, as now, blows from the west I hear the moaning and gnashing of toiling winches and cranes like in our home in Rome on the Aventine. I experience the noise of the daily activity in the harbor as well as the loud voices of fishermen and laborers as soothing and reassuring.

---

[3] According to Greek tradition, seven philosophers, statesmen, and law-givers from the sixth century BC who were renowned for their wisdom.

3.

Today, I received the death notice of the former Consul Gaius Lealius, reviving memories I did not wish to recollect. His obituary filled me with grim satisfaction that he who has enough time to live, survives all his enemies; a reprehensible sentiment, unworthy of his memory and that of my family. Laelius' father was a client of my father and as his son, he bestowed on my husband and me only the highest courtesy. The man was a prominent jurist and thanks to his efforts, I became familiar with the writings of the Greek Philosopher Panaetius,[4] whose ideas about life-long friendships appealed to me.

Unfortunately, I lost Laelius as a loyal friend of the family by his relentless fervor to pursue all followers of my son Tiberius after his murder, and even now, the man continues to haunt me. His obituary opened all my old wounds about the campaign of Tiberius.

Everyone remembers the shock wave that ran through Italy when Laelius proposed during his Consular election campaign a redistribution of public land to ensure our veterans could take up again their peasant life after their military service. Equestrians and Senators could not believe their ears. A storm of protest arose. Many had owned for generations the land, he reclaimed. They had paid for it and it housed their family graves. They had made investments in buildings, storehouses, and barracks for slaves, in planting vineyards and olive groves. They had bought expensive equipment for pressing olives and grapes. They had purchased herds of cattle, sheep, and goats. From the proceeds, they had contributed to the maintenance of our public roads. Their possession had served as collateral for borrowing and paying dowries. Had Laelius lost his mind?

---

[4] A philosopher from Rhodes (c. 185/180-110/109 BCE) who introduced Stoic philosophy to Rome. His most famous work was his *On Duties*.

The landowners of our allies in Italy also revolted. Anyone who had any influence in Rome, including me, received their supplications and at the Forum, they organized daily noisy gatherings where they gave speech after speech within sight of the Curia. I could hear the clamor of their demonstrations even on the Aventine. I had to listen to their speeches so often, in the end, I could repeat their arguments word by word. 'Was this their reward for their loyalty to Rome? Had a Censor ever taken the trouble to register the confiscation of their land? Captured ages ago, in wars no one alive today had witnessed. Many of their fellow citizens had simply continued to cultivate the land that had belonged to them for centuries. They had been ignorant of the fact this land was no longer theirs. Had there not been treaties with Rome, stipulating cities could take back the land in exchange for similar lease arrangements as Roman tenants? There had even been a decree of the Senate that anyone who wished to cultivate public land could do so in exchange for a certain percentage of the increased value. Forgotten? Were these levies ever administered by the Censors, let alone collected? Who would guarantee that they would not give the land first to Roman veterans, leaving their own veterans empty-handed? Soon they would lose their land as well as their rights because they would no longer be able to provide sufficient auxiliary troops.'

Scores of local magistrates, armed with maps of their area, visited Laelius daily, demanding him to specify exactly which piece of land was theirs and which part belonged to Rome, and to prove this by previous treaties. While Laelius increasingly regretted his proposal and desperately sought a way out, the veterans gathered in equally large numbers to show their support for his campaign. 'Finally, someone who cared about them! Finally, a Senator who proposed to recoup the land and lease it to those who were entitled!' They too organized large gatherings at the Forum. Sometimes clashes erupted between veterans and the Italian landowners when they demonstrated simultaneously on the Forum. The veterans assembled in front of Laelius' villa and as soon as they caught a glimpse of him, they began to shout encouraging slogans. The Roman and Latin veterans assured him, he could count on their votes if his election would require a vote from the lowest classes. I have never seen in my life a Consular candidate, receiving so many tokens of loyalty and support from the lower classes with such a sour expression on his face.

In a plenary session of the Senate, surrounded by hordes of veterans at the Forum, Laelius finally emerged. While everyone listened to him inside and outside the Curia in dead silence, he commenced his retreat under the argument his proposal would alienate the loyal allies of Rome and therefore it would not be in the public interest to pursue it further. A large number of Senators jumped up, applauding and stomping their feet, followed by a furious roar on the Forum. The Senators called him by exclamation 'Laelius the Sage', and his election as Consul proceeded smoothly, secured by an overwhelming majority in the highest classes.

Yet the unrest would remain. In the Italian and Latin cities, local landowners called on their political leaders to withhold any further military support to our campaigns in Spain, Africa, and Asia until the Consuls and the Senate had repealed the ancient confiscation of their lands, or granted them the Roman civil rights, so they could at least vote on the distribution of the public land. The veterans never forgot Laelius' campaign, nor forgave him for failing them. The damage was done and they were just waiting for a new champion to pick up their cause.

I blame neither Laelius nor Tiberius for tackling the unrestrained land grab by our Senators and Equestrians. All imaginable laws, adopted two hundred and fifty years ago and reconfirmed many times, had been violated. Everyone knew the Senators and Equestrians had bought out – in the beginning through intermediaries, later openly, first gently, then with force – the leaseholders and enlarged their properties many times the maximum permitted size of five hundred iugera.[5] Our soldiers had paid for this land with their lives. It is public property; many times promised to our veterans in exchange for their loyal service and he, who had appropriated more than permissible, should return it.

However, I do blame Laelius, my son, and the Senate for a lack of political leadership. Anyone who takes matters into his own hands must expect opposition. Laelius should have foreseen how fierce and unrelenting the resistance would be, and my son should have exercised moderation. Better than anyone else, my son knew that his proposal to include the estates near Rome in his redistribution plan would infuriate the most powerful families, but he deliberately ignored it and buried it under his election slogans. I have asked him numerous times what his goal was. More land for the veterans or the pursuit of personal vengeance. He could not achieve both, and if he aimed to obtain land for the veterans, then it was his responsibility to make sure they got it!

4.

Have I really been 'the female serpent whose tail rebelled against the head and demanded to go in front, with no eyes, nose, and tongue?' With his foresight, my husband predicted that the decisive moment in the life of my sons and me would occur after I had become their citizen. Depending on the state of our relationship at that moment, he envisioned the outcome either positive or negative, but never doubted my influence would be too great. In one of our marital quarrels, he bellowed once he

---

[5]A iugera was a Roman unit of area equal to rectangle of 240 Roman feet in length and 120 feet in width, the equivalent of about ¼ of a hectare or 0.623 acres.

owed the gods eternal gratitude I had been born a woman. I still remember the sparkle of genuine anger and pain in his eyes when he shouted that.

Sometimes, when I find the maelstrom of arguments, doubts and anxieties overwhelming, I choose the easy way out offered by the philosophers, and I put all the blame on the Fates. With iron logic, I argue, fate guided us through every step we made. Each time, or so it seemed, we made the correct move, well-balanced and motivated for the right reasons, while in reality, we were like blind horses who put the stone on top of the Aventine hill in motion and lost all control as it barreled down into the Tiber.

My husband and I fought a lot, but overall, I would say our marriage was a good one. Yet, I see now that the attempt by my eldest brother Publius Cornelius to forge an alliance between my family and the Sempronii also planted the seeds of our destruction.

Like Greece, our actual history is domineered by discord. In the city of Rome, we live our history; on the battlefields, we create our sagas of concord. Since the fratricide of Romulus and Remus, it has been the fate of our great houses to clash with each other. I do not think it was a coincidence that Remus took possession of the unruly Aventine and Romulus of the grand Palatine. From these two hills, my fellow citizens have contested each other since the founding of our city to gain control over the third hill, the Capitol. Many Tribunes hated my sons because their ancestors had ruled on all three hills. They were already mistrusted before they were born.

The position of my family, Cornelii, was undermined by the trials against my father and my uncle, designed to break our power, which, I admit, had gained almost regal status after my father had defeated our nemesis Carthage. Due to his weak health, my brother Publius was unable to play a leading role. Our father, the savior our Republic, had died as an exile, disgraced and humiliated. Through my marriage and the

adoption of my younger cousin Aemilianus, my brother Publius succeeded in one stroke to protect his legacy and build a bridge with the
Sempronii, securing his relationship with the allied families of the Claudii, Livii, and Lucci. Later, my husband strengthened the family ties by
marrying our oldest daughter, Sempronia, to Aemilianus.

The Cornelii and the Sempronii were families who had fiercely opposed one another in the past, but also joined forces against the monster
alliance of Carthaginian, Gaul, and Macedonian. The veto my husband
had imposed, against the wishes of all his fellow Tribunes, to end the trial
against my uncle, had brought our families together.

In anticipation of my wedding ceremony, I frequently stayed at the
house of my elder sister Cornelia. She subjected me to all those homely
pursuits in which she excelled and I thoroughly hated. While busy with
our hard-working chores like sewing, embroidering and arranging flowers, she regularly pointed out that my future husband came, granted,
from a Consular family, but was of plebeian descent. Her husband, Corculum Nasica, was a distant cousin of ours and like us, a patrician.

The enmity Corculum and I felt for each other, was there from the
start. Corculum found me a loud, flimsy, headstrong child and I still feel
his sour, disapproving look slide down my body. I found him cold, cruel
and full of conceit. My dislike for him found later its confirmation in the
gruesome massacres he allowed his soldiers to commit during the massive crackdown on Epirus in Greece. He even composed a book about
his, as he described it, 'heroic' role in this horrible campaign.

I agree with Panaetius that hatred is the greatest where first friendship prevailed. I am convinced this phenomenon occurs even stronger in
the case of family relations and good deeds often generate the highest
animosity.

Nasica Corculum and my sister never forgave my husband they
owed him gratitude for his veto in the trial of my uncle. They resented

our marriage and Corculum participated in the Senatorial Committee to investigate the public spending my husband had authorized as Aedilis[6] for the Ludi Romani. In his opinion, my husband had tricked many Italian cities in a financial disaster to secure his election as Praetor. I cannot deny the games had been magnificent with many public banquets, donations of meat to the poor, several gladiatorial games on one day, wild animal fights, and horse races. There had even been, for the first time in Rome, black panthers on display. The people had loved it. My husband brushed all the allegations with a broad smile aside – 'trust me, they would have done the same, they are just jealous, and this will be forgotten in a couple of months' – but I felt ashamed and saw it as a betrayal of my family. I reduced my visits to their homes. Thus, the street plan of Rome began to show a pattern of neighborhoods and streets I liked to go to and others I shunned. Without being aware of it, my exile had already begun.

Later my husband would retaliate, using his position as an Augur. After Corculum had won the Consulate, my husband reported from Sicily to his colleagues, that he had checked the protocols and concluded, to his utter dismay, he had committed some errors. His epistle contained a murky story about a tent he had not put up at the proper location and that he had forgotten to pray some prayers after crossing for the second time a tiny stream on the border of the Campus Martius. Everyone, including me, had second thoughts about his letter. Some Augurs even went to see for themselves and they had a hard time finding the little stream. However, since the word of an Augur was sacred, the College of Augurs was forced to advise the Senate nothing less than the annulment of the results of the Consular elections. Quite by accident, the re-election

---

[6]A public official responsible for maintenance of public buildings and regulation of public festivals.

delivered two of my husband's political allies a victory. From that moment, my sister and Corculum belonged to our archenemies. The poisonous seeds were germinating.

5.

Whenever the image of Tiberius' mutilated body looms before my eyes, I realize again that all his friends had abandoned him at that moment. At such instances, I tell myself how extraordinarily fortunate his life had been, however short; he counted less than three decades when he died. He had been blessed by his family lineage, the posts he held, the honors he received, and the friendships he gained. He was also richly endowed with personal qualities, smart, healthy, agile, strong and beautiful to look at.

Life was extremely good to him. From the moment he received his toga virilis,[7] he enjoyed one success after another. He was appointed as Augur at the earliest possible age and he experienced the joy of triumph when he received the Corona Muralis as a sixteen-year-old from the hands of my son-in-law Aemilianus in honor of the fact he had been one of the first to scale the wall of Carthage.

My ancestors, my husband, and Gaius all served with enthusiasm, but Tiberius truly embraced his military career with heart and soul. On certain days, women were allowed to watch the training of the young recruits from the sidelines of the Campus Martius and while I proudly followed the feats of my son, I noticed the rough fondness with which veterans treated him. In a Roman army, men touch each other constantly.

---

[7]A plain white toga, worn on formal occasions by adult male commoners and Senators not having a curule magistracy. It symbolized adult male citizenship and its attendant rights, freedoms, and responsibilities.

I always experienced a slight degree of jealousy when I saw them together. With slaps, hugs, pats on the head, a firm poke in the side, a bond was forged for life, one in which we women played no part. The attachment was so strong that Consuls often had to switch Centurions for fear they might lose the willpower to discipline their men.

The childlike enthusiasm and brassy behavior with which Tiberius had left for Africa, had given way to a serious sense of responsibility after his return. No trace of the pompous utterances like some of his friends. The war experience had matured him and a calm determination had settled in, which pleasantly surprised me.

He had received his Corona in front of the entire army and he had enjoyed his victory round while his fellow soldiers had cheered and clapped as he passed their lines. His name had been on everyone's lips, 'Tiberius, son of Tiberius Sempronius Gracchus, grandson of Scipio Cornelius Africanus!' It had made a huge impression when some soldiers had walked up to him and volunteered to serve under him, even in Spain, which they all hated. In the first few weeks, he could not stop talking about it.

6.

My son's first campaign had been a tough school. He had left with a mental picture of unreliable Carthaginian mercenaries versus patriotic Roman soldiers, but once in Africa, it had seemed the opposite. Our army in Africa had been little more than a loose horde of robbers while he was deeply impressed by the patriotism and bravery the Carthaginians demonstrated in their final hours. For three years, they had resisted our siege and many lost their lives when they swam across the waterways to set our siege engines on fire.

When he reported for duty, he swore, like the others, the sacred oath of our army. He pledged his allegiance to his commander and brother-in-law Aemilianus, and vowed not to commit a theft worth more than a silver sesterce within a circle of ten miles. Yet after spending a few days in the camp, he discovered the soldiers flouted their oath completely. During his nightly inspections, he overheard their muffled conversations. The camp had seemed more like a marketplace than an army base. Stocks of stolen goods exceeded the demand so much that prices fell by the day.

Aemilianus had taken care of my son as a father. He had invited Tiberius to come to Africa and he had welcomed him to stay in his tent; the highest honor a recruit could receive. My son asserted Aemilianus embodied all the virtues of a good commander. A man with an eye for details, athletic, tireless, equipped with a strategic insight, and always pushing to improve the condition of his soldiers. My son was adopted by the circle of faithful who had gathered around Aemilianus, like the Greek historian Polybius and Gaius Laelius. He had attended the meetings of the Centurions and taken part in their discussions about the well-being of the troops. He had heard their concerns about the morale of the soldiers and the need to do something after they had served their mandatory six years. During this campaign Gaius Laelius had developed with the support of Aemilianus his proposals for the land reform and my son had been full of praise.

It had pleased my son immensely when he learned that Aemilianus, after he had taken over the command, had chased everyone out of the camp who should not have been there; not only the many prostitutes, but also the fortunetellers soldiers consulted following a defeat. But even Aemilianus had been forced to interrupt one of the first attacks on Carthage because the soldiers had ignored his orders and first proceeded to plunder the temple of Apollo. It had been an outrageous scandal, talked about throughout the entire Mediterranean world.

7.

Tiberius spoke in awe of the scale of what he called the second army. His father had often elaborated on it, but his enthusiasm was so touching, I listened to him as if he opened a new world for me. Clerks helped soldiers write letters or draw up wills for their deceased comrades-in-arms. There were overseers, smiths – forging spears, arrows, helmets and swords – cooks, butchers, stonemasons, wheelwrights, supervisors for all the transports and special scouts for tracing water sources. My son had also been full of praise for our surgeons. Their skills with saw and pliers had saved many a soldier from gangrene. It had greatly affected him when they told him about a strange disorder by which soldiers continued experiencing pain in limbs after the amputation.

Our Centurions had impressed him the most. He developed with one of them, Gnaeus, a solid friendship and later, during dinners and in his speeches, my son loved recounting his life. To him, Gnaeus represented the epitome of loyalty and the irreplaceable value of the small farmer as a Roman soldier.

His father had left Gnaeus a piece of land and a small farmhouse where he had grown up. He had married his cousin and together they had seven children, three of whom survived childhood. His wife tended to their farm with her brother while Gnaeus was on campaign. All his children were married now. Gnaeus had started in the army as a foot soldier, but after three campaigns his commanders had noticed his insight and courage and promoted him to command the tenth company of spearmen. A few years later, he became commander of the first company of spearmen. When Tiberius met him, he had risen so far through the ranks that he was one the five senior Centurions of the first cohort.

On his arrival in Africa, Gnaeus had approached Tiberius out of respect for his father under whom he had served in Spain and Sardinia. His legs and arms bore the marks of many sword fights and due to a scar across cheek and mouth, he lisped, making it at first difficult for Tiberius to understand the man's dialect. With all his might of combat experience, Gnaeus volunteered to train my son and taught him how to strike out first at the legs of his opponent. As a result, my son endured his first encounters without any serious harm.

Gnaeus had made enough money from the spoils of war to retire, but he also offered Tiberius his services. When Tiberius asked him how old he was, Gnaeus had shrugged and with a grin, grabbed Tiberius' hand and put it in his mouth, so he could count the few remaining teeth.

8.

There are battles we hate to be reminded of – the one against the Sabines, at Trasumennus and above all at Cannae in the South. My grandfather Aemilius was one of the many who perished there. The defeat shook the foundations of our nation. It is hard to imagine now, but our very existence could have been wiped off the face of the earth. All our allies wavered and my father had to draw his sword, forcing his fellow Senators to remain loyal to Rome and not to hide in exile.

In the morning after our defeat, more than fifty thousand men and thousands of horses lay there in piles. Those who were still alive, begged our enemies to kill them. Many of the dead carried deep wounds in their backs and legs. Our enemies found soldiers who had buried their faces in holes to cut off their breath. Under a pile of dead Roman soldiers, they discovered a Numidian who was still breathing. After he had lost his arms, a Roman soldier had attacked him with his teeth and bitten off his ears and nose. In the aftermath, Hannibal, the Carthaginian commander, sent three bags full of gold rings – cut off from the fingers of Equestrians and Senators – to Carthage. At Cannae, we lost the flower of our generation. Eighty Senators died there and, according to my husband, we never recovered from this loss. The families replacing them were of a very different caliber than the ones who had perished.

Despite the horrors he had experienced at Cannae, my father had never hated Hannibal. On the contrary, he had always admired him for his courage and strategic thinking. In the eyes of my father, hatred belonged to the home front. His attitude had always confounded me until my son recounted the fall of Carthage. He had been convinced of the necessity to destroy Carthage. He regarded the revival of the town, fifty years after its defeat by my father, as a threat, which had to be nipped in the bud. The stories he had been told about Hannibal's crimes in Italy were reconfirmed by the cruelties perpetrated by the Carthaginian commander Hasdrubal. During the siege, they had watched helplessly as their captured comrades were tortured here. Hasdrubal had ordered to rip out their eyes, tongues, and private parts with iron hooks. Some friends of my son were thrown alive off the walls. He never forgot their screams.

But when my son faced the destruction of the town, he became overwhelmed with pity. He felt, he witnessed the same fate for Rome if Hannibal had persevered after his victory in the battle of Cannae. The demolishment of the citadel Byrsa to which the majority of the people had fled, had horrified him. Three long streets ran from the forum to the citadel and on both sides, there were houses, six stories high. Fighting from house to house, my son and his soldiers tried to ward off heavy stones and pieces of furniture the enemy threw down on them. Many of his fellow soldiers lost their lives. After they had captured the first rows of houses, they climbed to the roofs and connected them with bridges. A battle began on the ground and in the air. Citizens were stabbed to death or thrown alive from the roofs. The streets reverberated with the sound of collapsing houses and cries for help.

When the battle stalled and the casualties grew, Aemilianus ordered his troops to set fire to the houses they had seized. The fire spread rapidly, filling the air with the sickening smell of burning human flesh. Cleaners, who followed the battle on foot to clear the road of debris, threw survivors into ditches. Some still breathed, their limbs moving for hours, as they lay half-covered by the rubble. The streets were littered with human remains. The battle for Byrsa lasted six days and few of the soldiers could sleep, crazed by the rampage of burning, raping, looting and killing.

After the fall of Byrsa, the last group of Carthaginians and Roman defectors fled to the temple of Asclepius as their final refuge. Here they held out for three days until hunger drove them to the roof. At the very last moment, Hasdrubal escaped with his family from the temple and surrendered. Aemilianus ordered him to sit at his feet so everyone on top of the temple could see him. From the roof of the temple, his fellow citizens heaped curses on him. Then they set the temple ablaze.

Standing next to Aemilianus, Gaius Laelius, Polybius, and the Centurions, my son had looked straight into the eyes of Hasdrubal's children, filled with fear. He had watched with compassion as they had cried and pleaded. He told me one of them had been about the same age as Gaius, seven or eight. Stretching out their hands, the children had turned to their mother, begging her to save them. But she had struck at their arms, and cursing her husband, she had hoisted them up, one by one and thrown them into the fire. Calling him a coward and a traitor, she then flung herself into the abyss. No one had been able to hold back tears. My son had heard a weeping Aemilianus citing Homer, "A day will come when sacred Troy shall perish, and Priam and his people shall be slain." It had truly seemed to them that they had been reliving the destruction of Troy.

Aemilianus took Hasdrubal as a prisoner of war back to Rome. Chained, Hasdrubal walked behind Aemilianus' carriage in the triumphal march as onlookers mocked and spat on him. The State provided him with a house and a few slaves where he spent his remaining days. Hasdrubal's fate both fascinated and bewildered my son. He found it incomprehensible this man could carry on living. Every now and then, he would walk by Hasdrubal's house to catch a glimpse of him and each time, he was perplexed to see Hasdrubal shuffling through the front garden, looking fat and shabby and bereft of any sign of self-respect.

9.

Year after year, a river flows along a dike and undermines it bit-by-bit, imperceptible, inaudible, invisible until without warning or whisper in advance, the dike succumbs in a fraction of a moment and the river floods the land.

When the ship with the Carthaginian gold Aemilianus had sent ahead entered the port of Ostia and the rumor of the fall of Carthage spread, all of Rome came out. People flocked to the corners of the streets where they stayed up all night, sang songs, and celebrated. Veterans, surrounded at the squares by a bevy of young listeners and admirers, recounted their personal experiences and exploits. People recalled in tears the most critical moments, reminding each other of the farmlands, vineyards, and olive groves Hannibal had destroyed. They summed up the loss of our fleets, the power of the Carthaginian ballista's, the might of the elephants and the achievements of my father. We had lost three hundred thousand men, four hundred cities had been razed and we could not believe that it was all over. The Senate organized games and offered sacrifices in all the temples throughout Italy. Those were days – the last, I believe – when we Romans, young and old, rich and poor, were unified and we shared our sorrow, joy, and relief together in a true expression of cordial harmony.

Yet, in eight years much can change. When my son departed for Spain, following his successful election as Quaestor, he left behind a Rome very different from the one he had returned to after his first campaign. The brief period of unity was gone. The gold Aemilianus had sent was the last great war booty Rome received, and the Aqua Marcia was the last major construction undertaken in the city. The squares of Rome began to fill with men asking for work and food. The noise from construction activities disappeared and an eerie quiet descended on our city. I encountered beggars whom I had seen working a few weeks before. Traders and merchants could easily handle their businesses now with just a few freedmen and slaves. Soon others followed their example and people lost their jobs everywhere, in the public baths, tabernae, inns, workshops, granaries, and shipyards.

I noticed the crisis in our city through the behavior of the poorest among the old clients of my husband who had remained loyal to my household after his death. Earlier on, they had shown a preference to take the money and they left the bread, piled up in baskets in our hall, largely untouched. But during my monthly check of the household books with my stewards, I found the cost of bread had exploded, arousing my suspicion. I became worried Simo had embezzled money to gamble, a weakness shown by many Greeks. If it had been too much drinking, the other Greek ailment, I would have discovered it myself. With fear in my heart, I called him to account, but at first, he dodged my questions by pointing out the soaring wheat prices. After I had persisted, he revealed that he had steadily increased the amount of bread. Their children, other family members and friends of friends, he confessed, now accompanied our clients. My front door had taken on, in the morning, the appearance of a full-blown bakery. I reprimanded Simo for not telling me, but I also granted him permission to continue, provided they baked all the bread at home and stopped buying it from bakeries down the street. It forced him and others in my household to get up earlier, but the misery they witnessed in the morning was, apparently, so severe that none of them protested.

In the city, the situation deteriorated. Stories of violence and robberies became routine. Our streets were infested by a whole new generation of petty thieves; edgy, frightened, skinny children of four years and older, running up and down the crowded alleys and stealing everything from passers-by and open stalls. Angry slogans appeared on the walls of temples and public buildings. Senators were blocked in the streets, reviled, spat upon, and the labyrinth of alleys north of the Forum degenerated into an area where they were afraid to show their faces.

After the grain prices had begun to rise, people accused the owners of the granaries immediately of foul play. The rumor spread that they deliberately withheld grain to raise the prices. One of the Tribunes, Curiatus organized daily contios[8] on the Forum about the prices. He demanded the magistrates attend his meetings and he even summoned the Consul, in this case, none other than the son of my sister, Scipio Nasica Serapio. Serapio had succeeded his father as Pontifex Maximus after his death and grown into a man even more arrogant than him. While he ran for Aedileship, Serapio asked a man with whom he shook hands whether he had been walking on them. He dismissed it later as a light-hearted remark, but the people got the message and I was content to see he lost his elections in the Tribal Assembly as a result. Serapio was known to urge people to remain calm when he spoke. The Tribune Curiatus had ridiculed his condescending way of speaking by comparing it with the haughty behavior of another Serapio who was a well-known helper of

---

[8] A public forum or gathering where magistrates discussed proposed legislation and other matters of public interest.

the Augurs. I had been shocked when I first heard it. It had been an outrageous insult, drawing regrettably much laughter. This helper's main
task was to check in advance if the sacrificial animals carried any tape-
worms.

Curiatus demanded, with much approval from his supporters, that
the Senate should purchase grain at a reasonable price and resell it to the
needy. When Serapio did not immediately agree, people began to shout
that maybe the time had come to leave the city and occupy the Aventine
as in the days of old. Serapio shouted back that everyone should remain
calm and that he, as Consul, knew better than anyone else did what was
right for the Republic. His admonitions garnered him sneers, jeers, and
obscene gestures with fingers and arms. Some began to pick up pebbles,
and the lictors[9] had to move in to restrain the crowd.

When Serapio was even briefly incarcerated because of a lawsuit
brought by Curiatus on behalf of a dozen clients in relation to a conscription dispute, my son-in-law Aemilianus urged the Senate to appoint him
as dictator to restore order at the Forum. His proposal aroused immediate suspicion and the Senators rejected it. His initial support for Laelius'
proposals, even though they had been called off, had also weakened his
position in the Senate. While the people agitated at the Forum, our Republic was already in such a state of dissolution that friend and foe discredited any attempt at leadership in advance.

---

[9]An attendant or bodyguard to a magistrate.

10.

I have often wondered how the life of Tiberius and my family would have transpired if my husband had been his commander instead of Consul Mancinus. Spain is a treacherous country, and only a fool does not take the necessary precautions.

In their inimitable cynicism, the Fates determined that the place where my son would continue his military service would not be decided by lot, but in this exceptional case through a special assignment. The Senate expected much good of sending a Sempronius to Spain, and my son was delighted by the honor. His nomination was celebrated with a number of lavish parties. All his friends, sincere or feigned, congratulated him on his appointment.

He left on a brilliant morning, and it was a joy to see him; my young god with his shapely figure. His pleated leather armor shiny with grease. The cheek guards of his proud helmet accentuated his beautiful cheekbones. Sunlight danced over the polished shoulder and thigh plates of his armor and his decorated belt. His successful election as Quaestor had been the culmination of eight years of diligent service during which the Tribal Assembly had reelected him each year as their military Tribune. He had served in places where his father had previously established his patronage, in Sardinia, Pergamum and Greece. He had gathered a flock of admirers around him and he was one of the most sought after bachelors in Rome.

My son took his time. He had decided not to leave from Ostia, but to embark for Spain way up North so he could see with his own eyes what the situation of our farmers was. He had noticed many Senators hardly ever visited their lands, but preferred to remain in Rome and receive the proceeds of their farms through agents. He traveled via the Via Aurelia through Etruria, and from Alsium he followed the coastline, ending in Herakles Monoikos where he boarded his ship.

During his journey, he sent us letters, reporting that only north of Etruria he had found the small family farms, which had characterized our countryside for centuries. Before that, his trip had led him through vast farmlands where he had seen thousands of slaves working on the land, chained like herds of cattle. He wrote that it had felt as if he had been traveling through a real-life version of the handbook of Cato. As recommended by this self-proclaimed guardian of our mores, the estate holders had converted their grain fields into crop fields, growing profitable produce such as olives, figs, flowers, fruit and grapes, interspersed with pastures for cattle to supply our armies with wool, leather and pack animals. The production of our daily bread had been replaced by the pursuit of profit.

Tiberius' letters and the concerns he expressed, inspired my son Gaius to spread a pamphlet in which he called upon the Senate to reconsider Laelius' proposals for the redistribution of public land. I read his first public document with mixed feelings. It contained annoying passages written merely to show how much he knew about the history of our country, but also inspired parts in which his passion for our soldiers moved me. He recalled the origin of the public land. How we had seized it during the previous four centuries from the peoples of Italy before they had surrendered and become our allies in our struggles outside Italy. He also mentioned the colonies his father and grandparents had established on this land, in many parts of Italy, so that Rome could count on a steady influx of foot soldiers from its soil.

He described how our insatiable hunger for manpower in the last hundred years had driven us to reduce step by step the property requirements for military service. Until the mere possession of a pair of oxen and a few slaves allowed us to recruit even the poorest farmers, forcing them to serve for at least six years. Even I had been unaware of this. He mentioned how hard it had been on our peasants and pointed to the many conscription conflicts it had caused. In the old days, when wars took place in Italy, our farmers had been able to return in time to reap their harvest. But with distant wars in Spain, Greece, and Africa, and much longer campaigns, their small fields had become neglected, compelling many to sell, mainly to members of the Senate after our foresighted ancestors had forced the Senators to curb their mercantile activities.

It was a passionate pamphlet. I read with approval his quotations from Aristotle, who considered the existence of a prosperous middle class between the rich and the poor as the best guarantee for the well-being of a country. But did he really need to mention there were only 2,500 men in Rome who possessed sufficient resources to qualify for the class of Equestrians? I had to admit the small number amazed me too, but bringing it up could only arouse the jealousy of the lower classes. I read in his pamphlet not only a disguised attack on my father, but also on my husband when he argued that lowering the property requirements and allowing the number of volunteers to surpass many times the number of conscripts, had boosted the popularity of commanders whose campaigns promised to be profitable, eroding the authority of other commanders and the Senate. He also pointed to the danger of using mercenaries and the massive losses Carthage had suffered after their mercenaries had rebelled in a war that lasted years. The defense of our homeland, he concluded, had been replaced by the pursuit of spoils, echoing his brother's argument about our daily bread versus the pursuit of profit.

I had argued against a wide distribution of the pamphlet for fear it might harm his brother's career, but Gaius ignored my advice; the beginning of a bad habit that grew worse over time. For weeks, his document ruined many a dinner party in Rome, eliciting warm approval, as well as fierce criticism, especially from those who had resisted the proposals of Gaius Laelius.

11.

The army my son joined in Spain was notorious, but the reality defied his most gloomy expectations. The situation was even worse than in Africa. Not just the camp of his legion, but also the other Roman stations throughout Spain were in a state of neglect. After his first round of inspections, he estimated there were at least two thousand whores in the tents. Soldiers came and went whenever they pleased for expeditions to the surrounding villages where they often ransacked farms. During the march exercises, many stayed behind under the guise of all sorts of excuses. Horsemen rode next to sick soldiers without offering a hand. Most astonishing had been the use of slaves, which soldiers with some cash to spare had purchased to scrub their backs while bathing.

The financial administration was also in a state of chaos. My son was responsible for collecting the war indemnity and the correct handling of payments. The moment he arrived, he was overwhelmed by a barrage of grievances about payouts, inaccuracies in their saving accounts and the height of withholdings for housing, food, boots, clothes, weapons, and funeral costs. He complained it took him months to sort out all the personal accounts.

The physical condition of the soldiers alarmed him and the glaring poverty he found among most of them shocked him. They had stolen all their possessions from the surrounding villages and, during his first negotiations with the local population about the war indemnity, he encountered hatred that he had not experienced anywhere else.

From the sparse number of letters my son sent me about his Spanish campaign, I understood the Numantians successfully applied their standard tactic of small attacks, while avoiding a decisive confrontation. They gave our army not a moment's rest. One ambush after another followed, day and night. The losses became so severe that Mancinus decided to adopt the same course as pursued by his predecessors. He cut his campaign short and retreated into a fortress to wait for the arrival of his successor. But the army had not even been properly installed when a false rumor reached him that two other tribes had arrived to assist the Numantians and our brave Consul panicked. He ordered the men to extinguish all fires and after spending most of the night in darkness, they fled before dawn to a former camp at Nobilior. Here they paid the price for years of bad command and neglect. At daylight, they discovered the trenches had collapsed, the ramparts of peat had crumbled and there were no supplies. In the course of the day, the Numantians tracked them down and surrounded the camp. The army of my son was now completely trapped.

Mancinus sent envoys to the Numantians to propose a truce and a treaty, offering them the status of a friendly nation. But grown wise after many bitter experiences, the Numantians sent his envoys back. They had no confidence in Mancinus and demanded the presence of my son. He was the only one they trusted because of his correct valuation of the grain they had paid as their war indemnity. Some also remembered his father whose memory was still in high regard for the same reason. Although his position hardly allowed negotiations, my son ultimately succeeded in saving the lives of twenty thousand soldiers. In return, they had to transfer all their possessions, for the most part stolen from them anyway, the Numantians told my son. Furthermore, they insisted on coming to Rome to ratify the treaty with the Senate.

The goods and arms were handed over, but in the chaos of the transfer, my son lost sight of his financial records and the wax tablets, which contained all his notes, the receipts of the war indemnity and the accounts of the army. My son discovered his loss after they had left and while the army marched on, he returned to the Numantians.

The Numantian magistrates considered his unexpected return as an opportunity to strengthen their bond with him. They served him a lavish banquet, and not only did they return his records, but they also took him to the place where they had stored his army's possessions. With a sweeping gesture, they invited him to take anything he wanted. Thank God, my son was prudent enough to take only some incense he used as Augur for religious purposes. They parted with a gracious, friendly goodbye.

12.

As soon as news of the treaty reached Rome, the Senate deprived Mancinus of his command. They ordered him to return to Rome at once together with his staff and they set up a Senatorial Committee. At the bidding of my son-in-law Aemilianus, Furius Philus was appointed as president, who in turn appointed my son-in-law and Gaius Laelius as his fellow Committee members.

The treaty my son had brokered so skillfully was doomed from the beginning. At the start of the deliberations in the Senate, many Senators had clamored the whole thing reminded them of our defeat at the Caudine forks in the Samnite war, when all senior officers were stripped bare and handed over to the Samnites. I panicked when I heard it. Opponents in the lawsuit were Mancinus and my son. The relatives of the twenty thousand soldiers whose lives were at stake, watched in horror. It never became clear to me what the Numantian ambassadors thought of this whole charade. They had come to Rome in the illusion their agreement would be taken seriously by the Senate and they could sign a truce.

The debate about the treaty in the Senate soon degenerated into an adult version of musical chairs. In the allotment of the provinces, the Senate had assigned Spain Citerior to Furius Philus and it was not in his interest if my son kept the patronage of his father over the Numantians. His position as chair of the Committee also provided Furius the opportunity to settle his feud with his archenemy Mancinus. During my family visits to Aemilianus and my daughter Sempronia, I had gathered my son-in-law aimed to win a second Consulate, prohibited by law, and that he wanted to keep his future command over our troops in Spain free of any treaty. Then, last but not least, there was Gaius Laelius, our dear house friend who had been alarmed by the pamphlet of Gaius and the last person in Rome to welcome a revival of his land redistribution plans. A public humiliation of Tiberius would serve him well. Even Gaius had to admit now that the broad sharing of his pamphlet may not have been such a smart move.

The discussions, which dragged on for months, became downright ludicrous when Mancinus put all the blame on his predecessor, Pompeius. It had been Pompeius, he argued, who had left the army in disarray. The Senate summoned the presence of Pompeius, but Pompeius repeated in front of the entire Senate his assertion that his predecessor had neglected the army. Furthermore, he ended laconically; they had queried him once before about Spain and they could not try him twice for the same thing. Exit Pompeius.

In the meantime, Consul Lepidus, who had taken over the command from Mancinus in Spain, was waiting for a decision by the Senate. This man whose speeches Tiberius had analyzed on the advice of his father, carried the nickname Porcina because of his enormous body size. Tired of just waiting and sitting, Lepidus accused one of the tribes, which had reportedly assisted the Numantians, falsely of treason. He laid siege to their town of Pallantia. While the siege took place, envoys, sent by the Senate as soon as it had heard of his campaign, caught up with him, telling him what he already knew. The Senate had not granted him permission for a new war and would not do so, certainly not now. They ordered him in name of the Senate to end the siege at once. But Lepidus felt he could not withdraw. A retreat would lead to a loss of face and endanger the position of Rome in the whole of Spain. He told the envoys to go back under the pretense their mission had failed to reach him.

His siege became a disaster. He achieved nothing, ran out of supplies and his retreat proceeded so disorderly that the wounded and sick thought they would be left alone. They clung to anyone they saw, pleading for help. The Pallantines pursued his army, but before they could engage him in battle, the Senate had deprived Lepidus of his command and ordered to return to Rome.

By the time Lepidus arrived in Rome, the Senate had finally reached a decision on Tiberius' treaty. Because of a personal intervention by my son-in-law, they declared only Mancinus guilty and acquitted the others, leaving my son with no other option than to accept, under protest, the outcome. He had saved the lives of his soldiers and he escaped the humiliation that awaited Mancinus. However, his treaty was rejected, a public affront. Everybody, except my son, Mancinus, and the Numantians had gotten their way.

As former chairman, Furius Philus accompanied Mancinus to Spain. Their mutual animosity guaranteed the Senate its decision would be carried out to the full. Mancinus was stripped naked and handed over to the Numantians, but they refused to take him in, so he put his clothes back on and all returned to Rome without having accomplished anything. When the news spread, every man in Rome laughed his ass off.

13.

Convinced he had saved the lives of his fellow soldiers and before the Senate began its deliberations, my son had made a detour on his way back from Spain to visit the house of his friend Gnaeus, only to find out, to his great sadness, Gnaeus had passed away. His wife and her brother were still alive and they welcomed him as if he had been one of their own. They were doing well because Gnaeus had been able to leave them with enough money, but many of their family members were facing tough times. The crisis in Rome had struck here too. Numerous veterans, who hired themselves out as temporary farm workers, had lost their homes. They were worse off than many slaves Tiberius had met along the way and the depth and extent of their misery incensed him.

He bristled at the fact that the Senators saw their slaves as an invest-ment and made sure they retained their value by taking good care of them, but that the fate of temporary workers they hired during the peak season, left them cold. It made him furious to hear Consuls like Mancinus and Pompeius complain about the low level of our armies and shift their personal failure as commanders on their soldiers, while they exploited the same men as seasonal workers after they had left the army. He met with soldiers who had served under him and he experienced their silence and embarrassed looks as a personal reproach. They felt betrayed by their former commanders, including by him and the anger he experi-enced of seeing the humiliation of his fellow-soldiers, broke forth later in the speeches he gave during his election campaign.

"Is it not just that what belongs to the people should be shared by the people? Is a man with no capacity for fighting more useful to his country than a soldier is? Is a citizen inferior to a slave? Who is the best Roman, a man who only owns his body or one who owns some of his country's soil?

The wild beasts of Italy have their caves to crawl into, but the brave men who spill their blood in her cause have nothing left but air and light. Without houses, without settled habitations, they wander from place to place with their wives and children; and their commanders do but mock them when, at the head of their armies, they exhort their men to fight for their sepulchers and the gods of their hearths because among them, there is not one Roman who has an altar that has belonged to his ancestors or a sepulcher in which their ashes rest. Our soldiers fight and die to ad-vance the wealth and luxury of the great and they are called masters of the world without having a sod to call their own."

14.

The endless disputes about his treaty in the Senate and the travesties afterward tested my son to the extreme, resulting in a huge disillusionment. All his prospects for a successful career seemed to have disappeared in one blow. His position as guardian of his veterans and his standing as patron of the Numantians were impaired. He also noticed a change in the way his old friends treated him. They expressed their sympathy and shared his indignation in private conversations. But behind his back, quite a few mocked him, taking delight in his defeat, especially the son of my sister, Serapio. He portrayed my son during dinners as a failed leader who desperately tried to get even in Rome after he left the battlefield in disgrace.

The debate and its outcome reinforced my son's opinion about the Senate, which I deplored, but unfortunately never enough to raise the red flag. Even I could see the irony that lay hidden in the disputations my son and I carried on for days. Against every argument I put forward, he retaliated with everything I had taught him since childhood. Repeatedly he left me with the feeling what he said was correct, but that there was also something else going on.

In the eyes of my son, the Senate had become a private toy in the hands of a dozen corrupt families. He had been especially bitter about the way his brother-in-law Aemilianus had conducted himself throughout the whole affair. My son accused him, first indirectly and then openly, of forsaking his duty to address the abuses in the Senate and the army. Aemilianus responded first irritably and then angrily. My son-in-law was not the kind of man to stand for a young man like my son to hold him accountable and in the months thereafter, it became clear an irreparable fracture had developed.

For my daughter, the break between Aemilianus and Tiberius was a personal disaster. As his elder and only sister, she had always treasured their relationship and now she was torn between two camps. My quarrels with my son gained a bitter undertone after he demanded that I too should break with Aemilianus. He characterized my refusal as a lack of loyalty and accused me of betraying my family. The first time he berated me, he caught me completely off guard. I suddenly disliked the sheer sight of his face with those bulging eyes and his ugly twisted, childish mouth. A chill crept in my heart that I had only hitherto experienced when a child of mine had died before my eyes. My son had offended me to the very depths of my soul. Even my husband in his greatest rages had never doubted my loyalty.

My inability to respond immediately, made him assume he had struck a right note. However, when he repeated a second time his accusation, I snapped back with such anger, he did not have the nerve to bring it up again. Yet on his face, I read he had not changed his mind and I am sure he warned Gaius that if it really came down to it, he could not count on his mother; planting the next set of insidious seeds.

15.

It is true no one has offered my son Tiberius more resistance than I did when he unleashed his full-scale war on the Senate. I still consider it his greatest, fatal mistake. But to his defense and that of his brother, the Senate they inherited was the product of my generation and a shadow of what it once had been.

Gnaeus Manlius – may his family be cursed – sealed its fate. My husband and my uncle had loathed the Senate for granting this man permission to hold a triumphal march after his more than outrageous campaign against the Galatians. As a member of the Senatorial Committee, my uncle publicly rejected Manlius' argument that the victory over King Antiochus the Great in Syria would have been pointless without destroying the Galatians. In his arrogance, Manlius characterized the whole debate as a legalistic spat, but my uncle continued to uphold the sacred principle that only the Senate and the Comitia Centuriata could declare war. In an impassioned speech, I sometimes reread, my uncle condemned Manlius' campaign as a disgrace and nothing more than armed robbery. He had committed sacrilege, defenseless women and children had been slaughtered like animals and innocent people had been forced to pay war indemnities in the name of Rome.

Manlius created the precedent, but others needed very little incentive to follow his footsteps. My husband was appalled to discover that the people, who accompanied him at the start of a campaign, were so deeply indebted that they felt compelled to rob everyone blind. The prices they had paid for their homes and the extravagant designs of their gardens had stunned him.

While my sister's husband, Corculum, forbade the building of a Greek theater because it would corrupt our Roman values, he turned a blind eye to what went on behind the curtains in the Senate, things even our playwright Plautus could not have imagined in his most derisory plots. Consuls in their final months of office received donations from colluding candidates to manipulate the elections in exchange for a position as pro-Consul in the most lucrative provinces. Tribal leaders throughout the Mediterranean discovered they did not have to fight us. A payoff sufficed to get rid of us. Augurs were bribed to see good fortune in offerings that never took place. Permission to hold a triumphal march was bought from Tribunes in exchange for a higher share of the booty for the soldiers. This haggling deprived my uncle almost of his triumph after his victory over King Perseus.

After my uncle's victory, the Senate abolished under loud cheers the Tributum[10] for all Romans. In the past, we had paid these taxes to finance

---

[10]A tax imposed to finance the cost of war.

the build-up of our fleet against Carthage. It had been an expression of patriotism and a symbol of citizenship. The richest among us had conferred with pride their contributions and listed them on their tombstones. Now they perceived it as an assault on their private fortune and the abolishment made it clear the leading families attached more importance to their personal property than to the welfare of the State. The question was no longer how one could serve our Republic, but which position would yield the highest profit in the shortest amount of time. Our Republic had become a means and self-enrichment the goal.

The costs of the election campaigns rose to unprecedented levels with lavish banquets, free distribution of meat and bread, gifts, kickbacks, and spectacular gladiatorial shows.

With money provided by Equestrians, freedmen set up private enterprises. These people often got into fights about the value of their stakes if their enterprises unexpectedly had lost the bid at public auctions of contracts for the collection of tolls, construction and mining concessions. Under the watchful eye of Jupiter at the Forum, I witnessed nasty, ugly brawls in front of the stalls of the money traders if subcontractors changed the conditions of their verbal agreements and raised their prices after the main contractors had already submitted their tenders.

The dividing line between legislators and the negotiatores[11] – scrupulously observed by my husband and his colleagues despite all of their trickery during the election campaigns – got blurred when Senators gave money to middlemen who founded enterprises to secure the lending to City-States in Greece at usurious interest rates. They pushed in the Senate for the appointment of colluding colleagues and partners as local governors, so they could use our soldiers if the cities were unable to meet their obligations. Meanwhile Senators refused, as jurors of ad hoc courts established to compensate victims of extortion by Roman magistrates, to

---

[11]Money men that facilitated deals.

convict their fellow Senators. The first time my husband described this completely corrupted circus to me, I got so angry I made him stop talking about it.

My father's generation had robbed the Greeks of their works of art; my generation stole their bread.

16.

It got worse. While my son prepared during the day for his election as Tribune, the Fates pushed in the dark of the night a man in Sicily to the fore whose actions would turn everything in Rome upside down.

Landowners on Sicily had also bought scores of slaves and one of them, Damophilus, a resident of Enna, was a wealthy man. He owned many lands, large herds of cattle, and he behaved like a King. He moved in luxurious carriages, always accompanied by a host of slaves and his lavish meals were of Persian style.

Damophilus treated his slaves horribly. He had them branded like animals with hot irons, even though these men were often not home-born slaves, but prisoners of war who had been free in their own country. He kept them, shackled in chains, in animal cages and refused to give his shepherds extra clothes against the cold. His wife Megallis treated her slaves even more brutally. On top of randomly penalizing them with floggings, she lowered herself by abusing them for all sorts of debauchery.

Driven by exhaustion, hunger, and the hopelessness of their existence, the slaves began to conspire. They plotted to murder their masters and approached a Syrian, Eunus, who had the gift, or so he claimed, to communicate with the gods. Eunus was a runaway slave who had served his former master as a jester and who had cheered up his dinners with statements that he, Eunus, would one day be King. He had also warned, amid roaring laughter, to punish those who had been cruel to him and spare others who had been kind. After his escape, Eunus stole from farm to farm, telling slaves there would be a new Kingdom in which everyone would be free. To boost his story, he occasionally put something in his mouth, so he could breathe fire and he called himself a priest of the cult Dea Syria.

Eunus had little difficulty convincing the slaves of Damophilus their conspiracy had the blessing of the Gods. They were destined to own the land in and around Enna. Together they slipped in the middle of the night into the rooms of their masters, strangled Megallis, cut the throat of Damophilus and fled into the mountains. Here they made a pact with a brigand from Cilicia, Cleon, who led a free life in the mountains and valleys as a horse herder. Freedom is a powerful word and slaves from all over Sicily soon joined them. Their uprising grew into an army of more than seventy thousand men, forcing the Praetors to abandon their garrisons and flee to the mainland. Eunus, who had taken the name of Antiochus, anointed himself King of Sicily and he had free reign to fulfill his prophecies. Of the people he had known before, he released some, killed others and by this time, nobody in Sicily laughed anymore.

In the year my son canvassed, the uprising not only threatened Sicily, but also spread into the southern part of Italy. I received daily letters from friends from the Naples area, begging me to use my influence to help. Finally, after much delay and handwringing because the war would be costly without any profits, the Senate sent our Consul with two legions to the island, but due to its sluggish reaction, it took two years before the rebellion was crushed.

Because of the uprising, fewer grain ships from Sicily arrived in Rome. To convince people there was no question of speculation, the owners of the granaries threw the doors wide open so everyone could see the floors were bare. In our streets, grain had become truly scarce.

People undertook raids on farms near Rome and gangs plundered overnight the warehouses, where the grain for emergencies was stored. Friends of mine were burgled. Anyone who had any possessions hired guards and strengthened his home into a real fortification. The well-to-do were robbed in the streets in broad daylight, personal threats appeared on the walls of temples, and at the Forum protest meetings grew by the day, frightening us all. In the capital of the world, people were starving.

The first time my son came across dead infants with their gaunt faces and hollow eye sockets amid the dung heaps, he was deeply shocked. During his military campaigns, he had served in areas where food had been scarce, but it had never occurred in his life in Rome. In his daily rounds hunting for votes, he encountered clients aimlessly wandering through the alleys with dead children in their arms. He seized on the crisis in speeches to defend his land distribution program as a permanent solution. More Roman farmers would not only result in better soldiers, but also in more homegrown grain and fewer slaves to threaten our existence. "The dike along the Tiber," he warned, "was about to burst."

17.

According to the Greek philosopher, Heraclitus, water always flows and we can never step twice in the same river. Everything is in motion and the way we perceive our existence not only varies in time, but it is also different for each of us. Heraclitus advocated a fiery life and he asserted that if our souls became wet, they would extinguish, like fire.

His vision never stirred me more than when I beheld the Tiber for the first time after the murder of Tiberius. I suddenly hated the sight of its pale brown water, flowing so lively and aloof in front of my eyes as if nothing had happened. The water of the Tiber may fluctuate all the time, but for me, its riverbed had now forever assumed the makeup of a grave.

Just as I saw the Tiber in the course of time through different eyes, so did my point of view shift, each time I looked back on the meetings of Tiberius' election board. At first, when I attended their gatherings, feelings of excitement and pride prevailed. It was a gathering more than worthy of a son of Tiberius Sempronius Gracchus. These men, I thought, would bring my son to reason. After his death, my heart filled with anger and distrust. I became convinced they had used him for their political purposes and their betrayal was one of the key reasons I left Rome. Now, after so many years, my judgment has softened and I view them as the choir leaders in a tragedy.

My son made fatal errors of judgment, but is it too much to state his counselors failed too? They had more power than he did. Scaevola was Consul, Licinius was a Pontifex, as well as a leading Senator, and Appius Claudius was the first speaker of the Senate. What sense did it make to snub the Senate and directly submit the proposals to the People's Assembly if they could not control the Senators?

The clash with my son-in-law had driven Tiberius already a year before his election campaign into the arms of Aemilianus' archenemy. Appius Claudius had earlier on suggested a union between my son and his daughter Claudia, claiming he had reached an agreement about it with my husband before he had married me. However, my son had kept him tactfully at bay, partly on my insistence, but mostly out of respect for the feelings of his former commander.

As everyone else in Rome, Appius had closely followed the downturn in my son's relationship with Aemilianus and a few months after the decision of the Senatorial Committee on Tiberius' treaty, he had grabbed his chance at a banquet of the College of Augurs. Without consulting his wife Antistia or me, he had repeated his suggestion in the presence of all the other Augurs, and Tiberius had openly expressed his feelings for Claudia. I was furious, but after this public display, I had no other choice than to bow my head and pay my official introductory visit to my future in-laws. Standing in his vestibule, Appius welcomed me with a triumphant smirk on his face and he had been smart enough to make sure his wife and Claudia were standing next to him.

As I had predicted, Aemilianus immediately reacted to the announcement with two vengeful letters. In his letter to me, he accused me of betraying the alliance between my husband and him while he had remained faithful to my daughter Sempronia. He predicted the day would come when Appius would not only deceive me but also my son. In his letter to Tiberius, Aemilianus accused him of ingratitude and disloyalty to his former commander.

Not everyone carries an equal amount of moisture in his body and those, who hold a lot of water, are more prone to the mood swings this treacherous element educes. Perhaps Heraclitus is correct and their souls are already full of liquid. Appius was, in my opinion, an extremely watery man with his cold fisheyes and flabby skin. Even if you stood eye to eye with him, he seemed to avoid your gaze. He had the character of a sponge. He sucked up everything, but never seemed to add anything and when he came under pressure, precious little remained. His outbursts of anger, frequently with tears in his eyes, often came across as feigned.

Appius never used a nomenclator, but knew everyone in Rome by name, which secured his reelections. Despite fierce opposition from Aemilianus and his allies, he had managed to realize his dream and become the first speaker of the Senate where his opening sentences drew lots of laughter.

My son-in-law harbored only contempt for him. At his insistence, a Tribune had vetoed a triumphal of Appius since his victory over the Gallic tribe Salassi had not secured the required number of fatalities, but Appius had refused to receive a simple ovation. When they informed him of the Tribune's decision, he came up with a scheme only he could have concocted. He asked his eldest daughter, a vestal virgin, to veto on religious grounds the veto of the Tribune. After that, he still held a triumphal, paid for with his money. The people loved it.

Too much water in Appius, too little in Scaevola. Nothing seemed to flow in him. The quote from the Greek philosopher Hecaton, 'a wise man protects the interests of his family and does nothing contrary to the customs, laws, and institutions of his country,' seemed to have been etched in his dry skin. As it behooved a jurist, the *mos maiorum*[12] was sacred to him and his knowledge of our laws and customs served my son well. Each time Scaevola was able to provide Tiberius with a legal argument based on a precedent. His knowledge and rhetorical skills commanded respect, but I felt little affinity for the man. He hated to take decisions and his Consulship was marred by procrastination and passing on critical decisions to others.

His brother Licinius Crassus was his exact counterpart. He had been adopted by the Licinii, but he easily could have been a natural son of this illustrious family. He regularly quoted the many famous predecessors of this grand house and he enjoyed treating members of families who recently joined the Senate with disdain.

He was arrogant, provocative, intelligent and agile and with his delicate, ivory features one of the most attractive men I have ever met in my life. Licinius was known for his many extramarital affairs, putting a strain on his marriage with the sister of Appius Claudius. With glistening eyes, he portrayed himself as a follower of the Greek philosopher Anniceris. 'The only knowledge a man can collect, comes through sensory experiences, and the highest state that any man can achieve is when he experiences pleasure.' His speeches were famous and attracted thousands of spectators. Like me, he was a great admirer of Praxiteles and the New Greek poetry, which he frequently quoted from memory. When he

---

[12]Unwritten law in ancient Rome based on ancestral customs.

prepared himself for his campaign in Pergamum, he taught himself first the five Greek dialects people spoke there.

His great hero was Titus Quinctius Flamininus, the man who had freed Greece from the Macedonian yoke. Licinius told me the bizarre anecdote that when Titus announced the Greeks were free, the applause which rose was so powerful that it created a hole in the sky and overflying birds tumbled down. Titus, he told me after witnessing a fierce altercation between Tiberius and me, had distributed land among the veterans after the defeat of Hannibal and thanks to their support, he was elected Consul in spite of all opposition against him in the Senate. If I worried about Tiberius, he advised me to read more about Titus.

Diophanes, my son's teacher, our loyal family friend Fulvius Flaccus, and Blossius of Cumae regularly attended the group meetings. Fulvius was a flamboyant, high-spirited young man with a passion for history. He reminded me of my brother Publius but with a healthy body. Like my brother, he evoked the ire of people by his brusque manner of speaking and his impatience, but underneath he had a kind heart. At our first meeting, he praised the writings of my brother. According to him, if my brother had not been ill all the time, he could have become one of our finest orators.

In line with the tradition of his famous lineage, Fulvius had devoted his entire life to the well-being of all the different allies in Italy. According to him, we owed our victory over Hannibal solely to the loyalty of our allies. He constantly reminded everyone that the land distribution should benefit the Latin and Italian veterans too and we only could count on their continuing support if we offered them our civil rights. His knowledge of our bilateral treaties was stunning. It dazzled me when he said there were at least 150 different treaties between Rome and our allies. The Censors, the Praetor Peregrinus, and magistrates from all over Italy visited him regularly for assistance and advice.

Blossius was a guest of the house of Licinius Crassus. He was born to a wealthy family in Capua, one of the cities that had joined Hannibal. Blossius was a zealous democrat, like many spoiled sons of wealthy Greek families in southern Italy. The avowal that no one was above the law was his guiding principle. If the criminal law applied to everyone then so should the right to vote. He was an outspoken supporter of the secret ballot, the election of all religious functions and a fierce opponent of income and age weighted voting. In Athens, he was highly praised for his intellect.

It will be no surprise, I never trusted Blossius. The interest, which my sons expressed for some of his populist ideas to abolish the weighted voting in the Comitia Centuriata, reinforced my suspicion. It may be a trifle, but I have always seen it as a token that his table manners were so bad. The man ate like a ferret with short, vicious bites and each time something fell out of his mouth. Unfortunately, he refused to lie down, but ate upright in a chair so he towered over everyone else. He claimed he digested his food better that way and urged us to do the same; such rubbish. I always tried not to look and stay away from him as far as possible.

His family was known for its anti-Roman sentiments, and I have always suspected the only reason Licinius had invited him as his houseguest was to annoy and provoke his most conservative peers. With his quiet, clean-shaven face without any facial expression, Blossius often reminded me of a Greek masked actor. Later he would rip off his mask and join the slave revolt in Pergamum; the very same war in which his generous host lost his life. Do not ever let anyone tell you that you cannot judge a man's character by the way he eats!

18.

Water and fire, passion and cold calculation, sincere love and fanaticism, the clash between the opposing characters of Tiberius' advisers turned their discussions into mesmerizing events. The discussions often lasted late into the night and were always preceded by copious meals, generously graced with wine, especially if they occurred in the house of Licinius. I could never figure out where he got his wines, but his Mulsum was the best aperitif wine I have ever tasted.

My son's advisers agreed that given the outcome of the debate on Tiberius' treaty and the failure of Gaius Laelius, it was not wise to submit his bill to the Senate. They thought it would be better to gain first the approval of the People's Assembly and then, backed by this popular support, deal with the most influential Senators in person to ease the resistance. The strategy was not without risk, but there had been precedents and the damage would be manageable.

To the annoyance of Tiberius, I brought up the idea to see whether landowners were willing to give up their land voluntarily. I pleaded to hold preliminary consultations with the leaders of the great houses in the Senate and to reinstate the Tributum tax. The proceeds would cover the costs of the establishment of new colonies as well as the purchase of grain, selling it to the needy at a fixed price. My intervention was a bold move, but I had given it beforehand a lot of thought and I still believe it was a sound proposal. But except for Scaevola who had responded approvingly, everyone else had listened in silence, nodded politely, exchanged glances, and then continued where they had left off. From the corner of my eye, I watched Blossius shaking his head in disbelief.

They believed the opposition would come from three sides: from Tiberius' colleague-Tribunes, from leading Senators who ran the risk of losing a lot of land, and from the large landowners of our allies. If these three groups joined forces, all would be lost. The best would be if he got his bill passed within one year. The longer it took, the greater the chance the opposition would unite, and everyone agreed the food shortages required immediate action. As Tribune, Tiberius could lead the People's Assembly, set the agenda, and monitor the pace of proceedings. They drew up lists, just as my husband had always done, of opponents, doubters and proponents. Then they split the tasks. They asked Fulvius to appease the magistrates of our allies by continuing to promote their goal to obtain the Roman civil rights. Scaevola had to soothe the feelings in the Senate by offering earlier examples from his annals of precedents and practices. Claudius and Licinius would try to mollify the worst opponents by proposing to them, with the help of their friends, a number of compensating deals in exchange for their tacit consent. To me, they delegated the delicate task of inviting the wives of affected Senators for dinners, hear them out and report which households were most committed to put up a fight.

I cannot deny they had sweetened the bill with all kinds of mitigating measures. They allowed affected landowners to retain two times 250 iugera for their children. They would reimburse them for the improvements they had added to the land and the land, they were allowed to keep, would be assigned to them on the basis of a permanent lease with the right to sell or sublease. There would be a College of Three to regulate the distribution of the land and take care of the allocation. The presidency would rotate with Tiberius as President in the first year, Appius as second in command, and my son Gaius as third.

19.

As could be expected, my son's election in the People's Assembly was a resounding success. The enthusiasm had been so overwhelming, he was elected first out of his ten colleagues. It is now, in the light of subsequent events, almost unimaginable with how much joy and optimism the people embraced my son's campaign. I can still see the radiant and happy faces of veterans and relatives celebrating his victory in front of the temple of Ceres.

The campaign had been intense and all members of his team and household were exhausted. My son had worked like a horse and in accordance with the advice of his father, he had told himself every morning in front of a mirror, he was the best candidate for the position. He had mobilized his slaves and walked every day over the Forum in his toga candida, informing people about his plans. He had introduced himself to the heads and treasurers of the thirty-five tribes and the opinion leaders within the lower classes. He had approached the numerous associations, clubs, and guilds of Rome. He had entered the thresholds of many homes at dawn and he had been generous with dinners and gifts. His campaign had cost him a small fortune.

At my urgent request, my son had also devoted parts of his speeches to the achievements of his ancestors. He had been keenly aware of my misgivings about his Tribunate and he had outdone himself to appease me. He had reminded a frenzied crowd of the temples built by his family, the founding of the Basilica Sempronia by his father, his father's Tribunate, the triumphs of his forefathers, the colonies they had founded, their generous sharing of the spoils of war, the land they had distributed among the veterans, his ten years of service in the army, and his heroic feats on the walls of Carthage.

20.

Immediately after my son had taken office, he submitted the bill, Lex Sempronia Agriaria, to the People's Assembly and, as I had feared, his opponents responded immediately. They had followed his campaign and election with Argus' eyes and after his submission, they organized, first secretly, then openly, a series of meetings with his colleague-Tribunes.

Their choice fell on Marcus Octavius, one of Tiberius' best friends. Octavius had visited our house many times and he was one of Tiberius' witnesses at his marriage to Claudia. He was a studious, somewhat shy, discreet man, and very wealthy. I have to congratulate my son's enemies. They seem to have sensed a hidden streak in Octavius, I had noticed, when he was with Tiberius and his friends. This young man took himself far too seriously. When they teased him, he could grow very rigid with a white face and pinched lips and he often left, unable to relax or tease back, shunning our house for weeks.

Nevertheless, Octavius had always been full of admiration for Tiberius and when the Senators approached him, he reacted with indignation, refusing to be part of it. But once my son's enemies had made their choice, they did not leave Octavius alone and systematically increased their pressure. Invitation after invitation for dinners with prominent Senators followed during which they repeated all the arguments that were previously raised against Gaius Laelius' plans. In the end, Octavius succumbed.

My son has always claimed he had considered all potential threats, even a veto by one of his colleagues but never by his friend Octavius. Flabbergasted, he went to Octavius' house and tried to persuade him, but after three frustrating meetings, it finally dawned on him; Octavius could and would not pull back. My son countered by withdrawing his original law and releasing a second version in which all forms of compensation were gone. He hoped it offered Octavius a way out, arguing his veto had made the bill worse. But the opponents of my son told Octavius they were not impressed, urging him to ignore it, which he did.

Both ascended now, one after the other, the rostra and held daily contios, trying to convince their audience. It looked like a titanic oratorical struggle. Until that moment, my son had restrained himself, but after Octavius stubbornly persisted in his veto, my son offered him to compensate his losses with a personal payment. This deliberate affront earned him the eternal enmity of Octavius. My son had made it visible how much land he illegally possessed and, in the streets of Rome, Octavius was now depicted as someone who put his personal interests above the needs of the people. My son had openly discredited Octavius' position as Tribune.

Simultaneously, my son deployed the same strategy as his father once had done after a Tribune indicted my husband for high treason. He issued an edict in the Assembly in which he froze all public transactions and ordered the shutdown of the State Treasury. Anyone who would transgress this decree would face prosecution and receive a hefty fine. In the days that followed, I felt as if I was sleepwalking and reliving the worst of all my nightmares. Senators walked up and down the Forum, dressed in mourning gowns and stripped of their rings, yet this time, the Tribune was a son of mine and the Senators were the accused.

Public life in Rome came to a grinding halt. The conflict dominated all discussions on the squares, the street corners, in the public baths and latrines. People, waiting in the barbershops, got into heated arguments; in the tabernae, it came to blows. Combative slogans appeared on the walls of temples. Rumors spread in the public latrines that the enemies of my son had hired assassins. In reaction, my son began to wear a dagger under his toga and he gathered a group of armed followers around him. Many of them were well-trained veterans whose lives he had saved in Spain.

21.

On the day, the people would vote on the veto of Octavius, the first serious clashes took place. Supporters of my son's opponents grabbed some voting baskets. As a result, the proceedings for the tribal allotment went amiss, but since my son was sure of a large majority, he allowed the voting to proceed.

At that moment, two former Consuls intervened. Their unexpected action took place at my request. Tiberius, Gaius, and Claudia would later criticize me – Tiberius in an angry tone in front of my slaves, I cannot help to continue taking offense – for not having warned them about my conversations with these two old friends of my husband. I share their opinion now, I was wrong. I had compromised not only the entire campaign of my son but also his safety. On the other hand, I still believe that if I had managed to bring the parties closer together it would have saved our family and our Republic much grief and harm.

Unfortunately, my friends also turned their intervention into an overtly dramatic scene. They ascended the rostra, sank to the ground in front of my son, clung to his knees and begged him to halt the proceedings. Everyone was astounded to see two former Consuls kneeling before my son, a mere Tribune. Their action both angered and bewildered my son, but, as I had guessed correctly, the soldier in him made it impossible to ignore their Consular authority and he asked them what his next move should be. They answered they were unable to advise him, but they begged him to submit his law to the Senate. Looking at the startled faces of people in the crowd, my son felt he had no other option than to comply with their request. He grudgingly suspended the vote in the Assembly and summoned the Senate.

Here my strategy failed miserably. Despite all my preparations and numerous dinners, my son's enemies smelled victory and they commenced scheduling a series of formal debates, making it clear they would continue to discuss his bill for months. I had lost the war on three fronts. My relationship with Tiberius was now so impaired, he ignored all my concerns and recommendations. His counselors tried to keep me out of their meetings. My friends shunned me and my position within the circle of Matronae was compromised.

Scaevola agreed the obstinate reaction of Octavius was without precedent, but he could not offer a solution. The chosen strategy also prevented other Tribunes from helping my son. They refused to risk a conflict with the Senate on his behalf and their message was that if he knew it all so well, he should solve it himself. Some also secretly hoped he would fail, given his popularity among the people, which had become a threat to their standing.

My son had sworn not to end his campaign, as Gaius Laelius had done, and following the failure in Spain, he now faced the risk of losing his political career as well. Meanwhile, his supporters radicalized, which his enemies had been hoping. His personal attack on Octavius had tarnished the man in the eyes of many and my son was confronted with suggestions to use, if necessary, force to break his resistance. The meetings of his advisers grew grimmer in tone and I noticed a subtle shift in the speeches Scaevola and Appius held in the Senate. They still defended the bill, but they mentioned the name of my son less and less. The distance between him and his counselors grew wider and the first hard dividing lines became visible when the discussion focused on a possible way out: the impeachment of Octavius as Tribune.

22.

I cannot recall who came up with the idea, but my son's advisers were immediately divided. Scaevola and Appius opposed. Fulvius and

Diophanes had major doubts. Licinius and Blossius were the only ones in favor. While Scaevola and Appius even refused to be part of the discussions, Fulvius, Licinius and Diophanes managed to convince my son that he had to build in a number of intermediate steps. On their advice, my son first organized a contio to which he invited Octavius. In front of the public, he clasped his hands together, turned to Octavius, and begged him to lift his veto. Yet Octavius remained adamant.

My son addressed the crowd. Given that he and Octavius were colleagues, my son proposed they both would make their positions available and allow the people to choose between them. If he would lose the vote, he would immediately go into exile. But after Octavius had also rejected this proposal, my son raised his arms. He had done all he could do and now it was up to the people to decide. He dissolved the contio and announced for the next day a meeting of the People's Assembly.

On that morning, he made a last attempt to change Octavius' mind. After half of the votes had been cast, he ordered the counting to stop and walked over to his opponent. He threw his arms around him, kissed him in full view of everyone, begging him not to force his old friend and colleague to take a measure he utterly detested. Moved by his pleas, Octavius got tears in his eyes. He gazed helplessly around; his strength seemed finally broken, but after he had looked into the menacing eyes of the Senators and their supporters, he bowed his head and moved away from my son. The man caused my family and me immense suffering, but at that moment my heart went out to him. Anyone who watched realized there was no turning back and his fate was sealed. With a voice raw with emotion, Octavius challenged my son to do what he had intended to do all along.

After the eighteenth tribe had cast its vote, Octavius was again an ordinary citizen, but he refused to step down from the rostra and clung to it like a drowning man. It was terrible to see how this old family friend had lost all his dignity. To put an end to this shameful situation, my son made the mistake of sending his freedmen to him. To my horror, they began to pull at Octavius. The people were furious with Octavius and crowded around the rostra. I saw my son run forward to avoid further violence. People pulled, pushed, screamed and spat at each other. The Senators and supporters moved in and forced themselves between Octavius and the crowd, spreading their arms to protect him. A slave held bystanders off with his body, but one of my son's supporters gouged out his eyes. The man screamed like a pig in pain. Later my son's enemies would use his mutilation as an excuse that he had initiated the violence. They lifted Octavius into the air and followed by raging supporters, they carried him away as a hero. After they had left, calm slowly returned to the Assembly.

A few days later, my son submitted again his bill where it passed in the Assembly with an overwhelming majority, along with his nomination for a new Tribune, a loyal client of his. This time my son took no chances.

23.

Everyone came out damaged, Octavius, the Senate, the people, my son's advisers, but Tiberius most of all. The whole affair had dealt him a personal blow. Something had snapped. Unlike Gaius, Tiberius had always had a great disdain for fortunetellers. When he discovered them in the army, they were the first to go. Now he visited them almost daily. He avoided my house and the houses of the few friends he had left. He spent most of his time at home, with his veterans, or in the temples of Ceres and Libertas. He began, like Gaius later, to train his body excessively, and in the gym he sought out increasingly tougher opponents.

A man named Titus Annius personally attacked my son in the Senate. Titus enjoyed no reputation as a great orator, but he was a master at holding cross-examinations. The people hated and feared him for his brutal manner of interrogating. In a plenary session of the Senate, he loudly stated Tiberius had committed sacrilege by deposing Octavius. He had violated the office of Tribune. Many Senators began to applaud, the same people who had prompted Octavius' veto. My son walked out of the Curia and convened a People's Assembly to which he summoned Annius, so he could address his allegations in the presence of the people. But Annius, who knew he would not stand a chance in front of this forum, resorted to his proven tactic. He asked my son if he, before they would debate, could pose a question and unfortunately, my son agreed.

Annius asked. "Let's assume you want to remove me from my position. You threaten me; insult me, so I seek the help of one of your colleagues, as any Roman would. Your colleague ascends the rostra to defend me and you lose your patience. Are you going to impeach him too?"

It was a simple, open-ended question, which everyone easily grasped. All listeners turned their gaze on my son in the expectation that their hero, who always seemed to have an answer, would silence this man forever. People moved forward with grins on their faces to hear every word and recount the entire exchange at night to friends and family.

Never in my life did I experience a silence so deafening. My heart sank to my stomach and when I looked at the faces of Appius, Licinius, Scaevola, and Fulvius, I saw they were incredulous too. My son was unable to answer. He looked from face to face in the tense silence, moistened his lips and could not utter one word. The question had taken him completely by surprise. The worst thing was it seemed as if he only realized now what he had done. With a quiver in his voice and visibly upset, he dissolved the Assembly. After he had been gone, everyone began to talk at once. People, who previously had celebrated the deposition of Octavius as a victory, now wondered whether my son had inflicted irreparable harm to the office of Tribune, which would haunt them for years. His popularity had suffered a huge plunge.

Aware of the enormity he had committed, my son drummed up his counselors and worked with them for two days and nights on a long speech. They rewrote his speech many times, mainly due to disagreements between Scaevola and Licinius. It was, in the end, a compromise between the two extremes, polished by Diophanes and Licinius, and enhanced with quotes from my husband. My son managed to deliver it with verve and he won the argument, but in the fragments that I have, I still recognize all the compromises and adjustments they made. Deep in his heart, my son must have felt he had put something irrevocable in motion. To this day, I hear in his speech most of all an attempt to convince himself.

"A Tribune is sacred and inviolable because he is consecrated to the people and is a champion of the people. If, then, he would turn around, wrong the people, harm its power, and rob it of the privilege of voting, he has by his own acts deprived himself of his honorable office by not fulfilling the conditions on which he received it. For otherwise there would be no meddling with a Tribune, even though he should try to demolish the Capitol or set fire to the naval arsenal. If a Tribune does these things, he is a bad Tribune; but if he annuls the power of the people, he is no Tribune at all. Is it not, then, a monstrous thing that a Tribune should have power to incarcerate a Consul, while the people cannot deprive a Tribune of his power when he employs it against the very ones who bestowed it? For Consul and Tribune alike are elected by the people. And surely the Kingly office, besides comprehending in itself every civil function, is also consecrated to the Deity by the performance of the most solemn religious rites; and yet Tarquin was expelled by the city for his wrong-doing, and because of one man's insolence, the power which had founded Rome and descended from father to son was overthrown.

Again, what institution at Rome is as holy and venerable as that of the virgins who tend and watch the undying fire? And yet, if one of these breaks her vows, she is buried alive; for when they sin against the gods, they do not preserve that inviolable character which is given them for their service to the gods. Therefore, it is not fair that a Tribune who wrongs the people should retain that inviolable character which is given him for service to the people, since he is destroying the very power, which is the source of his own power. And surely, if it is right for him to be made Tribune by a majority of the votes of the tribes, it must be even more right for him to be deprived of his Tribunate by a unanimous vote."

24.

Once they had lost the battle over the veto, my son's enemies resorted to another proven tactic. Under the energetic leadership of my nephew Serapio, whose hostility against my son had degenerated into a public feud after the death of my sister, they argued that the treasury was almost empty and that they could not fund my son's program. They lowered his daily allowance to nine sesterces and deprived him of tents for his assistants, which slowed down the mapping of the public land.

For fear they would blame him for the delays, my son made sure to keep the veterans informed about the obstruction he faced, but his statements in the contios also aroused their emotions and they began to detect conspiracies in all sorts of random events.

After a friend of Tiberius died, a rumor immediately spread, he was poisoned. His body was laid on a bier and a large crowd gathered to pay their last respects. After the fire had been lit, bystanders watched in horror as the belly of the man snapped open. So much fluid and pus flowed out that the wood began to sizzle, extinguishing the fire. They had to build a new pyre, convincing many he had been murdered.

My son had given little credence to the story of the poisoning, but instead of openly contradicting it to calm things down, he used the incident to stir up the people even more. He appeared, accompanied by a pregnant Claudia and their two sons, a day later in mourning at the Forum, begging a furious crowd to take care of them if he was killed. His theatrical performance sickened me.

The obstruction of his enemies prevented my son from providing his veterans with land, but, truth be told, he had also never realized how much support they needed before they could go back to farming. If they were lucky, the land contained a small house, but to start, they also needed some simple agricultural tools, a few slaves, a pair of oxen, some furniture, and the first load of seed.

With only a few months to go before the end of his Tribunate, this time there seemed to be no way out, and no one in Rome harbored any illusions about the fate of my son when he, like Octavius, had become an ordinary citizen. His supporters saw this too and the whispering campaign, spread by his enemies, began to bear fruit. 'Perhaps there was some truth to the rumors. Maybe he was aiming for an autocracy and was not the man they could count on. What did he achieve? No veteran had received a plot of land.'

25.

My son Gaius had celebrated his brother's election as Tribune but soon after, he had left to serve under Aemilianus in Spain on his campaign against Numantia. I have always wondered if his absence in Rome had been a blessing or a curse. He might have convinced his brother to pursue a less radical course, but I doubt it, and it is more likely he would have perished alongside him.

I remember I read his letters from Spain, amid all the tumult in Rome, with a heavy heart. Because of the break with Tiberius, the relationship between Gaius and my son-in-law was cold and aloof, but Gaius too expressed his admiration for the strategic insights of Aemilianus. His reporting made it clear that my son-in-law would soon be able to hold a second triumph, which did not bode well for Tiberius. It would demote his earlier treaty with the Numantians even further.

Gaius described how Aemilianus delayed moving his camp near Numantia until his army was well trained and ready to face combat. After his arrival, he began methodically to burn all the food in the fields in the surrounding area of Numantia or seize it for his own use. He attacked nobody, but isolated the Numantians by countering attacks from allied tribes. Whenever he had averted an ambush, he would pull back and pursue no one, keeping his army intact and unharmed. In the course of time, he strengthened it with fresh troops and twelve elephants from Africa.

Following the reinforcement, he began the construction of seven major forts in a wide circle around the city. At the same time, he offered other Celtiberian tribes treaties and expanded his army with their auxiliaries. Once the seven forts were finished, Aemilianus built a connecting wall fortified with smaller towers close to each other. Whenever the Numantians attempted a breakout, the guards in the towers warned Aemilianus with red flags or torches, so he could quickly counter the raids with an elite unit of his cavalry.

The river Durius interrupted his wall and the Numantians used this waterway at night to supply themselves. Aemilianus built two towers on both sides of the river from which heavy beams were lowered into the river. They tied the beams together and equipped them with knives and spearheads. The turbulent flow of the river caused the trunks to dance wildly up and down, cutting off the last supply line for the Numantians.

Finally, catapults and ballistae were brought into position. By this time, Aemilianus' army numbered sixty thousand men.

After eight months of siege, famine struck the town. After all the inventories were exhausted, people first dismembered and cooked the dead who had died of starvation, but in the end, the stronger also assaulted the weakest. Every night, a few Numantians would attempt to scale the wall, but they were often caught and, by interrogating them, Aemilianus remained well informed about the increasingly dire circumstances in the city. After he had heard enough, he did not kill them, but sent them back, so their remaining inventories would be depleted quicker. The Numantians finally sent a delegation offering a truce, but he refused to sign a treaty. He demanded a full and unconditional surrender. The delegation returned empty-handed and its members were killed by their fellow citizens.

Because of the events in Rome, Gaius did not witness the eventual surrender of Numantia. As soon as the news of Tiberius' death reached him, he left his post and hurried back to Rome. From descriptions of his friends, I understood that the sight of the survivors must have been horrible. Many of these once proud, tall men and women were so emaciated that they could barely stand or walk. Their bodies and their clothes gave off an awful stench. They were filthy with long nails and matted hair full of vermin. Most gruesome had been the nervous glance with which the survivors avoided the gaze of our soldiers; the ashamed, guilt-ridden look of people who had eaten human flesh. While they were marched away, many of them committed suicide or killed each other. When the last survivors reached the borders of their beloved country, they fell to the ground and kissed the earth. Some gathered clods of soil and hid them in the folds of their robes.

Aemilianus' triumph, which we all had feared, turned out to be a shameful affair. The months-long siege had robbed the Numantians of everything of value and there remained precious little for the veterans.

Each soldier received only seven denarii, partly paid for by Aemilianus himself, which did not stop the families of veterans expressing their anger and dissatisfaction when his chariot passed them through the streets of Rome, calling him a liar and a cheat. Aemilianus had fifty Numantians run along his triumphal procession; He had sold the other four thousand in advance as slaves to reduce costs. Like Carthage, Numantia was razed to the ground, and my son added the honorific Numantius to his name. In the beginning, it made me nauseous to hear about it.

26.

Scaevola would later defend his final break with Tiberius on the basis that Tiberius had not notified him beforehand, as the ruling Consul, when my son broke the news to the People's Assembly about the will of the King of Pergamum. Tiberius had not only defiled his Consular dignity, but also breached their personal trust.

The envoy of Pergamum had first come to my son as the patron of his country. Given that, the King of Pergamum had designated the Roman people as his heir and not the Roman State, my son issued that morning an edict, placing a claim on the vast resources of that rich country. He also appointed himself as the executor of the will. He announced that he would use the funds to finance all the investments needed to house and equip the veterans. Finally, he declared he would propose to the People's Assembly to authorize the College of Three to decide on all disputes with the allies. The veterans were delirious with joy and the news spread immediately throughout Italy.

The Senate met in an emergency session on the same day. Many Senators, including members of supporting families, were enraged. All my son's old friends now openly distanced themselves from him. "Never in our centuries old history had a Tribune," they fumed, "threatened the power of the Senate so profoundly." By appointing himself as the executor of the will, my son had struck the Senate at its very heart. Hundreds of laws had to be drafted and adopted. People had to be appointed to city boards. Concessions had to be auctioned for the collection of local taxes, of tolls and the exploitation of the silver and gold mines. Until now, the Senate had performed all these tasks. For the first time in our history, the Equestrians, the publicani, and the money traders had to negotiate with a Tribune instead of the Senate. In one stroke, my son had become more important than the entire Senate.

Criticism erupted from all sides and the wildest rumors surfaced. His opponents succeeded in convincing nearly all Senators that my son had fallen under the influence of radical Greek democratic ideas; the same populist ideas which made the lives of many Roman authorities in the Greek cities so difficult. They mentioned the names of Blossius and Diophanes as the culprits. They claimed that my son had said that the People's Assembly could make, from now on, equally well, if not better, all the decisions the Senate had previously taken. Pompeius claimed he had heard, as Tiberius' neighbor, that the envoy from Pergamum had also brought a diadem and a purple robe from the estate of King Attalus. He had offered these to my son because he had understood that Tiberius would soon be the King of Rome, accusing my son for the first time of seeking a kingship, a mortal sin. His character was criticized, along with the pernicious influence he had on the people. My son behaved as if he was my father and the Republic his personal property, while he had achieved nothing in his life but a shameful treaty. All the Senators stamped their feet in approval after Quintus Caecilius Metellus had described how the people extinguished their torches to hide a party, when my husband returned home in the evening at the time he was a Censor, but when my son moved through Rome at night, candles were lit everywhere. My son was an utter disgrace.

At the same time, the Senators could not do much more than to swallow the decisions he took and bide their time until his Tribunate had ended. After the first funds out of the estate of Pergamum had been released, he engaged many slaves, speeding up the process of mapping and allocating the public land.

27.

His most loyal veterans were the first to urge my son to stand for re-election as Tribune. In their eyes, all the obstruction had prevented him carrying out his law to the full. The crisis in Rome and the country continued unabated and he ran too much risk without the protection of the office. He would be accused of high treason and face a trial in the Comitia Centuriata where his enemies held a majority.

Only Blossius still supported my son. Licinius and Appius vehemently opposed; Fulvius had major doubts. Scaevola no longer attended the deliberations. A fierce debate erupted in which Licinius, Appius, and Fulvius acknowledged all my son's arguments: yes, there had been precedents, Tribunes had been re-elected in the distant past; recently his brother-in-law was, against the law, re-appointed as Consul, and the Assembly was entitled to take any decision it wanted. Nevertheless, he would stir up so much resistance; it would destroy everything he had fought for. They urged him to transfer the execution of his law to a new Tribune, promising him that they would do everything in their power to protect him from any litigation. But my son declined their offer. The next day, he informed the People's Assembly that he would run for re-election. His announcement was received with roaring cheers.

With this step, the circle of his advisers broke down completely. Scaevola went so far as to attack my son in the Senate while Appius, Licinius, and Fulvius remained silent. No longer hindered by their assistance and advice, my son launched a frontal attack on the Senate. Later on, Gaius would go much further, so Tiberius' proposals seem less radical now, but at the time, I was speechless. It had been nothing less than a declaration of war. My son promised the People's Assembly not only an accelerated implementation of his land distribution, but he also proposed to limit the period of active service in the army, and above all to grant all of our allies in Italy Roman citizenship.

The reaction was swift and fierce. His enemies agreed that, if they did not thwart his reappointment now, they ran the risk of more reelections and, with the majority he held in the Assembly, he would continue confronting them with new assaults. They accused him of aiming to establish a permanent constituency of new voters with his proposal of granting citizenship rights to our allies. All of his fellow Tribunes turned against him. His isolation in the Senate was now complete, and I was so rattled by all his proposals that I was unable to defend him against the angry reactions of my friends and fellow Matronae.

When my son brought his reelection proposal to the People's Assembly for approval, his adversaries gathered all their supporters from the surrounding voting units, confident that many of Tiberius' supporters could not come to Rome because they were in the midst of the harvest.

It caught my son by surprise. With so many opponents present in the Assembly, he was suddenly in danger of losing the vote. Alarmed, his friends sent family members to all the voting units in the country to alert them. In the meantime, they stalled the voting process in the Assembly by giving long speeches in which they attacked his opponents. The deliberations dragged on. Finally, the meeting had to be postponed until the next morning.

When I returned late in the evening from the Forum, I received an unannounced visit from Claudius. He seemed very agitated. He did not want to eat something, a cup of diluted wine was enough, and he declined to enter to the reception hall and sit down. He had left his slaves outside, but I refused to be alone with him. This was a very unusual visit and I did not trust it. My slaves must have sensed it too. Three of my slaves positioned themselves in a corner, and I knew they had alerted Simo. He followed our conversation behind a curtain, accompanied by several of my guards.

After the usual compliments, Appius opened the attack. "Why do you hate your son," was his opening line, "and why do you hate me, my daughter, and my family?"

He reacted to my angry denial with a nod and continued his monologue, while avoiding to look me in the eye. I could only half-listen to him, preoccupied with the question of what could be lurking behind his inappropriate visit.

"We included Tiberius lovingly in our midst despite your opposition," he continued. "We have embraced and supported his program, but every time you thwarted our plans with your relentless meddling. Everyone in Rome knows you disapprove of his politics. Well, you will have your way. I do not expect Tiberius to be re-elected tomorrow. Through your actions, I am now forced to choose between your son and his program and the Republic requires me to choose the latter."

His last remark suddenly made it clear. He is going to betray my son, flashed through my mind. Aemilianus had been right! He is here to save his miserable skin. I stepped closer to him, seething with anger, which startled him. All the puffed-up air with which he had entered my house was gone and I realized how much I detested this man. I grimaced, which unsettled him even further. He turned away towards the hallway, stating he would leave Rome this evening. He did not wish to witness, what he dubbed to be, the result of my intrigues.

The moment he left, it occurred to me that he knew the Senators were planning something terrible, and a wave of panic struck me. "We need to go to Licinius," I stammered, "he is the only man who can save Tiberius."

I met with fierce resistance from Simo, but in the end, we went to the streets where my litter got stuck at the foot of the Aventine. There were thousands of people in the streets, carrying food and torches. Since the fall of Carthage, I had never seen so many people at night in Rome. Everyone we encountered spoke about rumors the enemies of my son were gearing up to murder him. There was no way we could get through and, to Simo's relief, I gave the order to return home where I spent the night fully awake.

The next morning, my son's supporters, who had rushed to Rome during the night, filled the Forum. While I was going down from the Aventine, people greeted and welcomed me from all sides. I heard the Senate had withdrawn into the Temple of Fides – as if Rome had been invaded by an enemy! It was a stirring sight at the Forum, people greeting one another with enthusiasm, slapping each other on the shoulders, embracing, singing songs. The atmosphere was alive with solidarity, determination, and hope.

My son arrived late. Only afterward I heard that he had encountered some bad omens after leaving his house. When he had hesitated to proceed, Blossius had mocked him, telling bystanders what a disgrace it would be if a bunch of crows had stopped the grandson of my father.

The voting in the Assembly was a disaster from the start. My son's opponents pushed through the crowd, trying to grab the voting baskets. Fighting broke out, with people pushing and pulling. Fulvius, who had left the temple of Fides to warn my son, climbed to a spot, where my son could see him. He waved his arms and my son ordered the crowd to let him pass. Fulvius told my son that his opponents were ready to kill him since they could not convince Scaevola to take action. They had assembled a large party of slaves and followers near the Forum, prepared to move in at a given signal.

My son informed his followers and everyone around him raised their tunics. They tore the maces out of the hands of the Lictors and passed them around. My son's supporters attacked the hostile Tribunes who fled the Assembly. In the great uproar, people who had been standing further away had been unable to hear my son. They called out to him and he held his hand above his head, signaling his life was in danger. When his enemies saw the gesture, they ran back to the temple of Fides. Later, Licinius told me they spread the lie that my son had asked for a crown, deposed all the Tribunes and appointed himself as a Tribune without an election. The deceits pushed the Senators to revolt. Serapio exclaimed Scaevola should act to protect the State against my son. Scaevola yelled back he would not be the one to use violence first without a fair trial; but if Tiberius had called upon the people to pass an unlawful resolution, he would declare it non-binding. At this, Serapio sprang to his feet and proclaimed, "Now the Consul has betrayed the Republic! Let every man follow me who wants to maintain law and order!" He threw his toga over his head and ran out of the temple, followed by a throng of Senators.

I still see them descending from the Capitol, Serapio at the front, followed by the Senators with their togas thrown over their left arms, wielding pieces of furniture taken from the temple. Like a massive spear, they drove through the crowd, straight for my son. Panic stricken, people scurried in all directions. A stampede bore down through the crowd and those who could not move were trampled. Men charged forward, screaming, hitting out with sticks and maces. In this rampage, I saw my son stumble, fall, rise, and fall again. He disappeared from my sight under a frenzy of arms, sticks, clubs, and table legs, raining down on him. The Tribune Publius Satyreius later bragged that he had been the first to deal my son a blow to his face with a table leg. Lucius Rufus dealt the second.

I fainted. My slaves carried me, still unconscious, to the house of Licinius on the Palatine. Later, I returned to the Forum; but lictors and followers of the Senators blocked my way. I saw my son from afar. He lay among many other bodies, his white toga covered with blood. When I begged for his body, they shouted me down and shoved me away. Fearing for my safety, Simo forced me to return home.

The city remained turbulent all night. Priests closed the doors of the temples. Enraged veterans set fire to public buildings. On the squares, my son's followers fought with organized gangs of the Tribunes and the Senators, both sides attacking each other with stones and clubs. The city was choked with smoke and thrumming with the sounds of buildings crashing, the stamp of marching boots and the echoes of people screaming. Apparently, lists had been prepared and throughout the whole night men were dragged out of their houses. Some were taken to isolated places where chest-high barrels awaited them, stuffed with vipers. After their deaths, their heads were displayed on long tables at the Forum as if they had been dangerous criminals.

To honor them in the name of my son, I forced myself to visit this portrait gallery of our dying Republic. I stopped in front of each one of them and prayed. I recognized some of them; loyal veterans who had worshipped my son and fought for our country for many years. Their frozen faces were slimy with spit from passersby, and the horrors they had endured in their final moments were still visible in strange grimaces. To our enemies, these men represented the past, but I had the feeling, I was facing those who had already witnessed our future.

PART 3
ALMA MATER
(NOURISHING MOTHER)

Roman Fresco, Stabiae
1st Century BCE

1.

There are days so serene that it seems as if the entire Gulf of Baiae bathes in the light of a Greek temple. The sea reflects the sunlight as a metalworker's anvil, matte glazed in the iron morning, fiery in the copper afternoon, and smoldering in the golden evening. The high ebullient rays of sunlight allure me into playing with my granddaughter a poorly matched game, which one of us can identify another blue-green mountain ridge in the far distance, until even she lost count. On days like these, I find complete solace in the memory of my sons. If I had the power to give them back one day here on earth, it would be a day like this.

My granddaughter Sempronia surprised me this morning on my terrace. A joyful infringement of the house rule, doubtless a result of the fact that her mother has gone for a few days to friends in Naples.

Of the three months my daughter-in-law Licinia had promised me, one has passed, and I have been counting my blessings every day. It is so gratifying to surround someone with care and such joy to see how she has flourished. The dark blue circles under her eyes have disappeared. A healthy pink-red glow graces her cheeks. The grief lines around her mouth are almost gone, and there is a bounce in her step again. Sometimes, in the homely intimacy, she takes off her mourning clothes, which she continues to wear to defy the prohibition of the Senate, and changes into a diaphanous, moss green robe, with her raven black hair trussed in a golden net, tiny curls cavorting on her forehead, and two golden earrings. It makes her look so lovely and pretty. Gaius often called her "my little water nymph."

Wrapped in a black amictus, my granddaughter gazed at the sea. As if in deep thought, she rested her chin on her hand and her forehead showed a shade of a childlike frown. She sat slightly bent over in a nearly perfect imitation of me, but I was astonished to recognize also my mother in her. As soon as she saw me, she straightened her back and blushed deeply.

She had surrounded herself with her dolls and, in an attempt to by-pass her sudden shyness, she invited me to look at them together. When I bent over to pick one up, she raised her hand and cautiously stroked my cheek in an affectionate gesture. Her spontaneous gesture startled her a bit and I pretended I had not felt it. There are times when I feel more affection for this child of Gaius than I have ever felt for my daughter Sempronia. Licinia told me my granddaughter had first attacked her when the news of Gaius' death had reached their home, and only after-ward she had started to cry. I immediately recognized myself in her irate reaction.

What I like about her is her doggedness. My daughter Sempronia was always too much impressed by the reaction of others. My criticism affects this child too, but she is ultimately not afraid of me and she re-mains very much herself. She has inherited from her grandmother the temper and volatility of the Claudii, but it is mitigated and enriched with intellectual prowess of the Mucii, and the compassion of the Sempronii. She is very restless and seems to be in need of a constant flow of external stimuli. As soon as the world around her falls flat and quiet, she descends into a morose, dark mood. She has still a long way to go. Much will de-pend on her future partner. I already receive requests from many fami-lies, but we have time. She is barely eight years old.

2.

The intimate encounter with my granddaughter recalled memories of the day when my mother, prior to my marriage, helped me – as I later did Sempronia – to bid farewell to my many dolls, rattles, marbles, and golden bulla. My dolls were like my children, but they belonged now to our house gods. I found the final goodbye difficult. My mother allowed me to hold each doll close to me, speak softly to it, caress its cheeks, kiss its lips, and put it away in the chest, but it is only now, at the end of my life, that I fully grasp the meaning of the ceremony. Marriage demands to say goodbye to your childhood and its symbols, but parting with my dolls was also my first exercise in paying a final farewell to my children. My collection was famous and envied by many. I possessed elaborate dolls made from cloth, ivory, and wood. Some had movable wooden arms and legs. I could make them walk, as I later guided my children in making their first hesitant, jerky steps.

My bulla contained a note with blessings from my mother and a small crystal rock, cast in gold. By entrusting my bulla and its contents to the house gods, I also lost the rainbows I captured with the crystal on sunny days. Sometimes I held it in front of my most beautiful ivory dolls so their eyes seem to come alive. I called my crystal petrified water. The rainbows reminded me of my swimming in the sea during a downpour when Iris pulled with her dewy wings high above me a bridge between heaven and sea.

Gaius is my only child whose passing I did not witness. With the others, I was present when their souls left their bodies. Half a year after the birth of Gaius, a plague took four of my children away, one after the other. Gradually the disease degraded their lovely features. In their restless sleep, the shadow of death became already visible around their eyes and open mouth. The incessant crying, the unquenchable thirst, the burning pain in the tongue and throat, the pimples and blisters on arms, legs, and genitals, the convulsions, the bent legs, the unnatural stand of their feet, the slow dying of fingers and toes, the eyes clouded with a milk-white fog without a spark of life, I hated all these signs and, above all, my ability to predict what the next stage would be.

A wife of a Centurion told me once that when she had arrived in Rome after a long journey and placed the urn with the ashes of her husband in their family grave, she felt as if she was losing her husband again. This was how I felt when I watched the leaden coffin with the feather-light body of my child sink into the ground. Of the nine children I lost, five were daughters. All of them had reached the age in which they could express their wishes. I have always made sure that their faces were turned toward their favorite doll and that they carried their bulla in their hands, with a crystal rock and note from me.

3.

Ah, that incredible moment when the first smile breaks through on the face of a newborn. In the first months, I just could not get enough of it. Each time I needed to take my child in my arms and watch it reappear.

Tenderness and discipline, those were my keywords. Tenderness embraces; discipline empowers. A child needs both. Tenderness caresses the soul. A child that has been treated with kindness radiates self-confidence. It loves its body in a natural way and it will never suffer Narcissus' fate. Only a child who loves himself is capable of loving others; a vital precondition to exert authority in a natural manner. I have seen children due to lack of affection change in a years' time from an open spontaneous individual into a hardened and gruff child. These children grow out to be resentful adults, who always hanker, consumed inside by a hunger that can never be stilled. They are in constant need of distractions and since nothing fulfills them, their yearning only intensifies. An excessive craving for eating, drinking, and debauchery overwhelms them. I was disgusted when the ever-growing number of binge parties among young Equestrians in Rome gave rise to the emergence of the abhorrent practice of induced vomiting so they could fill an empty stomach again with the next course. Fortunately, my house displayed enough civility and self-control that my table remained free from it, but I was less successful to prevent people wrapping secretly half of a meal in their napkin and carry it home.

Docendo discimus, by teaching, we learn. Only if parents spend enough time to teach their children, then their offspring will gain the inner strength and mental depth needed to play a leading role in our society. My daughter Sempronia was one of my first children and I never spent enough time with her. I was too busy with my husband's career. A friend, who felt sorry for her, compared her life to a seed of grain, pulverized between two millstones, my cousin Aemilianus and me. One of the real benefits of aging is that I realized immediately afterward that my passionate denial proved she had a point, although I still resent the way she phrased it.

For some reason, Mother Nature has been less kind for my daughter than for my sons who were both good-looking. I still have trouble recognizing in her face the features of my husband and me. The disease, which struck her around her fourteenth year, was so serious that I feared for her life. After her birth, I discovered her genitals were deformed and her marriage with my cousin Aemilianus remained childless. It gave Aemilianus a reason to divorce her, but he never did.

I always lost my patience with Sempronia. Her fragile condition and meek nature provoked an irritation in me that I was never able to control. She allowed everyone to bully her – her slaves, her freedmen, her friends, but above all, the natural mother of Aemilianus, Papiria, with whom she did not even have a proper daughter-in-law relationship. I found Papiria an insufferably vain and dim-witted woman.

In my annoyance with her inability to resist this woman, I once snarled at Sempronia, in front of everyone, on the day we were supposed to serve our freedmen and slaves, that she had better sit on the other side of the table. With a face turned ashen, she rose to move over, after which I yelled at her, if she had lost her mind. She ran off sobbing in tears. I have never forgiven myself. I was wrong in every aspect, but when I think back to that incident, I still get angry.

4.

A good education encompasses two fundamental aspects of the human existence, action and leisure. Both aspects reflect war and peace. I share the view that Sparta hastened its demise by its one-sided emphasis on action and war. In education, as in everything, the golden middle offers the best guidance.

I have strictly maintained the principle that children under the age of five years should not receive any serious teaching, avoiding the risk of hindering the growth of their body with too many burdens. Games and pleasure should prevail in their first years. As a child, I excelled in handling the yoyo and the toll, a pastime I still enjoy at my private terrace. I made sure my household was blessed with all kinds of balls, hoops, marbles and, above all, the rattle. I consider the rattle as a perfect toy. It allows small children to satisfy their natural need for movement and noise, and it prevents them from breaking things in the household. At the same time, I must admit there have been moments in which its simultaneous use by several children running around in my house, combined with the noise of the coppersmiths, drove me to the brink of insanity.

My mother left me too young alone in the company of slaves and I made sure this did not happen with my sons. Slaves and freedmen exhibit a tendency to involve children in the development of skills they themselves had to master to survive. However, it is not our role to make things. We have the responsibility to lead. Sometimes I wonder whether I have been strict enough. With Tiberius, the fight was about having too much physical exercise. If I had given him the chance, he would have developed the excessive muscular body of a gladiator. I insisted he spent as much time reading and writing as boxing and wrestling, his two favorite sports.

With Gaius, I had to ensure that his penchant for artisanship, in which he resembled his father, did not result in the fervor of a workman. I allowed Simo to teach Gaius general knowledge of the mathematical principles of mechanical tools such as winches, cranes, water screws, and ballistae. This knowledge served my son well in the army and helped him to negotiate the building costs of his roads and new granaries with the contractors. However, I made him stop when Simo began to teach him how to build the devices. In a charming attempt to bypass my veto, Simo took Gaius to a beekeeper to learn how bees build their honeycombs. Gaius was delighted.

Diophanes pointed out to me that when children enter the world, they are like spectators in a theater. They love the players or the stage sets they see for the first time. It is, therefore, important to protect young children against anything that might hamper the proper development of their sense of decorum like explicit images of human sexuality and foul language. A nearly impossible task to achieve on the Aventine and one of the reasons I spent the summer outside Rome at our residence in Praeneste.

Writing, reading, drawing, music, and physical exercise are at the core of what children must learn. These lessons should serve to train them, but in the case of drawing, music, and gymnastics, it is vital that these activities do not lead to an artisanal preoccupation. Children need to learn to draw sufficiently to develop an appreciation for our sculptures and paintings. The teaching of music is beneficial to train their ears in euphony and to appreciate the old songs of our ancestors. Gymnastics is necessary for the body to flourish in a natural, well-balanced way. Together, these activities should offer a harmonious, enjoyable pastime, thereby avoiding that they assume the character of relaxation after work. Rest after work is indispensable, but it is essential that children develop an appreciation for leisure not as a kind of counterbalance, but as a life-enriching experience worth pursuing for its own sake.

After my sons had sufficiently mastered reading and writing, they were ready to move to the next stage in their education. They were tutored in the life histories of their ancestors, the history of Rome, in delivering speeches, and in the teaching of good manners so that they would be able to exude authority and dignity in a natural way.

5.

Only he who speaks the language of a people understands its genius. My search in Italy, Greece, and Asia to find good teachers for my sons, brought me on the trail of the same bunglers that Plato had criticized. I came across sophists who promised everything. My sons would be able to look forward to a brilliant future. The only thing I needed to do was deposit a prepayment and the rest would follow by itself.

Of all the teachers, I have appointed for my sons, Diophanes was by far the best. During our first meeting, I could easily see how his big, beautiful, dark eyes, framed by the silvery-white hair, would capture the hearts and minds of my sons. He had such a warm, soothing voice. When he spoke, all chill vanished into the air. He came from the town of Mytilene, the beautiful port of my beloved island of Lesbos where his father owned a flourishing business in the export of amphorae, textiles, and terracotta. The man had exempted his son from his family business duties and Diophanes had written at a young age a great work about the lyric poet Alcaeus, whom we both loved. The moment he mentioned it, I knew he was the right man. He was an expert in the politics of Greek City-States – "snake pits" – and equaled Licinius in tactical skills.

Diophanes often called Tiberius his Greek Roman and Gaius his Roman Greek. As the final part of their teaching, Diophanes developed, together with them, a style of rhetoric in line with their personalities. For

Tiberius the quiet, graceful, albeit, given his age, somewhat pompous form of a Roman statesman. He taught him to hold his torso straight and tall with no excessive movements, pacing back and forth in a controlled, manly fashion. To keep his audience on its toes, he learned to insert timely breaks while holding the gaze of those who had listened approvingly and were waiting for him to deliver his next punch line.

For Gaius, he developed a lively and dynamic style. Many regarded Gaius as a reformer of our Roman speech making. His enemies compared him to the Greek demagogue Cleon. Like Cleon, Gaius walked briskly back and forth over the rostra. I found it far too theatrical, but the people loved it. Thank god, he refrained from exposing a bare thigh and slamming it from time to time as Cleon had done to the utter delight of his Athenian hotheads. Gaius commenced his speeches in a natural, conversational tone, gradually raising the pitch, but to avoid his voice becoming shrill, Diophanes introduced the deployment of a flute player, which I thought was brilliant. As soon as the tone of my son's voice became too high, his slave blew on his ivory flute. My son calmed down immediately and lowered his voice to match the tone of the flute.

6.

I recognized in both my sons all the good and bad traits of our ancestors. They displayed already at an early age the arrogance and willpower of the Cornelii, the tough decisiveness of the Aemilii and the wit and warmth of the Sempronii. Because it appears to have no consequence, it is tempting to allow a child to indulge in some of its bad habits and with hindsight; I could have done more to restrain them. Competition is beneficial among boys, but I fear my sons were not very good in taking their losses. They wanted to excel in everything and constantly challenged their rivals. Especially Tiberius could be so intense and rigid. If he felt, I had treated him unfairly, the conflicts immediately ran high, and a fight over principles soon overtook the initial cause. It was exhausting. His eyes became wild, his mouth twisted in a frenzy and afterward he wrapped himself for days in a cloud of self-pity and grief. His anger attacks reminded me of my father. I hate to say it, but he and his nemesis Octavius had more in common than he ever would have been willing to admit.

Gaius had an eye for beauty, but sometimes he indulged himself in extravagant behavior and his expensive purchases got him later into trouble. He had a sharp tongue and if he had outwitted someone with a hurtful response, a triumphant grin appeared on his face, infuriating people. From early on he was an incorrigible prankster with a knack for finding someone's most vulnerable spot. Pregnant slaves discovered in the morning feathers of an owl in their bedroom. Nuts to ward off the lightning were mysteriously replaced by black stones and he frightened illiterate slaves with werewolf claw scratches on the outside walls or with a nest of black cats in the utility rooms. It forced me many times to restore order in the household by making him apologize or clean up the mess he created. I do believe he often felt sorry when confronted with the anxieties he caused, but we all knew it he would do it again if the temptation became too strong.

When my sons grew up, their loving attention for me formed a gift, I had never expected. The affection with which Gaius held my hands, gave me the feeling to be the object of a loving attention, I had thought only I could show. They also began to observe and analyze me. It is the ironic, if not tragic fate of every parent that one day her children will return with interest all the things she has taught them with the best of her intentions. My sons expressed opinions about me, criticized me and tried to impose guidelines based on the very principles, I had urged them to follow. I miss Tiberius and Gaius as my sons, but I miss them perhaps the most as my guardians, and I treasure now the moments in which they thoroughly annoyed me with all their comments and lectures as my fondest memories.

PART 4
CORRUPTIO OPTIMI PESSIMA
(CORRUPTION OF THE BEST IS THE WORST)

Cornelia and the Grachii
Drawing by H. Vogel

1.

When I look back to the years between Tiberius' death and Gaius Quaestorship in Sardinia, they pass me like the rush of an autumnal storm. So many events crowd together in such a short period.

In the days when Claudia and Gaius spent all night ringed by hundreds of torchbearers, scouring the banks of the Tiber for any trace of Tiberius, my body was a prison to me. It was one of the rare times when I cursed the fact that I was born a woman. As those days passed, I was buffeted back and forth by feelings of hate and a banal inability to remember what had happened. Tiberius had awaited the arrival of the Senators in a state of near-paralysis, and for days after his death that same paralysis seemed to hold me in its grip. In endless conversation with my friends, we tried to reconstruct every event and arrive at a coherent whole, but all our attempts ended in bickering about who had said and done what, when, and where, and afterward, we felt we were drifting further apart.

Many times, I have been accused of inciting my sons to violence, but not on the one occasion, I truly considered it. The blood of my lineage was boiling in my veins and many of Tiberius' supporters were waiting in the alleyways of Rome to take their vengeance. They gathered in front of my house, prayed together, held speeches, and carved curses on temple walls and tablets, which they stuck between the crevices. When I stepped outside, men and women huddled around me. They embraced me, touched my hair and held my hands, calling me their Bona Dea! Strangely enough, all these expressions of grief and anger evoked feelings of consolation, but also of loneliness. The tumult and the anger in the streets of Rome were so great I feared our country was on the brink of a civil war. Everywhere I went, I urged the people to remain calm, but my speeches had little effect and I read in the eyes of my son's followers mostly disappointment and bitterness. They perceived my refusal to support them in their anger as a betrayal.

To maintain my own sanity, I silently nursed a daydream full of mayhem in which I merged the characters of my father, my husband, and Tiberius into one nameless hero. This alter ego was every bit as ruthless and unflinching as my father, as shrewd and diplomatic as my husband, and as passionate as my son. He carried through all the measures Tiberius had envisaged, but this time with a sword in his hand. He settled the score with my son's murderers, brought order to Rome, and claimed for his soldiers all the land that belonged to the State. If I had entered the Capitol at that time, my body would have cast two shadows.

I was also evenly torn about the attempts of my daughter-in-law Claudia and Gaius to retrieve Tiberius' body. I would have given everything to render my son a proper funeral and put his soul to rest. Yet I knew if he had been found, his supporters would have turned it into a major event with mass demonstrations at the Forum. After four days of searching, Claudia and Gaius called it off, making me feel both sad and relieved.

In the first session of the Senate after the murder of my son, Licinius delivered a forceful speech, attacking my nephew Serapio. The entire Senate listened to him in a grim, hostile silence. Licinius accused Serapio of having defiled the most sacred place of our Republic. By leading a violent mob, he had destroyed the little dignity and authority the Senate still had left. All the laws and attempts in the past to protect us from despotic and tyrannical behavior had been thrashed and he warned that violence would recur as the way to settle our disputes. At the end of his speech, he asked the Senate who the real traitor was. A Tribune who had tried through legal means to reclaim the land that belonged to the people or a Pontifex Maximus who abused the power of his office so he could keep the public land he possessed illegally. When he was done and everyone rose, many Senators left the Curia avoiding Serapio except for his most ardent followers who surrounded him in a show of support.

On the evening after his speech, Licinius came to my house. I could hear his arrival from afar. The moment he appeared in my street, hundreds of people rushed to my house to greet him, shouting his name in support and praising his speech in the Senate. Lighted by his torchbearers, he gave a short speech in which he promised he would never forget nor forgive the murder of Tiberius and that he would do everything to continue his land program. People applauded, jeered, and stamped their feet while he spoke.

He looked exhausted when he finally stepped inside and announced he could only stay for a brief moment. We had tears in our eyes when we hugged each other, but he could not help laughing about the ongoing clamor outside, knowing how much I detested all the noise on the Aventine. I asked him about his speech in the Senate and he shrugged his shoulders dismissively, contending it seemed to have served its purpose. He wrapped his arm around me, made me sit opposite of him and while holding my hands, he described the next steps he wanted to take. By his face, I could tell this would be a fateful evening, which would haunt me for the rest of my life.

"The Senate is afraid for the reaction of the people and we must act quickly to exploit their fears," he asserted.

"Tomorrow they will bring offerings to the temple of Ceres and maybe even send a delegation to the temple in Sicily. They profess it is to convey a message of reconciliation, but it feels more like they are warning the people they are just the limbs who cannot live without the stomach." He shook his head and mumbled some obscenities, which I pretended not to hear.

He told me Claudius had reached an agreement with Scaevola to install a Senatorial Commission to restore the authority and dignity of the Senate. He expected Scaevola to legitimize the murder of Tiberius as constitutional.

"We run the risk," he cautioned, "that Serapio and his followers will try to leave it at that and stop the land distribution. So I gave them my approval to inaugurate the Committee on the condition they will nominate me as the new chairman of the College of Three. Scaevola and Claudius have agreed, but it comes with a price, which brought me here tonight."

"What price?" I asked.

I felt my heart racing, thinking about a possible exile for Gaius or worse. He must have guessed it, shaking his head as if I had offended him.

"Not Gaius," he said crossly, giving me a sharp look. "Gaius will continue to be a board member of the College."

After a brief pause, he continued in a softer tone. "Serapio wants to interrogate our Greek friends. He is feeling cornered and wants to shift the blame. He claims that the Greeks poisoned Tiberius' mind and he also hopes to weaken our position as their patrons." He added that he had already notified Blossius to remain in Rome.

"But you have to inform Diophanes," he told me, "Serapio wants to interrogate him too and I agreed"

"And what will he do to him?" I asked

"I think we both know to expect the worst," he murmured and looked down, avoiding my gaze.

He left me facing a sleepless night in which I could not turn to anyone for consolation or advice. The idea to leave Diophanes, who had been Tiberius' mentor for almost his entire life, in the hands of his murderer, made me cringe with anger, followed by a nauseating feeling of utter injustice and powerlessness.

In the morning, I sent Simo to Diophanes and they returned together. Diophanes smiled when he entered my house, looking at me with his radiant eyes. The heat outside had exhausted him and he asked for some diluted wine. I let him sit and drink some wine without offering any explanation. There was something in his manner that told me he already knew.

"The only request I have is to choose the way I will die," was his first remark.

He glanced at me and shook his head when he saw my face.

"Do not be sad, my dear Cornelia. I am an old man and life has been extraordinarily good to me. Tyrants always want to hold cross-examination and cross-examinations are always about the past, so I will be the perfect witness. Maybe this old Greek can teach your nephew some lessons about politics. We Greeks have a talent for betraying each other he will never be able to match."

His second request was to speak with Gaius alone before it was too late. "I do not know when they will come to get me, so I would be grateful if you could ask Gaius to come today."

He looked at me with a loving stare and added, "When I talk to Gaius, I often have the feeling I'm talking to you. He has inherited all your strengths, but also some of your weaknesses, and we must make sure he will not do anything that would enable Serapio to harm him too."

Gaius and Diophanes spent the rest of that day and most of the night together. They came to get him early in the morning. Diophanes looked very calm and rested, as if he had enjoyed a good night sleep. I was very relieved and grateful to see how the soldiers treated him with respect and gentleness. It was clear on whose side they were and they allowed

Gaius and me to embrace him for the last time. Some of them became teary-eyed watching us.

Serapio and a number of his followers interrogated him for two days and then gave him a poison to drink. They never dared to harm him physically, which had been my greatest fear. I heard Serapio had been extremely disappointed and frustrated with his answers. Diophanes had outwitted him completely by referring constantly to earlier Roman laws and precedents. Diophanes had laughed a lot and even made some of them laugh too by recounting hilarious scenes from the turbulent history of Athens. When his death notice reached me, my last resistance broke and I could no longer hide my intense sorrow from Gaius and my slaves.

Later on, they also questioned Blossius. This brave champion of the people, who had ridiculed my son on the most fateful day of his life, asked his interrogators for clemency under the pretext that his love for Tiberius had been so great that he would have done everything my son might have asked. My former house friend Laelius, who assisted Serapio and the Consuls in their cross-examinations, reminded Blossius of the speech Tiberius had given after the impeachment of Octavius. Laelius asked Blossius what he would have done if my son had ordered him to set the Capitol on fire. I had to laugh when I heard it. The only reason my son had mentioned it was because it would have been such an insane thing to do. Blossius answered that Tiberius would never have given such an order, but since they had nothing else to prove my son's supposed demagoguery, they reiterated the question so many times that Blossius was forced to concede he would have carried out his command, which, as we all knew, proved nothing.

In the end, to everyone's surprise, the Consuls pardoned him. I felt completely betrayed when I heard it. Was it because Licinius had somehow managed to delay his interrogation until Serapio and his private warfare had begun to threaten the Senate's attempt to restore order? Why had Licinius not tried to do the same for Diophanes? Did he deceive me in sacrificing Diophanes for Blossius' sake? Did Blossius pay them a huge ransom or transfer some of his family land holdings here in the South? I never found out. A few days after his acquittal, Blossius was on his way to Pergamum where he continued to betray the Roman people until he ended his life.

The fates did, however, spare us a few morsels of justice. Fulvius had been pressing the Praetor to commence impeachment proceedings against Serapio. He was not successful, mostly because my son-in-law Aemilianus opposed it, but his relentless efforts did weaken Serapio's position. Everyone hated my nephew. Wherever he went, people walked up to him, spat on the ground in front of his feet, calling him a tyrant, and telling him that he carried a curse because he had shed the blood of a man who had been inviolable. Fearing his presence would keep the desire for revenge alive, the Senate appointed my nephew as Chairman of a Committee to reorganize Pergamum as our new province. It was forbidden for a Pontifex Maximus to leave Italy, but they decided to ignore the rule. He left Rome in secret and never returned. On his arrival, the slave rebellion broke out. He wandered as an exile from city to city until it became unbearable and he killed himself. Friend and foe celebrated his suicide in Rome with joy and relief. Diophanes was wrong. We Romans equal the Greeks in our ability to betray.

2.

As Licinius had predicted, Scaevola did give the murder of my son his Consular blessing, but he also kept his end of the bargain by nominating Licinius as the new chairman of the College of Three along with Claudius and Gaius; one of his last public acts. After his Consulship, he withdrew to the country and devoted himself for the rest of his life to writing histories and legal treatises. I have always wondered how he felt about his justification of my son's murder, but I am probably correct in assuming he buried his guilty feelings, if any, under a pile of legal deliberations.

After their election and under the energetic leadership of Licinius, the College of Three, assisted by a large group of slaves and freedmen, resumed the arduous labor of the registration, mapping, and redistribution of public lands. His leading role made Licinius so popular that he not only won the Consular elections, but also managed to become the Pontifex Maximus after Serapio had committed suicide.

Our joy over his double victory was enormous. Licinius was now one of the most powerful men in Rome and the tide finally seemed to turn in our favor until he obtained permission to lead the campaign against the slave rebellion in Pergamum. I pleaded with him not to go, but he insisted, arguing that the rebellion threatened the much-needed funding for the work of the College of Three. "All I need is to lay my hands on the royal treasury," he said with a grin.

His campaign began successfully, but he was ambushed and killed by Thracian warriors, who had joined the rebellion. Soldiers who survived the ambush later told me that Licinius had hidden his identity out of fear that the Thracians might have used him as a hostage. The devastating news of his death was the final straw. I left Rome shortly afterward.

I was already in Naples when Claudius died. His ambition to become the next champion of the people after Tiberius' death never materialized, partly as a result of Licinius' prominent role and partly because his health had already declined. I felt no emotion when they told me about his death, but I realized that the standing of the College of Three had now been greatly weakened. These setbacks made it easy for my son-in-law, Aemilianus, to thwart the attempt by the Tribune Carbo to legalize the re-election of Tribunes. Gaius had worked closely with Carbo to prepare his proposal, but I had my doubts about this man. He seemed to me one of those Tribunes who made use of the wave of popularity for my sons to further his own position.

Fulvius and Carbo replaced Licinius and Claudius as members of the College of Three and, unfortunately, this changing of the guard coincided with the beginning of the actual transfer of public lands to the veterans. It had taken nearly three years to prepare it, but now people had to give up their land. As was to be expected, it revived all the old conflicts and grievances. Some lost their orchards and were compensated with fallow land or stretches of a swamp. With each new allocation, the outrage of our allies increased and the new leaseholders faced a flood of hostilities. Their fields were dusted at night with salt, their tools and oxen were stolen, and their houses were set on fire. Delegations came again to Rome. When the Senate did not yield, they turned to my son-in-law. They reminded him of the faithful services they had offered him personally during his campaigns in Spain. They asked him to designate at least an impartial third party to settle the disputes between them and the College of Three. Once they heard about the request to Aemilianus, thousands of veterans flooded Rome where they held daily meetings at the Forum. The situation became so menacing that the Senate convened in an emergency session. Many feared for their lives and they called for Aemilianus to seize control and assume dictatorial powers.

In response, Aemilianus delivered a speech in the Senate in which he proposed to transfer the power of arbitration from the College of Three to the Senate, mandating the Consul to settle the disputed cases. His proposal received a majority. The Senators were so pleased with his intervention that they accompanied him in the evening, along with a large number of magistrates from all over Italy, on his way home. It became such a powerful procession that no veteran dared to intervene.

They authorized the Consul Tuditanus to supervise the land distribution and he did what they expected. He flipped through the hundreds of files and complaints for a few days, with a perfunctory glance, scraped some money together, and rushed off to Illyria with a small army, leaving the College of Three deprived of its arbitration power and without any further instructions. The veterans had lost again.

3.

At the time when Aemilianus was informed in Spain of the murder of Tiberius, he had turned around and quoted in front of Gaius and his men his beloved writer Homer, "so perish all others too who commit such mischief." His statement had grieved Gaius deeply, but since Aemilianus had been his commander, he was forced to remain silent and swallow the affront.

My son took his revenge in Rome when Aemilianus had to defend his intervention against the College of Three in the People's Assembly. My son and Fulvius quizzed him about the murder of Tiberius, and Aemilianus repeated his denunciation. While he spoke, the people started to heckle him, something they had never done before and it became an ugly scene with people hurling insults while Aemilianus shouted them down.

The public clash formed the beginning of a campaign against him, led by our veterans who turned their full fury on him. They gathered in front of the gates of his house and waited for him with clenched fists, bellowing that he had betrayed them each time he went to the Senate. A few days later, a rumor spread that Aemilianus was preparing a speech in which he would propose far-reaching reforms. The source of this story never became clear, but I suspect Aemilianus himself had started it. Nevertheless, the veterans suddenly had their hopes raised high up.

His slaves later asserted that he had set his tablet next to his bed to prepare his speech when they found him dead in the morning. It was immediately alleged that he was poisoned. As possible culprits, people pointed to Gaius, Fulvius, Carbo, and, to my astonishment, they also listed my daughter and me. Others claimed that he had committed suicide because he had been unable to live up to his words. Finally, there were people who contended that his slaves, after being tortured, had admitted that they had allowed strangers into his house, who strangled him, leaving bruises and small wounds around his neck. Yet, despite all these stories, no one found any evidence of a violent death and the Senate took no further action. For fear his death might provoke new disturbances, the Senate did not dare to give him a State funeral and he was quietly cremated as a man in disgrace.

4.

The death of my son-in-law moved me more than I had thought. I had every reason to salute it with a sense of relief, but my grief was great. The only bright spot was that my daughter Sempronia began to spend most of her time here with me in Miseno.

With his passing away, our last great commander had gone. As a patron of our society, he had been less successful. He started, during his Censorship, a campaign against the general deterioration of our morals and values, rebuking those who dared to yawn at public hearings. Rome, however, is not an army camp, and his campaign took on such a fanatical character that it became the target of ridicule and scorn. But I agreed with his loathing of the unbridled display of opulence at the dinner parties of young Patricians and Equestrians, and I shared his aversion for the heavily perfumed young men who, wrapped in transparent robes with long sleeves, paraded over the Forum in search of catamites with the smoothest hips.

One morning, while visiting my daughter at his house, we were both startled by a loud shouting and tumult. We rushed to the atrium where we witnessed my son-in-law chasing Gaius Laelius with a scroll, both roaring with laughter. I had never expected to witness such a cheerful scene in his house. Aemilianus was an excellent host, but he reserved his warmth and charm for a very select group of men. The moment he saw us, he ceased his game and fell back into his cold and distant demeanor.

Aemilianus was a born sword fighter and I believe he was happiest, like my father, when he was on a campaign – far away from Rome and all its political machinations. He accomplished one of his most famous feats, as a young military Tribune, barely seventeen, during one of the campaigns in Spain.

A tall, heavily-armed Celtiberian challenged our army, riding on his horse up and down in front of our lines. He shouted insults and challenged them to engage in a man-to-man combat. Our soldiers remained in line and stared at him silently until my son-in-law got tired of it and stepped forward. With a cry of joy, the Celtiberian dismounted, drew his sword, and started to swing it in the direction of the much smaller Aemilianus. He ducked and dodged the Celtiberian. While the man thought Aemilianus regretted his brash action, his fellow soldiers understood that he was only playing with the Celtiberian. The Celtiberian became impatient and lost sight of his defense. Suddenly, Aemilianus moved forward and drove his sword in a flash through the throat of the man. He pulled it out with such horrifying ease that even the most experienced veterans felt a cold shiver running over their spines. The Celtiberian collapsed with his face down in front of Aemilianus' feet. His death, witnessed in awe by both armies, offered our men such a morale boost that they defeated the enemy, despite their numerical superiority, without much difficulty.

Where my father and my husband had been cunning and subtle, Aemilianus had been coarse and overly forceful. His biggest frustration was that my father had already consumed the big meal, leaving him with just the crumbs. The way in which he destroyed Numantia appalled many of us.

In contrast to my brother-in-law, Corculum, he had an open mind and entertained many Greek philosophers and historians like Polybius and Panaetius. At the same time, his refusal to share power with our allies by withholding from them our civil rights prevented him from becoming the reformer he should have been. As happened to many men of my generation, his own ego ultimately defeated him.

Family ties were sacred to him and despite his misgivings about Tiberius' program, I am convinced that if he had been in Rome, Tiberius would not have been killed. Even after my husband had thwarted the Consulate of Nasica Corculum, Aemilianus continued to visit our house and pay his respects to my husband and me. When my mother died and the second part of the dowry had to be handed over to my husband, he did not hesitate for a moment and made it immediately available while he could have waited three years.

Aemilianus adored his natural mother, Papiria. Aemilianus' father had cast her aside "like an old boot" and, to compensate her loss, Aemilianus donated, after the death of my mother, all of her belongings to Papiria. It contained a series of exquisite vases from all over the Mediterranean, as well as a number of beautiful two-seaters, horses, gold, silver beakers, and exotic gifts my father had been given in Asia. When the valuables were carried in, Papiria held an open house for all of her friends. The Matronae praised Aemilianus for his generous gesture and wished that they had a son like him. Everyone told me I was just envious when I criticized Papiria for driving around Rome in her two-seater, cackling and beaming like a child, but the shame I felt for her had been genuine and sincere.

5.

Aemilianus' death invoked a deep desire to sever all my ties with the world for a time. My body and mind hungered for a surrounding that was still whole and unharmed. I found solace in the Asclepieum of Fregellae where I wandered through the fields and ornamental gardens like a child seeing the world for the first time. I enjoyed to be surrounded by fragrant blossoms and sit underneath the arched branches. The gardens were full of life with an abundance of snowy, winged petals, hovering over the white flowerbeds.

Resting during the days and taking baths in the evening had a beneficial, soothing effect. In the evening, surrounded by high, white plastered walls, far away from prying eyes, and after bringing sacrifices to Hygeia and Panacea, I was dressed in a white robe and stripped of all symbols that connected me to this world, my wedding ring, my belts, and my straps. Sometimes I drank a liquid enriched with the milky juice of the poppy.

Lying on a bed made of fragrant twigs with my arms stretched out and my palms unfolded, I gave myself in the night over to the healing care of the daughters of Asclepius whose spirits were invoked by the sacred rituals of the priestesses. In the beginning, my dreams were violent and hectic in which the nameless hero, who had accompanied me in my daydreams after Tiberius' death, featured regularly. He took all the shapes I had dreamed about as a child – a winged horse, a fish, a bird, a butterfly, a mouse, a deer. Sometimes the metamorphoses followed one another in such rapid and feverish succession that I woke up in a panic, drenched in sweat.

But after a month or two, my mind came to rest and my alter ego disappeared, making me feel whole again and strong enough to face whatever the fates had in store for my last surviving son.

6.

The building of my villa here in Miseno offered me a safe haven in the same manner that Gaius found harborage in the army and in his marriage with Licinia, which took place shortly after Licinius had died.

The campaigns allowed him to turn his back on Rome. He participated at the Campus Martius in the toughest training sessions for the new draftees; running with a full load of armament. He joined three times a month the marching days of thirty miles with the heaviest burden on his back. He became a master in chopping down trees. His fine hands were soon covered with calluses, resembling those of a workman, and he became one of the fastest sprinters. However, his attempts to disappear from the public eye by blending into the rows of the conscripts troubled me more than if he had plunged into the political fray. His frantic marching, exercising, and running around made him look like a panicky butterfly tangled in the sticky threads of life.

Between the campaigns, he stayed at home where he immersed himself in the simple pleasures that his wife Licinia and their newborn daughter Sempronia offered him; like a man with no political ambition. The attention he paid to the College of Three was minimal. The crisis in Rome had also lessened. The crushing of the rebellion in Sicily had restored the grain supply to our city. After the slave rebellion in Pergamum had been quelled, money began to flow in, allowing for the construction of the Aqua Tepula, our fourth aqueduct. In contrast to the Aqua Marcia, the water of the Tepula was lukewarm and murky, but the construction provided many men work and bread.

When supporters of Tiberius met him on the street, Gaius insisted he had not forsaken his brother's politics, but their reproaches made him withdraw even more. He lived frugally, took no part in dinners, and shunned all political gatherings.

Yet what no one saw at the time was that he very quietly not only trained his body, but also his mind and tongue. This became briefly visible on two separate occasions. Four years after the death of Aemilianus, he publicly gave his support to another attempt by Fulvius to grant citizenship to our allies, so they would cease opposing the land distribution and the power of the College of Three could be restored. Just as his campaign was gaining momentum, the Senate ordered him to leave Rome and undertake a campaign in the North. Fulvius obeyed faithfully and his proposal died a quiet death.

Fulvius' aborted attempt led to many bitter reactions throughout Italy and ultimately to a tragedy that I still consider as one of the worst atrocities we Romans ever committed. For centuries, my beloved Fregellae had enjoyed a Latin status. Samnitic families had used this status by moving into the city to register as Latins and later move on to Rome where they acquired the Roman citizenship. In the year of Fulvius' Consulate, a Tribune, at the request of the Senate, ended to this form of migration and ordered everyone to leave the city despite the fact they were law-abiding citizens who had done nothing wrong.

The Samnitic inhabitants of Fregellae suddenly saw themselves stripped of their ancient rights and, with the failure of Fulvius' proposals, their anger boiled over. They revolted against their own Latin magistrates in the vain hope Samnites from other cities would follow them. Opimius, who served at that time as Praetor, abused their rebellion to show that he was a man of law and order, even if it meant slaughtering defenseless men, women, and children. At the request of the magistrates of Fregellae, he gathered a large army and laid siege to this small town. His cruelty knew no limits. While preparing his siege, he had found a number of children playing outside the walls. He tied them together, placed them in front of the gate, and threatened to cut off their hands if they did not surrender, promising at the same time no one would be hurt. After they opened the gates, Opimius killed all the insurgents, including the women and children. The city was razed to the ground, together with my beloved Asclepieum. He rewarded the Latin magistrates with a new settlement and Roman citizenship.

Gaius organized together with Fulvius a contio at the Forum in which he attacked Opimius, demanding a trial, but the Senate ignored their protest and honored Opimius with a standing ovation.

On the other occasion, Vettius, a friend of my son, begged for his help after he was taken to court. Gaius defended him so eloquently that he won effortlessly. My son's intervention, brief and insignificant as it was, immediately raised suspicion, and the rumor spread that he was considering running for the office of Tribune.

7.

My son would later state that his decision to end his semi-retirement and run for the office of Quaestor had been inspired by a dream in which Tiberius had urged him to accept his destiny. 'Why hesitate, Gaius? There is no escape; one life is fated for both of us and one death as champions of the people.'

Friend and foe welcomed his election and appointment as Quaestor for Sardinia. The island had proven to be as treacherous as Spain. At dinner parties, many raised a goblet in anticipation that he would not return alive. The fact that my son had also been thrilled about his election and the post he was given should have warned his enemies, but they chose to ignore it.

Gaius knew Sardinia well. When the Carthaginians struggled to subdue the uprising of their mercenaries, Gaius' great-grandfather had snatched Sardinia from their hands, which, according to some, had given them every right to declare war on us. Thanks to my relentless zeal, Gaius had often frequented as a child the Temple of the Goddess of the Dawn and the map of Sardinia had been etched in his memory. He had served in a number of campaigns on the island, taking him to the same battle-grounds in the mountains where his father had been victorious. Sardinia was like a second home to him.

From letters my husband had sent me, I knew winters in Sardinia could be brutal. Gaius' Quaestorship coincided with an extremely severe winter. I remember that even the flanks of Mount Vesuvius remained covered in snow for weeks. Gaius' commander, the Consul Orestes, asked the cities to provide him with extra clothes and blankets for his soldiers and horses, but the wealthy citizens in the coastal towns turned down his request. After he commenced to pressure them, they sent en-voys to the Senate, pleading to be exempt from any claims. Gaius' ene-mies in the Senate handled the matter and they ordered Orestes to leave the cities in peace. The fate of our soldiers, often boys of barely seventeen years old, apparently left them cold.

My son took a number of them with him on a tour through the cities. He organized town meetings and placed them in front of him on the mar-ket squares, arguing they were here to protect the citizens and asking for a voluntary contribution. To the annoyance of the Senators in Rome, a large number of families immediately responded. Adding insult to in-jury, a message reached the Senate a few weeks later that King Micipsa of Numidia had sent, out of respect for Gaius, a shipment of grain to Sar-dinia. His generous gesture made the Senators so angry that they refused to receive the King's envoys.

When the Senate sent fresh troops to Sardinia, they ordered Orestes to remain, impeding Gaius from leaving his post as well. But as soon as my son heard it, he embarked for Rome. His unexpected return created an uproar. His enemies began a smear campaign in which they accused him of abandoning his duties as an elected official. He had to appear for the Censors in a public hearing. In his defense, my son pointed out that he had served twelve years in the army, while others had served only ten, and that he had remained for two years as a Quaestor, while the law had permitted him to return after only one year. The people who had listened to him began to shout that maybe they should try the Censors and not my son. Upset by this turn of events, the Censors attempted to call the meeting off, but my son turned around and addressed the indignant crowd. He told them that while he had been in Sardinia he had not once visited a tavern, no whore had crossed the threshold of his house, and he had not bribed even one slave. His purse and wine barrels had been empty when he returned and not chock-full of gold and silver as the casks of the Senators who had accused him. At this, the Censors got up and ordered everyone to leave the meeting, fearful that my son would commence listing some of the Senators' names.

Unable to find anything else, his enemies then blamed my son for the uprising of Fregellae. The charge was that his support for Fulvius' proposals had provoked the Samnitic immigrants to revolt. Whatever doubts and hesitations my son may have had – and there were many – this last allegation was so grotesque and outrageous that he made up his mind. His brother had been right; there was no escape.

Shortly after they had vented their accusations, he announced his candidacy for the Tribunate. His enemies got what they had dreaded the most, an immensely popular, brilliant Tribune; determined to restore our Republic as a union of free men and, yes, with a heart full of hatred, craving to revenge his brother. None boded well for them.

PART 5
Γνώθι σεαυτόν
(KNOW THYSELF)

Mosaic of a Roman Matrona

1.

Tonight, I received a message that the veterans had written, with charcoal slogans, – 'an act of insane discord produces a temple of Concord' – on the walls of the temple of the moon, urging their fellow citizens to continue opposing Consul Opimius' intention to build the Temple of Concordia. Their action pleased me, but I also found it worrisome. To whom can they turn, now they have lost all faith in our leaders? No country can survive without leadership. Woe to the land where its veterans and not its elected officials take the lead.

The Temple of the Moon is near our old House on the Aventine. It is of Latin origin and dates back to the time of the kings. Gaius sprained his ankle here when he jumped off the terrace, attempting to stay ahead of his pursuers to reach the bridge over the Tiber. It is not clear why the goddess of this heavenly body impeded his flight. My sons and I have always honored her faithfully with sacrifices.

Her full phase allows me to find my way easily on my terrace. Some claim that from time to time you can see a face on this celestial body, but I think the moon is just a mirror of stone, lifeless, and water cold. In her false light, the marble of my terrace looks like it is made from cobalt glass. The icy blue shade reminds me of the frozen face of a drowned wretch I once saw drifting by in the Tiber on a gray winter morning. I shudder at the memory.

On the watchtowers in front of me, night-watchmen have lit the fires to guide the fishermen, passing grain ships, and incoming naval vessels. The string of harbor lights along the coastline offers a spectacular show of man-sized flames and showers of glowing sparks. Patches of wind carry the crackling sounds and smell of burning branches. Towering over these, at the following inlet, loom the dark contours of the lighthouse of the gods, Vesuvius. Across the sky dome high above me, sudden flashes of light disappear as quickly as they came. Sometimes three or four at the same time, and I pray that the stellar rain will not turn out to be a harbinger of more bad tidings.

Below me, in the sea, something is stirring and to my utter delight. I spot a group of dolphins, a hopeful omen. They tumble up and down in the perfect cadence of small sea soldiers and, as if it finds their bouncy presence amusing, the sea beats against the rocks with upbeat drum rolls. In the moonlight, the dolphins' waterlogged backs are barely distinguishable from the rising and ebbing rows of waves. My night guards spot them too. They crowd together on the second terrace and point downwards. This is the only advantage of my sleepless nights. My unexpected visits ensure they remain on the alert. As a child, I would have woken now one of my younger slaves, forcing her to join me with a basket full of fish. With the increased use of the port and fishing along the coast, dolphins have become rare in the Bay of Baiae. Fishermen hate them and kill them whenever they can. Their bloodcurdling screams always fill me with great sadness.

On one of our first voyages, my husband and I were accompanied for days by a group of dolphins. Boatmen gave us silvery fish and we loved to hold competitions between the dolphins and seagulls, which would catch the fish in mid-air. My dolphins won more often than his seagulls. The sailors called the dolphins their pilots, and they claimed they had led many an amorous sailor to his sweetheart in the ports.

It is on nights like these, I miss my husband the most. I miss the warmth of his body, the smell of his hair, the raspy sound of his breathing, the touch of his warm hands on my midriff and breasts, his gentle, belly-cushioned thrust. I knew his body better than he did; the old and new scars formed a living map of his successful campaigns, gradually overgrown by the first signs of decline. I long at moments like these to hear his melodious voice, his compact Latin, and his fluent, poetic Greek.

I miss the loud talking in his sleep after we made love, and the messy sight of his tunics across all our private rooms. I miss his loving gaze with which he would follow me, to my growing annoyance, the whole day after he had returned from an extended mission abroad. I miss his elaborate, always balanced observations in which he identified new developments I had overlooked, and I miss his sudden outbursts after I had exhausted all his patience with my constant meddling and nagging. I miss his sad, melancholic glance with which he would withdraw in the morning after such an outburst, his days of silence like a sulking child, and I miss disrupting his sacred morning rituals with gossip and frivolities. I miss our family dinners where he sang old songs, accompanied by a flute player. I miss the grand state banquets with senior envoys from Spain, Pergamum, and Sardinia and the sense of power he had over these areas. I miss the moments during cheerful, lively dinners, watching the glances of warm affection his friends would bestow on him in the happy, proud knowledge that this was my husband. I miss his philosophical reflections on the functioning of Republic and the power and weakness of its organs. I miss his analyses of rivals, his joy when he outwitted them, and his sobering comments on his personal triumphs. I miss the meetings in the morning with his many clients as they came to pay their respects. I miss the casual encounters with admirers in the streets of Rome, who congratulated me, after he had held another speech in the Senate. His speeches had brought us together.

The poison cup in my bedroom is my last resort. My night guards offer some security, but I have no illusions they will stand if my enemies want to harm me. The goblet is my guarantee that I can determine the time and place of my death. In the darkest moments after the death of Gaius, the cup also offered an insidious temptation, but I managed to resist it. I wanted the attacks to stop; I did not wish to end my life. My enemies would have claimed victory and I would have betrayed everything my sons had stood for. If I am partly to blame for their demise –

and I believe, I am –, the least I can do is to keep their legacy alive. I consider it a sacred duty to extend my life as long as possible.

I have moved inside and sitting on my heels in front of my Sacellum, I behold the masks of my husband, his uncle, my father, and his ancestors. They are modeled and painted in the old, traditional style. The resemblance between my husband and his uncle – with their long faces, the deep lines on the forehead and around the mouth, the thin lips, and their challenging, energetic glance – is so striking that they could have been brothers. Tiberius wore the mask of his great-uncle during the funeral ceremony of his father.

The portraits fill me with a sense of shame. They were the silent witnesses of my insanity in the first weeks after Gaius' death. I carried the mask of my husband many times to my bedroom, placing it next to me. Sometimes I pressed my lips on the cold, clay mouth. A few times, I held the mask in front of my face while looking in the mirror. My eyes made it look alive, offering a weird, sickening kind of consolation. In the morning, Simo erased all traces of my tears without a word, but I know he must have been shocked.

For my guests from Greece, Asia, and Africa, the masks in my Sacellum symbolize the merger of two illustrious families. They regard my marriage as a highlight of the Republic. I do not contradict them, but when I am alone, I see only discord. I still fear the moment when they stop in front of the Sacellum to pay their respect to my husband and my ancestors; although the absence of portraits of my sons gives me some confidence that no sudden attack will occur. However, I know I must keep my distance and talk only about my father and his ancestors until the moment has passed and my guests have moved away.

In the flickering light of the oil lamp, the mask of my father casts off sharp-edged shadows. His fierce facial expression no longer inspires fear. My living remembrance of him has been replaced over the years by the inanimate image of his death mask. I regard him now as a tragic soldier in the service of our people. My father was thirty-three years old when he defeated Hannibal. After that, nothing remained but to live in the shadow of his achievements.

My husband was a young recruit present at the battle of Zama. He recounted how at a certain moment the armies were so packed together that no one could use his spear or sword. Carthaginian and Roman assaulted one another with daggers; in every single duel, the death struggle of two nations. The earth was so drenched with blood that men could no longer stand, slipping away over the red, slimy mud. An insane urge to kill or to get killed took hold of them and the front stalled. At that moment, my father intervened. Amid the loud blaring of horns, he ordered his soldiers to pull back, regroup, and carry the wounded out of the way. This decision earned him the most crucial victory achieved by any Roman. Later, most of the veterans looked back at that instant of madness with mortification, and it formed a memory they never wanted to talk about. For them, the conscription was an inescapable reality and if they were lucky, the spoils of war gave them enough to retire after six years. However, for some, a different outcome ensued. The life of a soldier, my husband contended, consisted mainly of marching and waiting, but some veterans repeatedly enlisted as volunteers because they could no longer exist without the frenzy of killing. My husband never lost sight of his goal. If achieving victory demanded a battle, he would enter it without hesitation, but if he could accomplish the same result through a ploy, he used that instead. Twice, he celebrated a triumph in the streets of Rome.

I will never forget the sight of the triumphs of my husband – wearing royal purple and welcomed by the entire Roman people – at the head of his troops. However, the ecstasy they provoke is treacherous. The taunts and insults traditionally shouted at the triumphant from the side of the road, warning him all glory is short-lived, do not impress anymore. Like many of our religious practices, they have assumed the character of hollow expressions, devoid of any real conviction. Dissatisfaction with the distribution of spoils increasingly forms the basis for the obscenities with which family members of veterans shower their former commander.

Pale morning light has entered my room. I watch it as it scales the wall, dyeing my Sacellum in shades of gray. I know I should get up, take charge, steer the household, but not today. Today, I will just sit here and look at the ashen masks until darkness has swallowed them up.

2.

'The island arched out of the sea like a craggy back of a donkey.' I am reminded of this line of verse as I look with some anxiety at the high mountains around me.

An earthquake hit my villa last night. The quake ran as a cold shiver over the entire backbone of my island. Everyone fled in great fear to the terraces and waited for the rest of the night in the open, dreading more aftershocks would occur, but it remained limited to one shudder and the damage to the villa was small.

I have attended this morning, at the request of members of my household, a service in honor of the earth-shaker Poseidon, despite the fact that they know I attach more credence to the explanation of Anaximenes, who believed variations in dry and wet weather fracture the earth. The language at the ceremony was Greek, but many of my Roman friends were also present, which made my heart feel good.

After the service, an unpleasant incident occurred. A slave of a Greek magistrate laid his hand very lightly on the shoulder of a Roman Senator who was here on holiday. The man turned around, walked without a word to his master, and struck the magistrate to the ground. Bystanders responded immediately. They rushed to the Greek, helped him to his feet, and asked him if he was well, but no one had the courage to approach the Senator. I felt deeply ashamed for the man's behavior and by urging my slaves to support the Greek, I made it visible how much I condemned his behavior. He avoided my angry stare and moved away quickly, making a throwaway gesture. The assault was outrageous and entirely in contrast to the way we live here.

The incident revived among my friends, during our ceremonial dinner, the old debate that Greek citizens are in no way protected against the arbitrariness and rude behavior of Roman authorities. Many of my friends from Rome were amazed to hear that my Greek friends had no interest in acquiring Roman civil rights, which annoyed me, since their position was well-known from all the discussions and writings. Nobody here in the South wants to give up his ancient city rights; everyone simply wishes to be protected. Without asking themselves if they were doing me a favor and devoid of my consent, my Greek friends recalled the speeches of Gaius during his second Tribunate in which he gave a series of harrowing examples of the rampant abuse of Senators. The heated exchanges back and forth took away our appetite. It became such a breach of my role as hostess, I got up and put an end to our gathering. Later, I reproached myself that I should have foreseen this. I could have known that people are tense after a tremor, often causing more damage to themselves than the aftershocks of the quake.

3.

Given the continuing turmoil in Rome and our provinces, I have sold many of my possessions in Asia Minor and Spain. According to my fidu-

ciaries, this was not the right time, but since they could not offer any further wisdom when I asked them how long I should wait, I decided to
ignore their advice. After an endless exchange of letters and the offer to
compensate them for losing a number of chargeable services, they ac-
ceded to my wishes. The whole transaction yielded me several million
sesterces; exceeding, they grudgingly admitted, all their expectations. It
is only regrettable that the interest rate of this month is so low. It would
have been much higher if they had followed my instructions immediately.

I thank the gods that my elder brother Publius insisted on keeping
the estate of my husband and me separate in our nuptial agreement, and
I have surrounded myself with several counselors. It still gives me immense pleasure that the ridiculous law of the Tribune Saxa and Cato,
prohibiting granting women a legacy of more than one hundred thousand sesterces, did not survive their death. I do not know of any other
law as quickly ignored as this one. Depending on their personal interests,
my counselors contradict one another, allowing me to make the final decisions. Also, potential buyers – friend or foe – offer me the opportunity
to put them under pressure if they try to thwart my wishes.

Ideally, I would like to get rid of the possessions in Rome I recently
acquired, but here I share the opinion of my guardians that it is too early.
My holdings constantly worry me. I have no control over the tenants my
supervisors put forward, and I distrust their willingness to ensure everything is done in compliance with the house rules. In the case of buildings higher than three floors, there is the constant danger of collapses and
the daily maintenance costs me hundreds of denarii. Furthermore, I suspect that many of my tenants split their living quarters and take in sub-
tenants while paying my supervisors hush money. I am told whole families with six or seven children are squeezed together in one room, where

they sleep, cook, eat, procreate, and work. Others huddle under staircases or block the escape routes, so I am frequently shaken by stories of fires and families killed by suffocation.

I agree with my husband that one should increase his estate only in a natural way. According to him, it was not correct to exist only from issuing loans. He who has money to spend should put it to work. Wealth is an elusive commodity over which one can exert only a limited amount of control. While it grows, you may deceive yourself into thinking you are in command, but after it has commenced to stall or decline, it melts away like snow under a hot sun. I see this obsession to acquire more money especially with the new rich. In their frenzy to continue to accumulate more money, they look as if they are trying to avert their fate through a desperate escape forward. No other free people are more enslaved by their work than money traders.

On the other hand, I also distrust men who claim that their finances are of no interest to them. In their contempt for a sound financial administration, they often build up such a huge amount of debt that they are eventually forced to spend more time and energy in saving their estate than those who take care of their finances.

I firmly believe that Mother Earth still offers the best investment. He who sows seed in her fertile furrows may sometimes lose a season, but over the years she will pay back everything with interest. Money traders may cherish the illusion that their livelihood has become independent of seasons, but ultimately harvests determine the wealth of a country and its people.

I have used a part of the proceeds of my transactions to expand my holdings in Praeneste. I have made donations for the construction of a temple in honor of the Dioscuri and for resurfacing a long stretch of the public road between Praeneste and Rome. The market for dried grapes is currently down, so I have made a one-time offer to the merchants to lower the previously agreed price to the current rate. I will lose a part of the profits I have made, but what would I gain in the long run by bank-rupting my trusted traders? Their gratitude was so great that they spontaneously offered to pay a higher price when the market rebounds. I appreciate their gesture, but sometimes I get the feeling I am the only one who looks beyond a single vintage year.

On the advice of my overseers, I had some fields plowed over, converted to pastures, and built new presses for olives. Both measures would have met stiff resistance from Tiberius and Gaius and, for a while, I felt guilty about it. According to the calculations of my overseers, we will recoup the investments in five years. With the proceeds, I could counterbalance my ongoing losses in Rome. I would be amazed if it did, but at least the investments have enhanced the value of my property, provided they keep a close eye on it. I have urged my agents in Rome to pay more visits to Praeneste, preferably unannounced. If they rise early enough, they could get there in one day, now that parts of the road are in a better shape. Here in Miseno, I do not want to own more land than I can cover in one walk.

4.

My transactions in Asia and Spain have brought me in touch again with communities that have tied their fate to my family and remained loyal even after the murder of Gaius. It pleases me immensely to receive almost daily letters from officials and individuals with requests to put in a good word for them. It involves the usual appeals: a personal recommendation for a son, mediation for a marriage or divorce, helping agents to retrieve late payments from communities where friends of mine recently have been appointed, or supporting requests for a temporary reduction in local taxes after my client community was struck by a natural disaster.

Unlike in the past, I do not ask my friends to inform my client communities their requests have been granted because of my appeals. Discretion is now more than ever my dictum. As I have become active again and my interventions are talked about in Rome – 'the siren from Naples sings again' – some of my Roman acquaintances take offense. They hold me partially responsible for the current crisis and, although none of them states this in so many words, they would rather have me pine away. My successful sale and proactive attitude are perceived by them as disrespectful to their suffering. It leads to anger and frustration. The weaker the other, the greater the indignation. I have no solution. The last thing I want is to hurt the feelings of others. Sometimes, I am just tired of people. I am often relieved when my Roman friends leave. Some come here just to pity me and leave again for Rome, uplifted by the thought how blessed their lives are in comparison.

I blame the tensions also on me. It is not that I am not able to separate appearance from reality. I know when I am dealing with real or perceived friends. But as soon as my friends depart, I commence imagining they have changed their opinion about me. Their personalities merge into an amorphous multitude of hostile voices, sentiments, views, and gossip. At night, I perceive in the howling wind their angry choirs, and when the waves rush over the pebble beaches at high tide, I hear the hissing of a thousand snakes' tongues.

When I watch people living together and witness the changes in their moods, I am often reminded of the delicate balance with which seagulls attempt to remain floating in the air. The slightest fluctuations in the wind force them to regain their balance and their wing movements seem to have a destabilizing effect on the birds next to them. In humans, the flow of the humors in their bodies appears to evoke the same effect as the invisible wind for the seagulls. It results in a prickliness that continuously disturbs the fragile balance in our family relationships and friendships. Sometimes it seems that we are doing nothing more in life than restoring our balance at the expense of others and vice versa.

5.

A willing horse loves to be spurred! My diligent life was a few days ago happily interrupted by the arrival of a good friend. How comforting it is to hear the voice of a sincere friend. Licinius had introduced Diantha to me years ago, and the moment we met, we became friends. Over the years, we have kept in touch, faithfully sending each other letters.

Diantha lives in Naples, and her family is of ancient Greek origin. She is a widow and about ten years younger than I am. My husband always called her 'the girl with the sparkling eyes.' She has a lovely round face, curly black hair, creamy, milky skin, and a slightly voluptuous body, which she has kept in perfect shape. She is quite agile, likes to live in her body, and her moves remind me of a cat. Her lively spirit exudes tender, intimate warmth that all men find very appealing.

Her letters often made me blush, embarrassing me by all the graphic details of her love life. She has quite a healthy appetite, whether she is alone, with another woman friend, or some freedman, but I do admit I learned a lot from her. She once even tried to seduce me. When she showed me her secret bedroom with mirrors on all four walls and love scenes on the ceiling, I was shocked, amused, and aroused all at the same time.

Diantha had barely arrived when she marched straight out of her guest room and pulled me out of my library. She took me by the hand as a child and led me through my own home, praising its openness and elegance. Many Greeks from Naples would love to live as you do, she assured me. From every room an unobstructed view of the sea.

Standing in front of the Sacellum she expressed in heartfelt terms her sadness over the loss of my sons. We both cried a little and she remained silent for a while, but then she burst out. Her message was I read too much. No wonder I was forgetful.

"Reading weakens the memory. The more you read, the more you forget," she argued, urging me to make short trips. "Exile is only evil if you make it so. We are not like immobile plants. My ancestors advised everyone to choose the best city with the best climate and time will eventually make everything familiar. If Miseno is your destiny," she exclaimed at the end of her monologue cheerfully, "then Miseno it is!"

One evening, she mentioned there had been a rumor in Naples that people in Egypt had seen the Phoenix again. Swarms of other birds had joined him in his flight to the city of Heliopolis just to catch a glimpse of him, darkening the skies for days. How I would have loved to see it! I do not know if I should give much credence to the story, but I am convinced the Phoenix exists and visits Egypt from time to time.

Her story inspired me, in a silly attempt to show off, to order a slave to bring me the sealed letter from King Philometer. Diantha had heard about it, but she was still impressed when she held the letter in her hand.

I had received the dispatch a few years after my husband's death. Accompanied by a large delegation of ambassadors, musicians, and gift bearers, the envoy of the King had handed me the letter from King Philometer in front of a crowd of curious bystanders. I had had the honor of meeting the King during his stay in Rome. The letter contained a graciously worded proposal to share the throne with him. It had been such an honorable proposal that I could not refuse it immediately, so I kept the envoy waiting for a week.

Once the news about the proposal spread in Rome, many friends came over to have a look at the letter. As could be expected, they extended their congratulations, with additional remarks about all the scandals that had rocked his family and how it would serve him politically well to have me next to him on the throne. My female slaves and I had a good laugh about every gossip that reached our ears.

Stimulated by Diantha's encouraging words, I forced a week ago Sempronia and my two daughters-in-law to accompany me for a visit to Poseidonia. My suggestion received a reluctant response. Simo was most concerned about our safety. It is true that our roads have become even less safe than they were in the past. Marauding bands of runaway slaves, who have nothing to lose and who are utterly desperate, increasingly plague us. But the ten heavily armed guards provided sufficient deterrence and nothing happened to us.

Poseidonia is one of my favorite cities in the area. Greeks, Samnites, and Romans live here in harmony with each other, and I enjoy hearing the old Oscan tongue. The Greeks founded this port many centuries ago, and I consider their three temples as a highlight of their culture. We Romans often boast that everything the Greeks did, we do better. This may be true as to the scale of our temples, but I doubt whether a larger structure also encompasses more beauty. The serene spaces, enclosed by tall columns, always fill me with great devotion. The entering light appears from a bygone era, as if from an ancient Greek spring, still full of promise, innocence, and strength. I also appreciate it greatly that these shrines – in contrast to Rome – are not surrounded by swarms of fortunetellers, snake charmers, and vendors of religious trinkets.

I have been told that in the far north, in the land of eternal winter, your breath freezes, and if you pronounce words and step back, their frozen echo falls apart like a whisper on your feet. The reverberation of the sound of my footsteps on the white marble steps of these temples always reminds me of that story: light and crystal clear.

One afternoon, we attended a play at the theater. It was a comedy by Terence and carried, ironically, the title 'Mother-in-law.' While I watched it, it dawned on me I had seen it before. The notion it must have been forty years ago, performed at the funeral of my uncle, made me feel old and melancholic. It was not a success, I remembered vaguely, and again I was not impressed. The other spectators also reacted rather subdued at the denouement. But the distraction it offered was welcome. It even elicited a faint smile from my daughter-in-law, Licinia.

The following days we spent in the baths for which Poseidonia is renowned. I could even seduce my daughters-in-law to join me in a full treatment at the beauty spa. For my grandchildren, our visit was a feast. They have wrestled, played trigon, and held underwater races in the labyrinth pool. Gaius' daughter was by far the best in archery, which she was allowed to try under supervision. I pray that Amor, once her husband is known, may strike both as accurately in their hearts.

It is always amusing to see how much less attention girls demand when they are playing. I believe my granddaughter only asked me twice to cast a glance at her, while my grandson begged me to watch him with every new attempt. I looked on as he aimed, saw the moment the arrow left the bow, and the tragic result. Sometimes the bow and not the arrow left his hands. Woe to me if I had the nerve to draw a comparison or express an opinion. If the glances his mother Claudia threw at me had been arrows, they would have killed me on the spot.

After the death of Gaius, our relationship has somewhat improved, but it remains precarious. Claudia has inherited her father's high-strung traits. She continues to visit me for her son's sake, but if he had not been there, I don't think we would have remained in touch. She still holds many grudges against me. All I can do is to pray my grandson will grow out to be more of a Sempronius than a Claudius.

6.

Last night, we were rocked by a domestic drama and I was grateful that my daughters-in-law had already left for Rome. The shouting and echoes of running footsteps were so loud that they penetrated my private rooms. When I got up, I found to my astonishment a group of armed guards in my library. They begged me not to go to further into my villa until Simo had returned. From their chaotic recounts, I gathered that some home-born slaves had attacked one of my newly appointed over-seers. I was upset, but not surprised. I had already warned Simo that this new man seemed to favor young, attractive female slaves, and failed to honor the privileges of the elders, like attending important dinners, keep-ing watch in my private rooms, and serving me breakfast. After waiting an hour, Simo finally appeared. With a sad face and downcast eyes, he reported that the new supervisor had been killed and my guards had chained the killers in one of the guestrooms. The question was what to do with them. If I reported them to the magistrates in Miseno, their fate was sealed. I was appalled when I heard their names. They had been part of my household for decades. However, I could not ignore their crime. I decided the best thing to do was to sell all three of them to millers in Naples who were always looking for fresh workforces and would take them in without asking questions. One of my guards had the insolence to remark in my presence that he would rather be put to death.

I waited to enter my villa until they were marched off. It made me sad not to be able to offer any relief or consolation. The corpse of the overseer was tied to a bag with stones and thrown into the sea. The ques-tion now is whether the rest of my servants will remain quiet. The inci-dent has severely disturbed the peace in my household and reignited an atmosphere of anger and resentment, just like after the death of Gaius.

7.

Of the three times – past, present, and future – that the gods gave us, I had in my younger years a preference for the future. I became a follower of the Greek philosopher Xenophanes who contended the gods had not given us from the start all there is to know. In the course of time, we mortals can learn through experience what is better. I remember the arrival of the first stone bridgeheads across the Tiber. These pillars seemed to sustain the optimistic vision of Xenophanes. Here, man, assisted by divine reason, created an overpass that Mother Nature had not provided. But the murder of my son Tiberius washed away all my faith in a hopeful future, along with his body in the Tiber. Now the past dictates the remainder of my life.

This last period in my life should have been the highlight of my existence. In times of great tension between my husband and me, I have always experienced our age difference as a solace. The gap held a promise of years of independence, of – why hesitate? – freedom. Liberated from daily concerns, I could devote myself to everything dear to me, my sons, my daughter, my memories, my books, my gardens, my clients, and guests. A serene, harmonious way of life blessed with wonderful memories, family, beauty, philosophy, literature, and friends; according to Plato the perfect path to happiness.

I had also hoped to be less of a burden to myself. To be liberated from my never-ending compulsion to meddle, model, force and judge. My husband surprised me once with his remark to a friend I was incapable of looking at something without judgment. 'My wife tastes and smells with her eyes.'

From my early childhood, I have carried on a dialogue with myself about my mental state, urging me to soften my stance, show more patience, and be less opinionated and more forgiving. It is the bitter but sweet bonus of aging that I could extend my inner dialogues with my loved ones after they had died. I first commenced conversing with my mother, my wet nurse Sila, and my husband. Now I speak with all those whom I survived and it is not just dialogues. I relive with my imaginary interlocutors the many situations we shared. These renewed exchanges often offer me more insight and guidance than when they occurred. The conversations with the dead fill my days and nights in a way that seems to make them more vivid than my dialogues with the living. I also appreciate how discreet the deceased are. As soon as someone interrupts my musings, my interlocutors vanish like Eurydice for the eyes of Orpheus.

8.

Know thyself! So simple, yet so hard. Even at my age, I find it impossible to answer. Memories of my childhood offer some insight. According to my mother, I was so busy in her womb that she called me her little belly dancer. From the day I was born, a zest for life bubbled in me. I have always enjoyed the pleasures of life, a good glass of wine, and all my guests praise my kitchen. I am an early riser, known to be cheerful and full of energy in the morning. I surprised many a slave by sitting all dressed up on the bed, waiting for them to get me. I loved the early morning hours at our old house in Rome the most. It had a large balcony from which I could overlook the lively Forum and the busy traffic around the old shops, watching passers-by who often waved back.

My childhood home in Liternum was, compared to our villa in Rome, like a tomb where my father moved around as a menacing ghost. He wore his skinny, wiry body like it was a poisonous cloak. Everything seemed sharp and angular, his arms, his legs, his chin, his long narrow face, his sunken cheeks, and his hollow eye sockets. A deep frown clouded his high forehead. His face showed a mixture of bitterness, rigor, and fierceness. A dull anger smoldered in his eyes, which suddenly could turn into a blind rage for no apparent reason. His voice became shrill and lost all its warmth. My husband told me when my uncle Lucius was accused of bribery and briefly incarcerated, my father drove to the prison and fought with the guards to liberate his brother, an act of sacrilege that astounded everyone. I fear that I may have inherited some of his inborn anger.

To escape the oppressive silence in the house, I spent hours at the beach, accompanied only by a few Greek slaves and guards. They surrounded me with long, saffron-colored screens to protect me from unwanted looks when I wished to bathe. Every time I see a young bride in Miseno wrapped in saffron, I am not only reminded of my wedding, but I also hear the sound of flapping screens in the wind and I feel the cool sea water sliding over my skin.

My wet nurse Sila told me that the Greeks believed men were originally born inside fish-like creatures. As evidence for this assertion, she contended infants calm down if one gently sways them back and forth, as if they are floating.

She also told me the tale about the dolphin that fell in love with a boy. The story made me cry at night. I would later use it as a theme for some of the murals in my baths. The dolphin had allowed the boy to climb on his back. Every day they swam and played together for hours. People came to watch them and their friendship became known in the wider area. Visitors flocked from everywhere until the authorities of the town decided it attracted too many spectators. They asked the parents to keep the boy inside one morning and waited for the dolphin to appear. It was easy to catch it and kill it. The next morning, the boy waited in vain for his arrival. He returned every morning, calling for his friend until an old fisherwoman from the village took pity on him and told him what had happened. When his parents came to his room the next morning, they found his bed empty. Later that day, a piece of his clothing washed ashore. Sila smiled and nodded when I assured her that I would have done the same.

The sea was my passion. My favorite spot was to sit between the gray-white rocks that colored the blue-green water, a dazzling tint crowned with white froth that I was never able to catch in my hands. To find out how our ancestors viewed the world, I sometimes opened my eyes under water to see what the sky looked like if the surface of the sea was my first firmament. I loved swimming during a heavy downpour. I imagined being part of the sea, comforting my extended body while it was hammered by a sister element. The lashing raindrops beat small dimples in the skin of the sea, which dissolved faster than my eyes could follow, leaving no scars. It felt like I was swimming in two animated elements, the living sea and the living air.

9.

My visits to the beach must have been a real ordeal for my slaves. Burdened with all kinds of rules and restrictions my mother imposed, they tried to keep me in line, but the power struggle was uneven. Cocky and imperious as I was, I cut them off – 'who is the slave here, you, or me?'– with warnings if they contradicted me. None of them dared to approach my mother about it, fearing they would lose their privileged position and be sent to the mills. Their downcast eyes, submissive muttering, and beads of sweat sparkling on their lips as I threatened them with flogging or degradation in the household, filled me with a physical sensation of power, which in turn scared and thrilled me.

On one occasion, I caused so much anxiety that one of my youngest slaves, barely older than I was, suddenly broke out in heaving sobs. The next day, she was gone. My mother enlisted the assistance of slave hunters who found her in a neighboring village. They brought her back and my mother ordered them to give her some strokes of the cane as a warning to her and other slaves. Her screams pierced into my room.

For my mother, the incident was almost a daily occurrence; slaves often ran away, but it made an ineradicable impression on me. What had seemed to be just an exciting exchange of words and a harmless competition in willpower had suddenly turned into a serious event with a horrible outcome. In the following weeks, I was greeted in the morning by a wall of hostile silence. It was a decisive moment in which I had the choice to harden my attitude or give in. I chose the latter. I stopped making threats and followed the gentle path of persuasion, which they all welcomed with a sigh of relief.

I have seen in my life similar interactions between children and their slaves in which, due to a lack of self-discipline and absence of parental oversight, slaves are exposed to all kinds of inhumane treatments. Such households are increasingly ruled by violence, poisoning the life of the master and the slave alike. I hear more and more stories about families where slaves revolted and ran off after murdering their masters.

My mother ruled our household with a stern hand, but she was never cruel. If she had caught me making the lives of the slaves miserable and sad, she immediately would have disciplined me. She forbade anyone to raise a hand in anger against a slave. To assure domestic peace, she purchased slaves from all corners of the world because the use of many languages lowered the risk of a conspiracy.

My mother was also very forgiving. Later, I was told that my father had a romantic relationship for years with one of the young slaves. My mother ignored it and, after the death of my father, she manumitted the young woman and married her off to one of our freedmen whom she loved.

Following her example, I urged my sons and daughters at a very early age to be aware of their obligation to protect all those who are in their power, slave, freed, or subordinate. I am convinced that the root of the crisis Rome now faces, lies in the upbringing of its children. Legislation will accomplish little if there is no self-discipline. People in Rome are advocating now to declare all decrees, which have been introduced forcefully, as nonbinding, and to impose this order if necessary, by force. Our world has been turned upside down.

10.

After my wet nurse Sila had told me the story about the Centaur Chiron, I conjured a dream to help me fall asleep in which Chiron adopted me as his pupil, sharing my role as my interlocutor and educator. My phantasy became an obsession and, to attract his attention, I had my Greek slaves scratch my name in Greek on trees, a request, which, in my eyes, they never took seriously enough. I even suspected them of extending my pleas with highly inappropriate additions after I noticed their suppressed giggles and chuckles when we came across old carvings. They denied it all vigorously. I bet it must have felt like a sweet revenge.

Chiron never made his appearance, but my eldest brother Publius played for many years a comparable role, serving as my best teacher. He even looked a bit like Chiron with his round beard, deeply lined face, and longish hair.

Publius was the first man I met who never participated in a military campaign, but spent his days reading, writing, and offering lectures. His poor health – I do not believe he was even for a moment in his life free of pain in his joints – prevented him from obtaining a leading position in Rome. The only title he ever held was that of Augur. Instead, he became a man of the arts. He wrote some speeches that were widely praised, and a historical work in Greek, a language he loved.

My brother lived in the most fragrant house I have ever entered. All his tunics and gowns were pregnant with the aroma of oils that were used for his daily massage, but most dominant were the fragrances that came out of his library; a sweet bouquet of scents from glue, leather, papyrus, parchment, ink, mold, and molten wax. Hold a scroll in front of my nose and I can tell you with closed eyes whether it is a new one or an old work.

His library was one of the largest in Rome. According to him, it counted more than six hundred copies. His home contained two reading rooms, one for Greek and one for Latin. The rooms were on the East side of his domus, with floor-to-ceiling windows. The floors were tiled with green marble, so occasionally one could redirect one's gaze toward the floor, giving tired eyes a moment's rest. I discovered it really helped and I had the same marble installed on the floor in my library here in Miseno. Fifteen slaves and freedmen worked daily on the collection, copying old works and protecting it against fungi and worms. Only my uncle would surpass him when he brought over the library of King Perseus. I am eternally grateful to both of them for leaving me many scrolls after they had died.

The persistent pain made my brother short-tempered, and he had no patience for girls. Expressions of compassion to soften his mood were resolutely cut off. I felt defenseless against his sardonic remarks and incapable of making him revise his opinion about me. As a token of his disdain, he gave me lyric poetry and silly novels to read.

Publius administered his estate like no other, but when it came to art and books, he lost all self-control. He closely watched the proceedings of the assignments in the Senate for positions in Greece and Asia Minor and as soon as the appointment was announced, he contacted the appointee with a whole slew of requests to assist him in finding certain works. He had been cheated a number of times into handing a slave or freedman a significant amount of cash to purchase an artwork or a book, but if his friends tried to warn him against his lack of restraint, he denied to their great amusement the upfront payment or claimed the man was still searching.

One morning I witnessed a conversation between him and a freed-man. In contrast to Publius, who hardly noticed me, my presence bothered the man. His shabby appearance, edgy behavior, and the boastful manner in which he recommended his contacts in Greece aroused my suspicion. After he had left, I advised my brother to hand the man only a small amount of money and pay the remainder after he had returned with the requested work. Annoyed, Publius waved my comments away. I had already forgotten the incident when, one day, he approached me about it. With averted gaze, he admitted he had never heard from the man again, and he recently discovered that the man was known to be a notorious swindler who had also deluded some of his friends. I expressed a few words of sympathy and moved away without offering any further comment. I think my discrete reaction formed a decisive moment in our relationship. In any case, from that time onward, he asked me to attend, hidden behind a curtain, his negotiations and to offer my advice.

After this incident, Publius introduced me under the watchful eye of my mother to the richness of the Greek language and literature. At regular intervals, he admitted me to his reading rooms where slaves brought me from his library the scrolls he had chosen for me in consultation with my mother. I received these lessons, in addition to the usual instructions in spinning and weaving, but after I had told him how much I detested those domestic chores, Publius decided my education no longer needed the supervision of my mother. From then on, I could order whatever I wanted.

As I became more familiar with the various Greek dialects and writers, I was able to develop preferences, enhancing my ability to discuss with the librarians which other writers might interest me. It gave me great pleasure when I began to discern all the hidden allusions with which playwrights like Menander and Aristophanes attacked or ridiculed the works of their predecessors and contemporaries. Pleased by the reports of his librarians about my growing insight and eagerness to learn, Publius laid the foundation for a tradition I also continued with my children. Before I read a new comedy or tragedy, Publius hired a few Greeks actors to perform the play for us in his garden. Some comedies gave me so much pleasure that after Publius had left, I asked the players to show it again, cheering up his otherwise quiet and dignified atrium with croaky frog sounds – 'brekekekex koax koax' - or jolly grunts of piglets - 'oink, oink.'

If he was in the right mood, my brother enriched my reading with history lessons about events surrounding the plays. After watching Aristophanes' play about the Athenian women, Publius told me that my mother had initiated a rebellion of women in Rome. He mentioned it in his typical, offhand manner with a sly grin on his face, and I thought he was just making fun of me. But after I had gathered enough courage to ask my mother about it, her eyes immediately lit up and a proud smile appeared on her face. She became so excited that she forgot to ask me how I knew. She made me sit down in front of her and told me that the freedom I was about to enjoy as an adult woman in Rome was the result of their struggle. She predicted that I would be told they revolted because they wanted to display their jewelry in public, but for her and her friends, the real issue had been that they did not want to be curbed like Greek women.

She described how they had organized parades in the Forum and occupied the Capitol, blocking access to the Senate. She emphasized it was all done in a lighthearted manner, avoiding any harsh confrontations. Accompanied by flute players, they had formed long lines and thrown flattering looks at passing Senators, begging them as they passed that since the private fortunes of all men were daily increasing, they should allow the women to have their fair share too. During the day, they withheld from their husbands their food, and in the night their love, but whenever they sensed their revolt became too offensive, they reduced the pressure by resuming some of their daily and nightly duties.

My mother had even saved excerpts from the speech the Consul at that time, Cato, had given in the Senate. Her private secretary had no trouble finding it, and she read parts of the speech aloud to me, imitating Cato's high and mighty manner of speaking with a sparkle in her eyes. "The liberty of men, already destroyed at home by female violence, was now crushed and trodden underfoot in the Forum. What sort of practice is this of running out into the streets and blocking the roads and speaking to other women's husbands? If the women win this, what will they not attempt? The moment the women begin to be your equal, they will be your superiors." While laughing aloud, my mother repeated the final words of his speech several times. I had never seen her so animated and cheery.

Step by step, my mother told me, the resistance in Senate had crumbled and, in the end, they had been granted the right to wear jewelry as they pleased, ride in carriages, and be borne through the city, gaining a public freedom that no Greek woman had ever enjoyed. It had been her biggest victory, she stated proudly. Her story made a lifelong impression on me.

Like Publius, I was struck by the light and cheerful tenor in which the plays were written at a time when Athens was ravaged by one catastrophe after another. The lamentations of the playwrights about the lack of money for sets and costumes made me dream of becoming a patroness of the arts, a wish I have been able to fulfill here in my little wooden theater.

The plays and the stories of my brother aroused my interest in the writings of the Greek historians Herodotus and Thucydides. On his advice, I read them simultaneously, alternating between myths and analyses. The narrative by Thucydides about the war between the Greek cities made me share his immense grief over the collective suicide his beloved cities committed.

In retrospect, I wonder if Publius, by introducing me to Herodotus, also meant to prepare me for my future. I read Herodotus while my body matured and many suitors asked my mother and my brother for an introduction. In his digressions about the wedding rituals of other cultures, I found answers to questions that would never have crossed my mind. Although I am grateful to my brother for the freedom he gave me, I later imposed more restrictions on the reading of my daughter Sempronia.

I read Herodotus with an intensity that is typical for a girl of that age who takes any writings about marriage far too personal. Some habits perturbed me, like the public auctioning of marriageable women in Babylon. The most beautiful brides went first and, with the proceeds, the auctioneer was able to pay the dowry for the least attractive girls. I pictured myself at the Forum, auctioned like a slave, and shuddered at the thought, but there is no denying that such an arrangement would have saved many a poor girl in Rome. They are often forced to prostitute themselves to gather enough money for paying their dowry. I even heard horror stories about girls who were rejected after the gifts had been paid because the prospective husbands had changed their minds and suddenly objected to the fact that they had been prostitutes.

With the image of my obese mother for my eyes, I had to giggle when I read about the bizarre custom of the Massagetae who killed their elderly parents and ate them. Herodotus claimed that they regarded it as the best death and that they faulted family members who became ill and had to be buried before they could be eaten. But I was upset for days after reading that families in Egypt sometimes waited three days before handing the body of a beautiful woman to the embalmers to avoid the risk, that they would violate her body.

After his introduction of the historians and playwrights, Publius dropped with a dull thump some scrolls of Aristotle in front of my nose, with the condescending remark he did not expect they would appeal to me. As if to prove his point, dust swirled around me and I broke out into a sneezing fit. He gazed at me with a pitying look and walked away while shaking his head, muttering something on his way out about philosophy and witless girls, which I happily ignored in my excitement to unwrap the first role. I was convinced that neither my mother, nor my older sister Cornelia, nor any of my girlfriends had ever read anything of him.

Aristotle's extensive comments opened my eyes to a completely new group of philosophers. His range made a huge impression on me. After all the oddities of Herodotus, his detailed *Problemata* offered a wealth of knowledge and insight. I recognized many of the physical symptoms he described and his analyses have been of great value for me in my married life. They contain nothing that can shock the soul of a married woman. His advice to breathe deeply while in labor has served me extremely well.

Under his influence, my interests shifted. After reading yet another comprehensive explanation about the origin of life, I lost my interest in the ancient philosophers while the writings of their successors about politics, ethics, the soul, and health never ceased to fascinate me.

Has there ever been a race that has shown more intellectual prowess and original thinking than the Greeks? Take Krates, who wrote a comedy about animals who refused to be eaten by humans and a time when all the work will be done automatically? Or Eratosthenes who calculated the circumference of the Earth and distanced himself from the haughty distinction between Greek and barbarian. He held a futile plea to treat Romans, Persians, Indians, and Carthaginians as equals, given their advanced forms of governance. Or Erasistratus who claimed that there are valves in our hearts, which cause the blood to flow in the same direction through our veins and argued that there are no specific female illnesses.

I have never fully shared his opinion that bloodletting worsens the disease, but to err on the side of caution, I did follow his advice when my children fell ill. His view was confirmed by the success my husband always had when he punished soldiers through bloodletting. For days, they felt weak and vulnerable, frightening them more than a flogging.

Or take Aristarchus who contended that the sun and the stars stand still and that the earth circles around the sun. His most perplexing claim was that the earth itself rotates, explaining the difference in day and night. During dinners when I wanted to tease my Greek friends or end another tediously long discussion, I made everyone laugh when I reminded them of his dizzying theory.

Discussions about our soul and senses kept me for a long time in their grip. Plato moved me by his observation that anything that needs food, whether humans, animals, or plants, harbors a craving and therefore experiences pain when left hungry. I found the refutation by Aristotle that animals can only taste, smell, and touch unconvincing. I do believe that animals, as well as plants, harbor feelings as Empedocles had asserted.

My brother and I also had lengthy discussions about the gods. He confounded me with his confession that he did not believe the Gods cared about the fate of individuals. In a discussion about our temples, he shocked me with a quote from Xenophanes who had stated that if horses could sculpt they would have created holy idols that would have looked like horses.

11.

As I got older, Publius allowed me to attend his dinners, behind a curtain, so that I could hear poets in person or listen to his table talks when he discussed prominent writers that he thought I should read with his friends. Sometimes, the conversations wandered off and they talked about issues that I was not supposed to hear, but if I remained quiet enough, Publius would forget my presence in the heat of the discussion.

As a result, I could surprise my older sister Cornelia with shocking details about a Consul whom a concubine had contacted. Defying the danger of getting killed for her betrayal as an ex-initiate, the woman had been the first to warn the Consul about the Bacchanalia, which held Rome at that time in its grip. She had taken the step to protect her young patrician client out of fear he might be dragged into it, and Publius' guests praised her courage. They recounted stories about nocturnal events, debauchery, rape, orgies, and torches that were thrown into the Tiber, yet continued to burn! The perpetrators concealed the screams of their victims with loud noise from drums and cymbals. My ears glowed.

At a very young age, I had noticed some of the agitation among the adults, but it was only after hearing their stories that I began to realize how grave the crisis must have been. Publius' friends estimated thousands had been involved. By order of the Consul, every Roman citizen was instructed to reveal the names of those who had taken part in the nightly gatherings. They caught the priests quickly and put them to death. Hundreds committed suicide or fled the city to escape their punishments. A large number of men and women, from all walks of life, were publicly executed. Others were transferred to families outside Rome and placed under the parental supervision. The stories filled me with disgust and excitement, coloring forever my image of religious sects as cruel and fanatical.

My voracious reading habits, lack of enthusiasm for the traditional domestic chores, and the fact that I knew so many shocking details about the Bacchanalia, incurred the ire of my sister. She alerted my mother who was already upset with me after I had corrected several times guests at the dinner table with quotations from Aristotle. My mother reprimanded me in the presence of my sister and, while she watched me with a triumphant smirk on her face, my mother lectured me about all my shortcomings and flaws. 'I was loud, rude and spoke too much. I did not cast my eyes down in time when guests talked to me. I laughed with my mouth wide open and, on top of it all, I used the Greek language in the presence of others. No honorable girl did that!' My mother notified Publius and warned him that if he did not impose more restrictions on me, he would endanger not only my position as a young bride but also that of my sister.

My mother's disapproval and my sister's condescending attitude struck me like a whip. I felt for a long time hurt and humiliated. But over the years I have come to appreciate their concerns and learned to apply the required silence in my favor. If I have to, I can use many types of silences, a shy silence, a confused silence, a reproachful silence, or an icy silence. For a while, I even used silence as a weapon, noticing how quickly men lost their self-confidence when I countered a token of affection with an icy silence.

Of all the things I have been accused, there is one I immediately admit. I have not taught my sons enough suppleness. The story my mother told me about her rebellion is a case in point. We women are like tall grass. Where a tall tree crashes in a storm, we bend unharmed until the winds have died down. In our ability to bend lies a hidden force that scares men more than the sight of a screaming Greek Hoplite.

12.

My father had pledged in his will a dowry of fifty Athenian talents for my wedding and after Publius, my mother, and my future husband had agreed to the nuptial conditions and I – after three encounters – had given my consent, I paid farewell to my beloved beaches. I experienced the transition despite all preparations as abrupt, and, in the beginning, I dearly missed my old girlfriends and slaves.

At the very last moment, just before I closed the curtain of my litter, Sila came rushing out. With her face wet from tears, she overwhelmed me in her agitation and distress with a whole slew of advice, so mundane and so incoherent that they stuck with me for years as if they had been jewels of profound wisdom. 'If I had eaten leeks, I had better keep my mouth closed when kissing. Wild asparagus from Ravenna was the best. It is better to eat salad at the beginning of a meal than at the end. Apples tasted best if I first dipped them in honey. Figs work well against constipation. It helps to eat many onions if the conjugal fire in my marriage had diminished.'

I have eaten many onions in my life, but never for that reason. When I think back to my childhood, the young Cornelia seems like a stranger, but the people who took care of her look all the more real. This is true for my mother, for Sila, but most of all for my brother Publius. There are days when I have the feeling that he follows all of my movements with a loving gaze. His tortured face lights up when I answer him in my thoughts, and his warm smile makes me want him to talk to me in a patronizing, sarcastic tone.

13.

There is a short period in the life of every woman, beautiful to look at or not, when her body is in perfect condition. The skin tight and shiny, her breasts full and robust, rosy cheeks, and a glance full of life. People talk about me now in the same manner that I had heard my mother speak about some of her friends: 'you can still see that she must have been beautiful.' It always aroused my curiosity, but when I saw the woman, I was disappointed. What I saw in my youthful haughtiness was just age and decay.

My old skin still remembers the tingling sensation in my fingertips when I put down for the last time my trusted toga praetexta and pulled the white, seamless tunic over my head. Four slaves assisted me and my mother watched us from a distance with a smile on her face. She held her hand over her mouth and the memory of her teary eyes still moves me.

Under cheerful, half-suppressed giggles, the slaves fastened a woolen belt round my waist, tying it with a double knot, and covered me with a bright, saffron robe. On my feet, I wore soft leather sandals in the same color. They secured my black hair together with six locks of blond wool and over my head, I wore a veil in bright, fiery shades, covering half of my face. The wreath on my head carried the fragrance of marjoram. If I pull now the moth-eaten faded locks out of my chest and hold them next my hair, it is almost impossible to see the difference.

My husband arrived at dawn, accompanied by all his friends. Gaius Claudius, with whom he later would share his Consulate as well as his Censorship, was his witness. My family had already gathered under a bright June sky in the atrium. My husband and I offered the Pontifex Maximus a spelt cake. A pig was sacrificed and Publius studied the omens in his capacity as Augur. After we had received his blessing, my husband offered me a series of gifts, including the golden ring, which he put on my ring finger, connecting it via the vena amoris straight to my heart.

When he attached the ring, my husband and I uttered at the same time the words "Ubi tu Gaius, ego Gaia," while everyone shouted "Feliciter." Amid loud cheering, my husband took my face in his hands and kissed me for the first time on my lips. We spent the rest of the day in the atrium where we received the felicitations of many guests and dignitaries from all over Italy, Spain, Greece, and Asia Minor.

In the evening, after the banquet, my husband rushed with his friends along the Palatine Hill and Circus Maximus to our house on the Aventine. I followed later, accompanied by all our guests. Flute players danced in front of us. To ward off the danger of premature death, three boys whose parents were still alive walked next to me. Scores of torch carriers lighted our way. Everyone sang songs and threw walnuts into the streets. My husband had played with them as a child and stowed away for his wedding day. The rattling sounds of the nuts on the boulders were meant to bring me the blessing of many children. People came out of their houses to wish me luck and children kicked the nuts up and down the streets. It looked as if whole Rome was celebrating.

My husband waited for me at the doorway of our house and lifted me, to loud roars, over the threshold. Inside, we first made a tour through the house where my husband held out a bowl with water and a small cauldron with burning charcoals. After I had touched both, servants took my sandals off and washed my feet. Accompanied by the oldest slaves of my mother's household, who had shared the bed with only one man, I entered our bedroom. Here they stripped me of my cloak and veil, while my mother, my sister, and friends watched me, standing in the doorway. Friends slapped my husband on the shoulders and, under frolicsome encouragements, they ushered him into the bedroom where he joined me on the bed. With a last look at the two of us, lying deftly next to one another, everyone left the house to rejoin the banquet that would last well into the morning.

For the first time in our lives next to each other, we looked back to the day and all the guests who had come to congratulate us. My husband portrayed their influence in the Senate and its numerous Committees. Gradually, we grew quiet, listening to the sounds, coming from the streets and finally just to our breathing. I felt my heart pounding in my throat in anticipation of the moment that I had feared throughout the entire day. But after my husband had unraveled the knot of the woolen band and I had pulled my tunic over my head, his soft, shy tenderness formed a revelation. It became apparent, he had been equally as nervous. The harmony I immediately felt put an end to all the bizarre fears I had had for months in advance. I know that for many of my fellow Matronae marriage is like a prison, but I experienced our first intimacies that night as a complete liberation.

14.

In Liternum, the gentle swishing sounds of the waves had woken me up and my mother had instructed the slaves inside our villa on the Palatine to use only small brooms and dusters in the morning. When I think back to our house on the Aventine, I think of noise. There was such a sea of noise on the very first morning after our wedding night, I clapped my hands over my ears and my husband, laughing aloud, had to pull them away to kiss me good morning.

It commenced with the noise of our slaves who, under lively chatter, banged the buckets down onto the marble floors and began to mop them. I put an end to that the very next day, but the noise they had made, was soon drowned out by a cacophony of sounds from the outside; the jeering of passersby; the laughter and loud talking of the first clients of my husband at the front door; the monotonous goat-like bleating of the shopkeepers around the corner, but above all the knocking, tapping, and clanking of the coppersmiths. As soon as the first rays of sunlight hit the rooftops of the insulae on our hill, their Vulcanian racket took off and these metal workers never seemed to sleep. Sometimes the banging and hammering of six or seven different workshops penetrated simultaneously from all sides our house.

Darkness brought no relief. Immediately after the sun had set, cackling and chiding women from the alleys swarmed in groups into the streets on their way to the latrines. Their shouting, name-calling and squabbles brought me in touch with all the woes of Rome's love life. Unwanted pregnancies as a result of leaking sheep casings, adultery, dildos of absurd dimensions, bleeding hemorrhoids, stretched arse holes, rampant worms, the list of gruesome details with which they attacked each other and their husbands was endless. Even if I believed only a tenth of what I heard, more than half of all Roman women were less than whores, suffering from the most horrific infections in and around all their body openings. In Liternum, I fled my home because of the silence. In Rome, the noise drove me into the streets.

To make up for his refusal to leave the Aventine and move to one of the villas on the Palatine, my husband gave me a free hand in furnishing our domus. Besides the workspaces of the coppersmiths, there were many other shops on the Aventine where I could get everything, I needed. The task required a delicate balancing act between the austere taste of my husband and my wish to create a warm, welcoming and elegant atmosphere.

Our house encompassed three floors of adjoining rooms, all centered on an open atrium. Two dining rooms, one for the winter with a fireplace and one for the summer, flanked the reception hall, which gave access to the atrium. The quarters for the slaves were on the ground floor in front of the house, which also contained the kitchens, the latrines and inventory rooms. Our private living rooms, library, bedrooms and bathrooms were upstairs, as far away as possible from the street noise. Adjacent to the guestrooms was a second, smaller atrium.

The fate of Rome is decided on two kinds of battlefields. In Spain, Africa, Illyria, Macedonia or elsewhere our armies force a decision. At the dinner tables in Rome, we wage the other battles and both my husband and I attached great importance to the layout of our reception and dining rooms. My uncle Aemilius Paullus always claimed there was no difference in preparing a banquet or a battle. In both cases, a thorough preparation will determine the outcome.

While visiting the workspaces on the Aventine, I discovered a studio run by a Greek carpenter from Epirus who had had a furniture workshop before he was taken to Rome. My eyes fell on his young son Simo. His open countenance and lively intelligent eyes struck me immediately. This young lad of barely twelve years listened intently to me during my first visit. When I returned, he had prepared some drawings, which his father, with great trepidation and trembling hands, passed on to me. Simo suggested I should choose for our dining room a circular rather than a traditional four-sided table. The boy managed to convince me I could equally well create the formal seating order of an official banquet at a round table. I had not consulted my husband in advance and when the superbly polished cherry-wood table with inlaid walnut ornaments arrived, I dreaded his comments, but he was delighted. Simo was also helpful in choosing the fabric and colors for the semi-circular couches.

After I had recognized my husband hated expensive luxury, but appreciated craftsmanship and natural materials, it became easier for me to choose. I took my time, step by step enriching each floor with red and green marble from Greece, fragrant citrus and ebony wood from Egypt, and ivory from Africa. I had the walls plastered, painted in soft green and ochre tones, and decorated with hunting scenes with stags, boars, dogs, lions, and hares; the tiled floors became covered with Arabic rugs. As for the seating areas, I choose large cushions in warm, dark red, and purple tones.

The result of all my efforts was a home that offered comfort, domestic happiness, and a discrete kind of natural grace that family members, friends, and acquaintances loved and praised. I purchased many items in that period, including the table, the rugs, and the cushions that now decorate my villa here in Miseno. I pray I may also have taken with me the same spirit of warmth and hospitality.

15.

In the first years of my marriage, I hardly distinguished myself from my fellow Matronae. Like them, I paid little attention to the obsessive need of Greek philosophers to explain the meteoric rise of Rome or to their endless debate about whether our constitution offered the right balance between monarchy, aristocracy, and the voice of the people. I had my eyes solely fixed on strengthening the position of our family. The Senate, the Assemblies, and the contios were like marketplaces for me where people of flesh and blood gathered to buy and sell influence, prestige, favors, positions, and power.

I was, at the start, not free of shyness and anxieties, but as I grew more accustomed to the many unwritten rules and practices, I plunged with all my youthful energy into the political power game that held Rome day and night in its sway.

Ah, the titillating thrills of power running through my veins! Even now after so many years and so many disillusions, I still feel its heavenly intoxicating rush. How I treasured all the trophies that the triumphs of my husband yielded. Just as Senators venerated former Consuls in the Senate, so too their wives idolized Consular Matronae. I had twice the honor of leading them as Bona Dea in the annual nightly celebration. It gave me great pleasure to enter a room where everyone bowed to me or having people stop and move aside in the narrow alleys as I passed. I loved seeing the mixture of curiosity, admiration, jealousy, and awe on their faces.

I became a frequent visitor to the site near the Sundial on the Forum to catch the latest gossip and I kept a journal recording who received the longest applause when entering the Circus Maximus. I was thrilled when a public meeting of an opponent was canceled, giving priority to my husband or one of his friends. I closely followed the proceedings in the Senate, taking note of who spoke first and whose interventions had made the biggest impression. I sent slaves to the most-visited hairdressers, bathhouses, restaurants, shopping arcades, and latrines to remain informed about any coalitions between this or that family. I maintained a close relationship with copyists so I could intercept letters of our adversaries and prepare my counterattack even before they had sent them out. I initiated whisper campaigns during elections and I became a master in telling stories while omitting half of the truth. Sometimes I dictated to four slaves at the same time. The city of Rome became like a carriage with multiple wheels and my husband and I formed such a splendid span of horses, with him holding the reins and me behind the scenes.

My husband would never submit a proposal to the Senate while it was still boiling hot. Everything was prepared far in advance with a cool head. Like a farmer can stand on a hill, gazing over his fields, herds, and orchards, so could my husband stand in the doorway of the Curia and let his eyes slide over the heads of the Senators. I could hear him count softly. Eternal optimist as he was, he would first tick off his most loyal supporters; family members of the Fulvii, Flacci, Licinii, Mucii, and Claudii. He then went home to compose, with the assistance of his nomenclator, several lists of doubters. Some were up for grabs. On others, he would have to exert more pressure or offer deals in exchange for their support for which he needed the backing of third parties. He sent friends to the chairpersons of the numerous societies, guilds, and the centuriae in Rome to see if they would be willing to persuade opposing Senators. Each time, he would update his lists until he was convinced he had enough votes. I am afraid he even lowered himself to the reprehensible practice of snatching existing clients from his opponents to weaken their influence if the voting appeared too close.

Except for horseracing, nothing in Rome arouses such strong feelings as the elections. Even when my husband was not a candidate, I attended many Consular elections in the Comitia Centuriata from the sidelines at the Campus Martius. To this day, the memory evokes a longing in me to go back to Rome and witness it again. Days ahead, thousands of voters from all over Italy swamped our city. All hostels and guesthouses were filled to the rafters. The alleys were packed with supporters who marched up and down the narrow passages, chanting the names of their favorite candidates and challenging their opponents at the squares in the evening. In the case of Consular elections, the exhausted candidates, whose voices by this time had become fatigued and hoarse, were allowed to campaign in the last three days at the Forum. On the Election Day, the clamor of the crowd filled the air of Rome with a reverberating, solid roar as if the Gauls had returned.

My husband and I managed twice to seize the highest price, including the positions of Praetors and Censors for our associates. The posts of the first speaker in the Senate, the military Tribunes and the Rogatores[13] then fell like ripe apples in our voting basket. For years, the city lay at our feet and I received daily requests for support, advice, recommendations and personal appointments.

16.

Was it Plato who once remarked that if one loses sight of the right proportions and designates something for which it actually is too large – a huge sail for a small ship, a big meal for a tiny body, too much power for a little soul – everything is torn apart?

When the Senate accused my father and my uncle Lucius of having accepted a payment by the Syrian King Antiochus of four million sesterces, my father tore the scrolls with the financial records of that campaign to pieces in his anger. He stamped on it with his feet, yelling at the shocked Senators to come and see for themselves if they could find the

---

[13]Election officials in ancient Rome.

payment. He declined to answer any further inquiries, claiming he had enriched the Treasury with 200 million sesterces and marched out of the Curia, bristling with anger. It was the wrong reaction to a false accusation, but the fact is that my family has awarded our Republic with hundreds of millions of sesterces.

I do not believe there has ever been in the long history of Rome a generation, which witnessed so many changes in our capital as mine. After the victory of my father at Zama, Rome became the belly of the Mediterranean world, our roads its veins, our armies its blood, and while it was spilled in Spain, Africa, Greece, and Asia, the veterans, Roman or ally, flocked to the city where their victories were digested. Our Italian and Latin allies protested against the depopulation of their towns and villages. At their request, my husband's co-sensor, Gaius Claudius, ordered twelve thousand Latins to leave Rome, but this one-time measure had barely any effect. By the time I left the city, it had grown so much that only Antiochia and Alexandria could match it in size.

The many newcomers had to be housed and their massive inpouring unleashed a building frenzy of insulae all across town. My husband hated them. Driven by the insane rise in rent prices, contractors built the apartment blocks to ever-greater heights, four to five floors, adding on top of all the noise a new racket, the echoes of their building and collapses. Somewhere every month an insula[14] imploded, burying its residents under the rubble, while builders stood by looking for parts of the debris they might use again. Our city burst at its seams. The height of the rent also drove many a veteran into the streets. It broke my husband's heart when he recognized one of his former soldiers living the life of a homeless in one of the alleys.

Among the more than fifteen temples that were built with public money after Zama, changing the appearance of our seven hills forever, I

---

[14] A type of Roman apartment building for the lower classes.

regularly visited four. In the spring, I loved to stroll along the banks of the Tiber and visit the small, defiant island in its middle where an enchanting little temple was founded in honor of Faunus. It was financed with the proceeds of fines imposed on farmers who had let their herds graze illegally on public land. I went there before my marriage, offering sacrifices to ensure the horny Faunus would not adulterate my dreams, but I remained a loyal visitor after my wedding. To pray for the soul of my father, I turned to the temple dedicated to Pietas. It contained the first gold-plated statue that appeared in our temples. With Tiberius and Gaius, I regularly visited the Temple of Iuventas and the shrine in the Temple of Jupiter where they sacrificed a coin on the day they received their toga virilis.

The splendor of Praxiteles' sculptures – Rome's finest spoils of war – brought me to the Temple of Felicitas. In front of his exquisite Thespian muses and Venus, I asked the blessing over my epigrams and writings. The nude Venus with her lush hips, small breasts, oval face, high cheekbones, and tightly strung hair became the most sought-after beauty icon in Rome. They say his mistress Phryne had been his source of inspiration. My vanity was handsomely soothed when my husband remarked in one of his amorous effusions that I could have been her twin sister.

On the Aventine, I visited the older temples, dedicated to the goddesses Ceres and Diana. Diana offered in her compassionate wisdom a safe haven to all women who were vulnerable or on the run, freeborn and slave alike. Her sanctuary dated from the time of the Kings and a weathered stone reminded us of old treaties between Rome and the most powerful Latin cities. Gaius took shelter here on the last day of his life, near his old family home, before he made his desperate escape in the direction of the Tiber. If I ever return to Rome, I will bring her my sacrifices of praise for the protection, no matter how short, she offered him.

They say the effigy of the goddess Ceres in her temple near the Circus Maximus, at the foot of the Aventine, is the oldest bronze statue in

Rome. Her temple was one of the main meeting places of my sons and their followers. Their Aediles kept office here and from this temple, they carried out the food distribution programs for the needy. It drew large crowds and with its heavy, sturdy construction and the dark terracotta statues on its roof, this temple resembled a kind of earthen sanctuary. After the advent of so much smoothly polished marble elsewhere in Rome, I began to appreciate its rustic simplicity of dark red bricks. The priestesses came from Naples or Velia and they held their services in Greek. In times of famine, they offered sacrifices of spelt wheat and like Diana, Ceres offered protection for all those who fled to her sanctuary. Ceres' celebrations always took place at the height of the summer and I have many fond memories of these cheerful gatherings, graced with diluted wine and food for the poor. Lamentably, on the last day of the celebrations, foxes with burning torches on their backs were set loose at nightfall in the Circus Maximus. The people enjoyed this spectacle immensely, but I always felt sorry for these poor, distraught animals, and I regarded it as a barbarous, cruel entertainment.

17.

After he had withdrawn from active life, my husband and I often walked together to the Temple of the goddess Libertas, which was built by his grandfather and where his uncle had commissioned a mural painting in celebration of his victory over the Carthaginian commander Hanno. The temple later became one of the favorite spots of Tiberius to which he withdrew early in the morning or late at night at the height of his campaign, meditating and plotting his next moves in front of the victorious scenes of his ancestor.

As Censor, my husband restored the Forum in all its previous glory as the beating heart of our city. Through his efforts, I developed an appreciation for the many great public works he and his colleagues undertook. The streets and alleys around the Forum, which in the autumn and winter degraded into life-threatening mud trenches, were, for the first time, paved over. The city walls were reinforced and enhanced with many new gates. They even made an attempt – unfortunately often ignored, which use to drive me crazy – to earmark each new bridge for only one kind of goods, so that the supply of slaves, cattle, fish, wheat, flowers, fruit, and vegetables entered the city as close as possible to the designated markets, which were built at intersections near the walls. The Circus Maximus became equipped with stone trackside seating for the Senators, with covered spectator seating for the well-to-do, with iron cages for the lions and with giant oval eggs, straddling on the middle barrier, which turned each time the horseracing carts had completed a lap. Quay walls were built to protect us from the eternal flooding during spring and our water supply improved dramatically by the renovation of the aqueduct of Appius and the construction of the Aqua Marcia and Aqua Tepula. Gaius, who continued the building tradition of his father during his first and second Tribunate, regarded the Aqua Marcia as a masterpiece. He praised the quality of its water, contending that the 60 miles long aqueduct was the largest structure ever accomplished in the world. In addition, as if there was not already enough noise, they built more grain warehouses on the Aventine and new ports along the Tiber.

I still consider the reconstruction of the Forum as the highlight of my husband's work. The Senate provided him with the means to buy the old house of my father and the neighboring shops and stables of the butchers. My husband had the house and shops demolished, building in their place a new basilica, the Basilica Sempronia. A few years earlier, the Basilica Fulvia et Aemilia on the north side of the Forum was finished and with the construction of the Basilica Sempronia on the South side, a huge space in the middle was created. Just as my husband approached every-thing that crossed his path with an open mind, so it seemed as if the Fo-rum, after his reconstruction, could breathe again. My husband also added a series of new traders' shops along the Via Sacra and from the spacious balconies above these shops I have watched many festivities with my sons and friends.

18.

Everybody knows I have always hated the office of Tribune. It is a function born out of discontent, a product of distrust, a tool to arouse popular agitation. Tribunes betrayed my father, my husband, and my sons. I loved my husband dearly, but I cannot deny there have been quite a few moments when I wished I had married a Patrician like my sister. Then my husband, as well as my sons, would have been barred from that ruinous office.

My husband and my sons loved their Tribunate and they have al-ways defended it. My husband saw it as a token of my inferior female intellect that I was unable to make a distinction between the institution and the behavior of an individual Tribune. A wise Tribune tempers the fickleness of the masses, realizing that after one year, he is no longer in-violable. The introduction of the Tribunate centuries ago had been a great success. No major conflicts had occurred since then and it was good that the power of the Praetor Urbanus had been challenged. We have two Consuls and two Censors to check and balance their power, but we had only one Praetor until the arrival of the Tribune.

I was never able to counter the arguments of my husband ade-quately, but he shared my view that the Tribunate had fallen increasingly into the hands of those who were only driven by a personal opportunism. As an unintended consequence, his reconstruction of the Forum had also given the Tribunes the space to move their popular meetings to the center of the Forum and their contios had become true political spectacles, drawing thousands of followers. I regret to say that Gaius even went so far as to avert his gaze from the Senate house when he addressed the crowd, one of his cheap tokens of defiance just to please the masses.

The enemies of my husband had successfully delayed his election as a Censor, but, five years after his first Consulate, no one could stop him anymore and he was elected together with his former co-Consul Gaius Claudius. My husband regarded his nomination as his last and only chance to oust the most corrupt members of the Equestrian class. As soon as he and Gaius took office, they held public hearings at the Forum to purge the list. As many had feared, they degraded a large number of Equestrians to the lowest voting ranks and quite a few incumbent Senators searched in vain for their names on the new list of the Senate. Furthermore, they blacklisted all the tax collectors and contractors their predecessors had engaged. The livid contractors first appealed to the Senate with the absurd request to restrict the power of the Censors. When the Senate rejected their pleas, they enlisted the support of Rutilius, a Tribune.

Publius Rutilius was exactly the kind of man about whom I had been talking. He was a small, pugnacious, obese thug with thickset lips, pig eyes, and a high-pitched voice. He was so full of himself, marching through Rome with his huge belly in front of him and a nasty smirk on his face. Each time I saw him, he made me cringe. An acquaintance of this rabble-rouser operated an insula alongside the Via Sacra, opposite the public shrines near the Forum. As one could expect of the likes of him, he started without permission an extension, building a wall up against public property. My husband ordered him to bring it down. When he refused, my husband sent his men to him, imposing a lien on his property to secure the fine. The freedman appealed to Rutilius and his plea offered Rutilius the pretext to intervene not only on his behalf, but also on behalf of the contractors. He submitted a plebiscite to the People's Assembly in which he accused the Censors of tyrannical behavior and abuse of their power. They were ordered to remove the lien and cancel all new building contracts, including the one of the Basilica Sempronia. A new round of calls for tender had to be held, this time without excluding anyone.

My husband notified Rutilius that he would ignore his plebiscite and Rutilius summoned the Censors to the People's Assembly. Alarmed by this sudden turn of events, I accompanied my husband to the Capitol. The people remained respectful when my husband spoke, but as soon as Gaius Claudius addressed the crowd, the Assembly became unruly and noisy. The haughty manner with which he treated the people – so typical of a member of the Claudian gens – now worked against him. Nevertheless, the whole affair would have fizzled out if Gaius Claudius had not lost his temper. He allowed himself to be drawn in by ordering his men to silence the Assembly. I still see how Rutilius, who had been waiting for it to happen, rushed forward yelling with his hysterical voice that Claudius had robbed him of his sacred dignity as chairman of the Assembly. His Office had been breached. The next day my husband and Claudius were indicted by Rutilius for high treason and their case would be tried in the Comitia Centuriata. All our possessions were to be confiscated and the Praetor was asked to set the date for their impeachment. My husband and Gaius had twenty-four days to prepare their defense, and the atmosphere in Rome suddenly grew grim. I was enraged; my husband, who had celebrated two triumphs, accused of treason! For the first time, I began to understand how my father must have felt.

To step up the pressure on Rutilius, my husband and Claudius banned all public transactions. They closed the treasury in the temple of Saturn, as well as their office at the Forum, sending all the slaves home. They let their beards grow and appeared at the Forum dressed in the white robe of an accused together with some Senators who, in a show of heartwarming support, had taken off their rings and wore mourning gowns.

We lost the vote in the class of the Equestrians, but the lower classes saved us. I heard people call out to my husband that he had nothing to fear. My husband responded that if they convicted Claudius, he would go into exile too. I nearly fainted when he said that, but his unwavering loyalty carried the vote. Later on, my husband dealt with Rutilius. After he had finished his term as Tribune, my husband removed him from the list of Equestrians.

Still, there was damage. When my husband and Claudius submitted the customary request to finish the second half of their term, another Tribune vetoed their bid because my husband had kept him out of the Senate. It grieved him deeply that he was unable to guide the construction of his Basilica to the end. I felt sorry for him but secretly, I was very relieved we no longer ran the risk of any new confrontations. Tribunes!

19.

One morning my husband found two venomous snakes in his bedroom. He consulted immediately his Augur colleagues and they instructed him, in their unrivaled wisdom, that he should neither kill them nor let them escape, adding, that if the male serpent was killed, he would die, and if the female perished, his wife would die. Therefore, he decapitated the male adder, allowing the other to escape. A year later, my husband died.

On the eve of our worst naval defeat against Carthage, our commander, Claudius Pulcher, became furious when the sacrificial chickens refused to eat. He grabbed them by their feet and threw them overboard while execrating, "Let them drink if they don't want to eat."

When the commander of my son Tiberius, the Consul Mancinus, embarked with his troops for Spain, everyone suddenly heard the fierce cry, "Stay, Mancinus, stay!" Mancinus looked around, but he saw only the blue sky and after a brief hesitation, he boarded.

When my son Tiberius left his house on the fatal day of his re-election, the birds refused to leave their cage and eat, even after the birdwatcher had shaken their crates. When he walked out of his house, he stepped on a nail protruding from a piece of wood and blood seeped through his sandal. On his way to the Forum, a flock of crows stirred up a pile of stones on a roof, causing one to roll off and hit his injured foot.

No one can accuse the gods of being ambiguous. Their signs surround us daily, but it is our doom to ignore their messages. Each generation grows up in a world the previous one left behind, and the achievements of the former are taken for granted by the latter. The struggles it took and the people who made the effort are no longer visible. My grandchildren merely see an old woman. The image of a young Cornelia full of energy and actively pursuing opportunities to strengthen the position of the family never reaches their eyes. The long, arduous existence of one person is just an epitaph for the other, barely noticed in passing – one knows the old inscriptions:

'Greetings traveler, ye who passeth here with a carefree look. Stop for a moment and look at my headstone. My name was known. For my husband, I was a good wife, for my sons a good mother. Death took my breath away. Enough. Pray the soil rests softly upon me and continue your journey. Goodbye to all of you above the ground.'

Know thyself! Do we Romans really know who we are? What made us the masters of our world? Is it possible for an entire nation to know itself, understand its history and what lies ahead, when it is virtually impossible for an individual to do so? Strangely enough, it seems easier for me to answer this question about the Greeks than my own people. I oc-

casionally find on deserted beaches the helmets of restless Greek warriors from a distant past. Like a wavering memory of their craving for ev-
erlastingness, the dented remains of their iron masks still swayed back
and forth to the rhythm of the waves washing ashore. No writer has captured the genius of the Greek people better than Homer has done in his
story about Odysseus. For the Greeks, the wine-red sea was their ulti-
mate province. Here they sowed the best of their dragon seed. Here they
drew their last breath.

This is what I know about us. In contrast to the spirited, seafaring
Greeks, we Romans are a down to earth race. We lack imagination and
we perceive our lives as lines of march. After centuries of warfare and
burdened like pack animals with our fate on our backs, we prefer to
move directly from A to B. The proverb "a straight road is the safest
road" decorates many a Roman fireplace. Friend and foe still praise
Gaius' orderly layout of our roads. Recta Linea!

We experience the movement of the foot as natural and of ships and
carriages as unnatural. As soon as we lose solid ground under our feet,
we become frightened and nothing terrifies us more than an earthquake.
We prefer to man our ships with slaves and freedmen. After the fall of
Carthage, pirates again rule the waves. Many a grain ship from Egypt
falls into their hands before it reaches our shores.

They say our country bears the resemblance of an army boot. It is
blessed with vast forests, mountains, rivers, lakes, and fertile valleys. It
carries the name the Greeks gave it, Italy, land of cattle, our oldest source
of revenue. The stride of our farmer-soldiers is like their beasts of burden,
the humor of our people is boorish, and our dishes are so plain, one can
still taste the soil. Of all the conflicts dividing my people, there have been
two which shook our foundations to the core; the height of the grain price
and the distribution of our public land.

We have founded colonies in Asia, Spain, Africa, and Greece, which
can best be described as the footprint of an army camp. A visitor will

encounter the same layout, the same streets, the same angles, the same fora, and the same street numbers. In all these different places, it is possible to step out of the exact same shadow into the sunlight.

My husband saw it as the cornerstone of our civilization and a guarantee for our survival. In the eyes of my husband, the street plan of his colony Grachurrius in Spain represented exactly how a State should function. He made people laugh when he recounted how barbarians, entering his colony for the first time, acted like foreigners in their own country. "With a shy look and staying close to the façades, they tiptoe through the streets, overwhelmed by the height of our temples, basilicas, theaters, and baths, the neat appearance of our cobblestone streets and squares, the well-designed ease of our food and beverage stores. In these streets, the heart of our civilization beats and whoever has felt its pulse can no longer live without it."

I never had the heart to challenge my husband's vision while he was alive. Yet over the years, I have come to wonder what kind of legacy we will leave behind once we are gone. Will it be more than our drains, roads and aqueducts?

In private conversations, my Greek friends confided to me that we Romans scare them. They had expected us to surrender after our horrendous defeat at Cannae, and the fact that we continued to fight, ultimately annihilating Carthage, terrified them, just as the destruction of Numantia. They contended that we were different from any of the people they knew. "We Greeks may be obsessed with immortality, but you Romans are obsessed with killing. Others would have been satisfied with surrender, but you had to wipe out their very existence."

My brother Publius, who never minced words, spoke about our overseas campaigns in the way he would talk on rare occasions about his aches and pains. "We have tied our people on the bed of Procrustes, stretching them out until they have no limbs left. We Romans possess

only two skills, agriculture and fighting, and if we abandon the first, robbery remains." Because no one could accuse him of articulating a personal ambition, my brother felt free to express a preference for the Kingship.

"Kings go through periods of inaction so the people can catch their
breath and dedicate themselves to other things than war. A peace treaty
with a country ruled by a King carries the character of a personal com-
mitment, which only ends after his death. By electing our Consuls for
only one year, our Kings die every year, and we never leave our people
in peace."

My brother-in-law, Corculum Nasica, belonged to those prominent
Romans who believed cultures that owed their emergence to the sea were
inferior and he despised everything that was Greek. Yet, ironically, his
campaign in Epirus resulted in the largest influx of Greeks into Italy ever.
We enslaved hundred and fifty thousand of its inhabitants, and the
Greek language began to rule our hallways, storage rooms, kitchens, and
fields. The thousand hostages, he had seized to prevent another uprising,
had been legislators, historians, and philosophers, and they were appointed in Rome as teachers. Anyone who passed the open schools on
the squares in Rome could easily imagine that he was walking through a
second Greek capital.

When the Consul Opimius gave his orders to kill my son Gaius and
our fellow citizens, he had to use archers from Crete for fear our free Roman soldiers would refuse. Ah Rome, know thyself!

20.

I have always been convinced that my husband knew he was dying
when he lectured Tiberius in the last year of his life, during hours-long
sessions, about the workings of our Republic and the irreplaceable value

of the Senate. He often used the metaphor of our body as the Consul Agrippa had resorted to in our distant past. Weakened, and with a barely audible voice, my husband recounted how the plebeians had withdrawn en masse onto the Aventine as a result of a conflict with the Patricians over the grain prices. Agrippa succeeded in persuading the plebeians to return by telling them what happens to a body if the limbs revolt. He described how the limbs had turned against the stomach because it only consumed while they were doing all the hard work. To force the stomach into submission, the limbs withheld it its food, but by doing so, they also weakened themselves. They discovered, the stomach played an important role by distributing the blood, enriched with digested food, through the veins to all the other parts of the body. No one could survive without the other.

My husband talked about the Republic, but he could have spoken equally well about himself. Whatever food we gave him, his stomach refused to hold it. In the end, he could barely move his limbs. As a physician of our Republic, he had given everything to keep our Senate healthy, but he knew our vital organ was beyond recovery, and I think he welcomed his own death as a salvation.

PART 6
QUIS CUSTODIET IPSOS CUSTODES?
(WHO WILL GUARD THE GUARDS THEM-
SELVES?)

Gaius Gracchus addresses the Roman People
(Silvestre David Mirys (1742-1810))

1.

"These men beat my brother before your eyes with clubs to death, dragged his body from the Capitol through the midst of the city and threw him into the Tiber. They murdered his friends without any trial. There is an ancient rule that if someone is accused of a capital offense and does not respond to the summons, a trumpeter shall go in the morning to his house and order him to appear by the sound of the trumpet and the judges shall not rule on his case until this is done. This is how judicious and scrupulous we dealt with capital cases in the past. But where can I turn my eyes? To the Curia, to the murderers of my brother or to the Aventine where my mother is buried under her grief?"

Ah, my eloquent son! While you paced back and forth on the rostra, you whipped the people up with your trembling voice and hatred in your eyes. Who could resist you? You moved even your enemies to tears.

All the pent-up hatred, anger, and sadness boiling inside him for ten years burst loose after he had announced his candidacy for the Tribunate. The news spread like a wildfire throughout Italy and beyond. Couriers, on foot or horseback, rushed from town to town to alert friend and foe. From everywhere people poured into Rome. They had to move the election to the Campus Martius, but even then there was not enough space. Thousands of supporters followed the elections from the rooftops. Because of a last desperate attempt by his opponents to stop him, my son did not succeed to become the first elected Tribune. He came out fourth, but from that moment onward he surpassed all nine of his other colleagues in popularity and legislation.

Socrates once touched upon the similarities between a written text and a sculpture. No matter how convincingly a writer may have penned down his description or how truthfully a sculptor may have portrayed a person, in the end, both encompass just surrogates, which can never match the merit of a personal exchange. He, who addresses a scroll or a sculpture, will never receive a reply. When my son stood on the penultimate day of his life in front of his father's statue, he entered a dialogue with a father he had never known. He spoke to an idealized image his brother that I had sketched him. I fear the image we conjured has been far too flawless. It put my son under so much more pressure than if he had been able to speak with his father in person and learned how to handle personal flaws and shortcomings, making his fate more bearable.

The dead letter of his laws has now replaced my memory of the living spirit of my son, and with each passing day, the distance between him and me grows. My son weighed every word, every phrase, and every paragraph carefully, but I am left with the result, and the many considerations that preceded them are gone.

My Greek friends keep telling me it is not the letter, but the spirit of the law that matters. Gaius would have agreed only partially. Our laws of the Twelve Tables were drawn up in such a way that many a workman could recite whole sections as if they were nursery rhymes. Gaius was always thrilled about that and, following this tradition, he made sure that his laws and decrees, etched in bronze placards, were displayed in such a way that it was easy for everyone to read. On holidays, he had literate slaves standing next to them so they could read them aloud, clarifying their meaning to the common people. He argued that an illiterate man who could cast a vote in the People's Assembly may be less knowledgeable about politics than a seasoned Senator, but that the sum of many could lead to more wisdom than that of a few. Yes, there was anger, but I wonder if anyone of the Roman people ever fully appreciated the love and devotion with which my son worked day and night for our common good.

I fear one can read the answer in the never-ending stream of anonymous hate letters I receive to this day. I recognize in the caricatures little of Gaius, but all the more of the worldview of these brave authors.

'In his relentless fury to attack our leaders and to establish a reign of terror, your son conspired to obtain the support from all sections of our population. They were not only his supporters, but also became the driving forces behind all his plans and laws. Motivated by their own selfish needs, they ignored every risk to defend the laws he introduced. By denying the Senators, the right to sit as jurors and appointing Equestrians in their place, your son allowed the inferior element to prevail over the superior. Your son destroyed willfully the harmony that had existed between the Senate and Equestrians. Both were now exposed to the whims of the common people. Your son split our society in two to pave his own ruinous pathway. He wasted the money of our State by handing out briberies and through ill-advised spending just to ensure all eyes were turned on him. By exposing our provinces to the greed of the publicani, your son caused the nations we govern to develop justified hatred against us. To pander our soldiers, he introduced laws that undermined the ancient discipline and opened the gates to anarchy and rebellion. For someone who no longer respects his superiors will also lose the respect for the law itself and all of this will lead to a fatal disorder and destruction of the State.'

In our Republic, we constantly misrepresent our adversaries. We conjure shallow images of each other that have little to do with reality. I have been guilty of it too, but I never went as far as the enemies of my sons. Tiberius was vilified as a man trying to become King; Gaius as a perfidious demagogue, consumed by anger and hatred. If someone wants to destroy his opponent, the best option is to tarnish his image. Public images are elusive, but once they have settled in the minds of people, they are ineffaceable. One can demolish a prison made from stone, but a prison made from imagery never.

2.

Even though I reject the falsehoods of my son's enemies, I must confess, I found it hard to support some of Gaius' legislative programs. Did the blood of my Patrician lineage revolt? His supporters called him a far-sighted statesman, steering the ship of our State into safety, but I continued to be haunted by the image of a desperate shipwright, running in the face of a growing storm from one gaping hole to another.

My inner struggle deepens when I go through Gaius' writings, speeches, and decrees. The scope of his legislation fills me again with awe. His first Tribunate resulted in a breathtaking stream of proposals and laws. While his enemies were still trying to determine the implications of a ruling, he had confronted them already with a new one. Nothing escaped his attention, the size of the proletariat in Rome, the fate of our soldiers, the new colonies, the food distributions in Rome, our judiciary, our State finances, the governing of our provinces, the political status of our allies. The list is endless.

According to my Greek friends, I am also too harsh and critical in my judgment of the various measures my son took. They point out that the latest census displayed an uptick in the number of small farmers. Not as many as hoped for but still an increase. They praise Gaius for restoring the status of the Comitia Centuriata by ordering that only the Roman People could prosecute capital cases and not an ad hoc Senatorial Committee. With the re-establishment of the Comitia Centuriata as the proper legislative body, they argue, he not only overturned Scaevola's decision to declare the murder of Tiberius legal, but also shielded his enemies in the Senate from malicious prosecution by their colleagues. They estimate that our Treasury receives every year millions of denarii more after he had taken the tax collection in Asia out of the hands of our local commanders and consigned it to the Censors.

When I listen to their uplifting assertions, they fill my heart with joy, but as soon as I am alone, all my previous doubts return. Why do I hear this praise only from the lips of my Greek friends and almost never from my fellow Romans? Cui bono? Our country as a whole or only a limited group of beneficiaries? If it is the latter, where were those publicani who acquired the rights to collect the taxes in Asia when the Consul Opimius ordered the attack on my son? Where were the needy after my son had installed a bottom price for the grain, built granaries and new roads? Where were the Senators after he had protected them against bogus lawsuits in which colleagues could accuse one another arbitrarily of conspiracies? Where were the soldiers for whom my son arranged extra clothing and raised the legal minimum age for their first call? Where were the veterans after he had restored the powers of the College of Three, founded new colonies, and ensured that they could elect the military Tribunes of the first four legions again freely? My son died, like his brother, the death of a lonely man.

3.

I think that of all the measures and legislation my son initiated, he loved his building activities the most. He built his roads to facilitate and speed up the supply of animals for slaughter, grain and vegetables from the Italian countryside to Rome, reducing its dependency on imports from Sicily and Egypt. The construction provided many families in Rome and Italy work and bread and the new warehouses he built on the Aventine secured a steady supply of grain for the needy.

Sometimes, I came unannounced to Rome. During one of these unexpected visits, I had the pleasure to observe him from a distance. Surrounded by a group of architects and builders, he inspected the construction of a granary and it was such a joy to see with how much warmth and respect everyone treated him. They all followed closely his directions, made jokes or weighed the pros and cons of his comments with serious faces. As soon as my son stepped down from the rostra and moved among the people, he became a different man. In his personal contacts, he could be warm, charming, funny, and free from any kind of posturing.

The roads he built were stunningly beautiful. On a brilliant summer day, he took me out to the country to show me a section they were working on, just as my husband had taken me once to the Forum to view the progress. I could see his road already from afar, carrying like a grey-white line through the country without any deviation. He had all the holes filled up, torrents or ravines were bridged over and both sides of the roads were of equal, corresponding height so it radiated an elegant image of symmetry and precision. When I walked over it and gazed ahead, the straight line of the road had a spellbinding effect on me and the surrounding nature suddenly looked coarse and outlandish. I got excited when Gaius pictured a whole network of roads throughout Italy. He was also looking at the viability of running a regular courier service over the roads.

After completion, he had every road measured off by miles and planted stone pillars in the ground to mark the distances so travelers knew exactly where they were and how many miles they had covered. On shorter distances, he installed smaller stones, allowing riders to dismount without the help of third parties. My Roman Pericles had created a thoroughfare worthy of the gods.

4.

My greatest disappointment in life has been Gaius' failure to harness his accomplishments as a Tribune that would have launched him on a career of unparalleled success. Life rarely offers an opportunity to influence one's fate, and my son was the last person in Rome to miss it. Ultimately, his enemies offered him only two choices – which came down to the same thing – death or the Tribunate.

The people presented no problem. The first half of Gaius' first Tribunate had progressed so miraculously well that they would have granted him anything. His land distribution law, his compensations for the soldiers, and the banning of the ad hoc Senatorial Committees had been highly praised. They were especially excited he not only restored the judicial power of the College of Three, but also extended it. The College was now authorized to found new colonies, not just in Italy but also overseas. It permitted my son to claim land beyond the mere redistribution of the public land in Italy and do more for the non-Roman veterans, which greatly reduced the resistance of our allies. He even secured the support of the Equestrian class by issuing, for the first time in our history, large tracts of land that they could purchase and sublease in smaller lots to the poorest among the veterans. It was a brilliant move, solving in one stroke all the major obstacles that had cost his brother his life. My letters to Gaius congratulating him on this bold initiative incurred anger from Claudia who perceived my praise as a criticism of Tiberius' policies. I answered her letter by stating that it had not been my intention, but that I continued to believe my eldest son had made serious mistakes that not only cost him his life, but also threatened Gaius' life. I never received a reply.

In the period that the candidates for the Consulate had to file their names, Gaius delivered a speech asking the people a favor. His modest tone – if granted, he would value it immensely, but if they refused it, he would find no fault with them – made me laugh. People interpreted his remarks as a sign, he would try to run for the Consulship maybe even in combination with a Tribunate. However, when the Consular elections drew near and everybody was on the tiptoe of expectation, they saw him leading Fannius down into the Campus Martius and joining him in the canvass with his friends. It turned the tide in favor of Fannius and he was elected as Consul.

I harbored friendly feelings for Fannius. Fannius had scaled the wall of Carthage together with Tiberius, and he was one of the many house friends Tiberius had lost in the course of his campaign. Supporters of Gaius would later accuse him of treason. Yet Fannius has always been straightforward so that while he had been pleasantly surprised by the support of Gaius, he was also aware of the fact that Gaius had done so to prevent the election of Opimius, who was looking for revenge after my son had tried to sue him over his horrible campaign against Fregellae. It had been a strategic move, not a token of friendship.

I had been disappointed about Gaius' decision not to run for the Consulship, but my regret turned into anger after I received a message that he had accepted a second Tribunate. I could not believe my ears. After everything that had happened to our family! First, he pretended in response to my letters that it had been a spontaneous action of the people, which had surprised him too. However, when he was with me, he admitted he had had some hand in it. With a wide grin, he recounted how the people, to the bewilderment of his enemies, had simply stopped the voting after they had elected the ninth Tribune, appointing him as the last of the ten. Fulvius Flaccus had already preceded him, making him the first Tribune who had previously served as a Consul.

5.

Solon once compared the fate of citizens, ruled by tyrants, with beads on an abacus. Just as the numerical value of a bead randomly varies due to its position, so will a tyrant capriciously favor or dishonor a citizen from one moment to another. He, who allows the Roman mob to rule, installs a despot fickler and more deceitful than any Greek tyrant I know.

For those who believe I am too harsh, take the reaction of the people when Calpurnius Piso – known for his wealth as well as his stinginess – came all the way to the temple of Ceres with the aim to discredit my son's grain law. After the law had passed, Gaius spotted Piso with a large group of slaves, standing in line for the allocation of grain. My son asked him why he was there since he had disapproved the measure. "I don't care, Gracchus, for your little game," Piso had replied tersely, "but if you are handing out grain from my tax money to everyone then I'll take my cut too."

To my son's astonishment, bystanders did not fault Piso but him. The fact that a wealthy man like Piso bought the subsidized grain immediately aroused their suspicion. Never mind that he violated the qualification threshold. Blinded by their jealousy, they suddenly shared Piso's view that my son had only initiated the grain law to buy votes and this came from the lips of the very same people he had tried to help. Their reaction baffled my son and left him speechless, probably for the first time in his life.

My husband has always praised the instincts of the Roman people, but never trusted them, contending that for a person who faced the choice between his back or the whip loyalty embodied an unaffordable good. Gaius could have learned so much from him.

His unexpected re-election allowed my son to launch his most controversial rulings, fixing two thorny issues, which had infuriated his father. In the first decree, he banned all Senators and ex-magistrates from the juries of the courts, established to compensate victims of extortion by officials in non-Roman territories, replacing them with members of the Equestrian class. In the second one, he authorized the Censors to collect the taxes in Asia. Both were approved in the People's Assembly but barely. They won a majority of only one voting tribe, with seventeen against and eighteen in favor. My son had been quite fearful about the outcome and, after they were accepted, he exclaimed that the sword of Damocles now hung over the heads of his enemies and that he finally felt at peace to face whatever fate had in store. It made me flinch when I heard that.

My son had illustrated the need for more control over the Senatorial class by attacking the behavior of certain magistrates and officers of the State and the people, always ready to be fired up, had loved it. I hated every word of it, but there is no denying his examples had been devastating. He mentioned the wife of a Consul who had insisted on taking a bath in the male section in the city of Teanum Sidicinum. The Consul ordered the local Quaestor, Marcus Marius, to clear the pools. The woman had complained to her husband that the bath had not been vacated quickly enough and not properly cleaned. Our brave Consul had the Quaestor tied naked to a pole in the middle of the town square and had him flogged until he had succumbed to his injuries. In another town, our Praetor had ordered without any trial the arrest of two Quaestors, prompting them to commit suicide. When a young officer, on his way to Asia, passed an innocent farmer and the farmer, after seeing his closed litter, had asked with a chuckle if there had been a funeral, the officer had the man lashed and dumped on the side of the road where he bled to death.

The rulings and his speeches destroyed whatever goodwill my son had left in the Senate, including that of Fannius. The Senators had done everything in their power to stop him and his victory in the People's Assembly had shaken them. His enemies now gained the upper hand, convincing the remaining few, who had given my son the benefit of the doubt, that he was worse than his brother had been. They began to plot his downfall, making sure not to repeat the mistakes they had made in the past with Tiberius. They found in Livius Drusus the perfect candidate for their campaign.

Livius Drusus was an eloquent, powerful, and wealthy Tribune. He had also been, like Fannius, an early supporter of Tiberius. He was a rather vain man, less bright than my son, trusting, and known for a kind of doggish stubbornness, which made him both annoying as well as reliable. Once you had pushed him to pursue a certain policy, he stuck to it and did not let go.

Drusus wisely refrained from attacking Gaius directly, but launched a charm offensive in which he promoted himself as the true champion of the people; however, in his case, with the full support of the Senate. He emphasized repeatedly that the welfare of the people was his highest priority and that his own position was subordinate.

When Gaius proposed to found new colonies in Latium, Etruria and Campania, the Senate's reaction was cold and dismissive. But when Drusus outdid my son's proposal by suggesting to establish twelve, the Senators welcomed it as if it had been their own initiative. When my son charged the leaseholders the usual amount of rent, the Senate brushed all its complaints about the costs of his land programs aside and supported Drusus in his absurd proposal of leasing the land without a fee.

Flimsy and see-through as these tactics may have been, gradually the mood changed and the whisper campaign my son's enemies had launched found more ears willing to listen each day in the alleys of Rome. 'Gaius just provokes resistance while Drusus gets things done. Gaius always promotes himself, but Drusus shares his position with others. When Gaius talks about what the Roman people wants, he means what Gaius wants. He has a smooth tongue, but what we do we buy for all his fine words? There is no difference between him and his brother and what did his brother accomplish? Only strife and conflict.'

The colonies proposed by Drusus were never founded, and now that Gaius is gone, I do not expect they will be. The Senate certainly never meant to establish them, and the distribution of land has come to another standstill. Every nation gets the government it deserves, while the veterans, for whom it all had begun, were left again with empty hands. Hail Drusus!

6.

The time had now arrived for the fates to show my son what they had in store for him by delivering their final masterstroke. There is an old rule that a Tribune may not leave Rome, but since my son was elected only at the very last moment, and his departure as Chairman of the College of Three to oversee the founding of the new colony in Africa had already been confirmed, he left Rome at a time when he should never have gone away.

He gave this new Roman settlement near Carthage the name Iunonia, and from the start, the omens were terrible. A storm rose during the initiation ceremony. The wind destroyed the standards, blew the sacrifices from the altars, and a pack of wolves tore the border stakes to pieces.

To make matters worse, Fulvius reinvigorated in Rome his campaign to obtain the Roman civil rights for our allies with all his usual energy, haughtiness, and lack of diplomacy, making him an easy target for the Senate. In a counterattack, Drusus proposed immunity for our Latin allies from corporal punishment even during military service. It offered them more protection from abuses by Roman magistrates than even Roman citizens enjoyed. A Senatorial Committee was set up to look into it, but just as in the case of Drusus' colonies, they never carried the ruling through. Yet it was a shrewd move and served its purpose by creating a division between the Latins and the veterans of the other allies, weakening the positions of both Fulvius and my son.

Alarmed by the bad news that reached him daily, my son did everything he could to finish his work for the colony as fast as possible. It must have been a horrible period for him. He never wasted time, but now he even surpassed himself, and, after seventy days, he sailed back, exhausted, and feeling deeply troubled. In his tunic was a letter from a courier warning him that his enemy Opimius had a good chance of winning the Consular election.

After his return, my son discovered, to his great disillusionment, that the support he had enjoyed among members of the Equestrian class had completely eroded. The news about the bad omens at the inauguration of his colony Iunonia had spread and it had rattled the first participants, making it suddenly look like a doomed project.

Many of them had also become quite wary of the duties they had to perform as jurors in the extortion courts, loathing the fact that they could not refuse. A summon from the Praetor was not something they dared to ignore. Better than anyone else, the Equestrians had understood my son had not really trusted them to perform any better than their Senatorial predecessors had. They recognized that all the rules in which he had hemmed their duties served two purposes. They offered protection, but also kept them in check. The meetings had to be done in public which they thought was good, and they liked the fact that the voting was kept secret, but they were very scared of the hefty fines they would face if they were caught cheating. The penalties could ruin them and who could guarantee that they would receive a fair trial? My son? The same man who had burdened them with all this, and who would likely be indicted after his Tribunate or worse clubbed to death like his brother.

They also found the frequency in which they had to show up, deeply troubling. Everybody knew how corrupt a lot of Senators and magistrates were, but why did they have to function as the guardians of those whose job it was to guard over us all? Most of them just wanted to live their lives, take care of their families and personal interests and stay away from all the political intrigues and haggling. The last thing they wanted was to be crushed between my son and the Senate. The name Gracchus had contracted a bad smell. It meant trouble and risks they did not want to run and the sooner he was gone, the better.

Their reaction made me upset, but came as no surprise. It confirmed the remarks my Greek friends made. They never believed it had been my son's intention to drive a wedge between the Senators and the Equestrians. When some of my Roman acquaintances suggested that he had appointed the Equestrians to win their votes, they just laughed. They called it an artful smear, skillfully planted by his enemies and designed to make my son look bad, but without any substance since there was very little if anything the Equestrians had gained. My son had appointed them as jurors for the simple reason there had been nobody else to take their place.

My Greek friends laughed, but when they were alone with me, they also expressed their sadness about the fact my son's enemies had been so successful in corrupting his legacy. They observed it was partly my son's own fault, contending that his angry forewarnings had tarnished the real value of his intents and accomplishments. My son was their hero. In their eyes, his key objective had been to ensure that victims of extortion could recover their losses and they were eternally grateful for his efforts.

I agree with every word my friends uttered, but I have noticed a change in the attitude of the Equestrians that I deal with in my transactions. They feel burdened and complain about it, but their new responsibilities and enhanced status have also made them more self-assured, more aware of the common interests they share with other non-Senatorial Equestrians, and less inclined to view their peers as rivals. I do not believe my son wanted to split our society into two warring groups; he loved our country too much for that. However, I do believe he considered it a healthy development if the Equestrians would challenge the Senators more as a political force for the same reason my husband had praised the fact that we have two Consuls or two Censors. If so, it is all the more tragic that the growing awareness of their new role made the Equestrians distance themselves from my son.

Gaius had criticized his brother posthumously for failing to secure a broad power base, but he had become just as isolated. His support came now mainly from by the poorest of the Roman veterans, from the non-Latin veterans, and the fickle masses in Rome; in short from those who were the most vulnerable and easy to frighten.

Hubris precedes the fall. I have always understood this Greek proverb to mean that if a man feels he is falling, he responds by exhibiting an arrogant and brazen behavior, thus accelerating his demise. Much to the sadness and anger of my daughter-in-law Licinia, who had lost all control over him, my son moved after his return from Africa to a house in the alleys near the Forum to show the people he was their true champion. It was a shameful and empty gesture, awarding him only scorn and disbelief. Was this the same Gaius who had purchased some silver dolphins at twelve hundred and fifty drachmas the pound?

It was under these terrible circumstances that he and Fulvius released their proposal to settle once and for all the long-standing issue of the civil rights. By that time, I was almost as sick and tired of hearing about it, as I was when somebody mentioned the words public land and distribution. As usual, the lower classes throughout Italy welcomed their proposal with great enthusiasm and my son had prepared it well. To bypass the opposition, he and Fulvius offered our full civil rights to the Latins and to the other allies the rights of the Latins. Out of respect for the feelings of those who did not want to give up the rights of their beloved hometown, they built in a provision that each city could opt out, with the guarantee that all the existing treaties would remain intact. When the news spread in Miseno and Naples, people in the streets congratulated me and showered me with expressions of joy, which I humbly accepted, barely able to hide my disbelief in the outcome.

To hear the speeches and follow the voting, thousands of Latins and Italians flocked to Rome where they witnessed, to their shock and disillusionment, how Fannius and Drusus told the Roman voters that they could only lose if they voted in favor. Surrounded by numerous Senators at the Forum, they warned them that Rome would be flooded by poor, needy families, who would buy their grain, by alien freedmen who would marry their daughters and steal their jobs, and by greedy publicani who would undercut the bids of their Roman competitors.

Skirmishes broke out between the different population groups, which provided the Senate the excuse for issuing an edict that all non-Romans had to leave the city, an unprecedented move in our history. My son brought out a counter edict, denouncing the Consul and promising the allies his support in case they refused to leave, but Fannius ignored his edict. People were rounded up and driven outside the city walls. For fear of more violence, my son did not intervene, not even when the lictors of Fannius dragged a friend of his away in front of his eyes. He had lost all control over events.

The fearmongering by Fannius and Drusus had been so successful that the People's Assembly rejected my son's proposal with an overwhelming majority. I am convinced our allies will obtain one day our rights, but it will come at a huge cost and only by the sword.

7.

When my son, in a last desperate attempt, decided to run for a third term as Tribune, I wrote him a letter, which led to an irreparable breach between him and me. I wrote the letter in great anger, and I used my position as his mother, knowing this would hurt him the most. I kept a copy and my hands start to shake when I read it again. Each word cuts through my soul like a knife.

'You will say it is a beautiful thing to take revenge on our enemies. To no one does this seem either greater or more beautiful than to me, but only if it is possible to pursue these aims without harming our country. But seeing that this cannot be done, that our enemies will not perish for a long time, I would rather have them as they are now than have our country be destroyed.

I would dare to swear solemnly that, except for those who have murdered Tiberius Gracchus, no enemy has imposed so much difficulty and so much distress on me as you have. You should have shouldered the responsibilities of all the children I had in the past. You should have made sure that I have the least anxiety in my old age. You should consider it sacrilegious to do anything of great significance contrary to my feelings, especially as I am someone with only a short portion of my life left. Cannot even that time span, as brief as it is, be of help in keeping you from opposing me and destroying our country? In the final analysis, what end will there be? When will our family stop this madness? When will we cease insisting on troubles, suffering as well as causing them? When will we begin to feel shame about disrupting our country? But if this is altogether impossible, seek the office of Tribune when I am dead! Do what pleases you, when I will no longer have to witness it. May Jupiter not for a single instant allow you to continue these actions or permit such madness to cross your mind. If you persist, I fear that, by your own fault, you may incur such trouble that at no time in your entire life you will be able to find peace.'

Gaius never answered my letter and, unfortunately, the content of it leaked in Rome. When the rumor of my writing spread, many faulted him. My opinion about his candidacy did not surprise him, but I know he experienced my letter in the midst of all his setbacks as a stab in the back.

Just before the elections, my son made his last major mistake. A number of Senators and Tribunes had commissioned as part of the festivities the construction of a wooden theater from where people could watch the gladiator games. They had done this every year and it had earned them some extra denarii by renting out the front seats to the well-to-do. To gratify the masses, my son issued an edict to take it down so the poorest would have a clear view on the games. After his colleagues ignored his edict, he instructed some laborers of his public works to demolish the theater in the night. The people loved him for it, but it incensed his colleagues and there are many who assert it cost him his life. They claim he won the election, but that his colleagues committed fraud in their proclamation of the ballot results. Others state he simply lost. I have never been able to find out what really happened, but I suspect he won the popular vote by such a small margin that it was easy for the Tribunes to lower the number of tribes, he had won. I also believe it did not matter anymore. My son had incurred so much hatred that his enemies probably would have killed him in the course of his third Tribunate or shortly afterward. As for his supporters who cried foul, they should have known by now that no matter how just the losing cause may be, fortune favors the victors and no group reaps more derision and contempt than those who lose ungraciously.

At the same time, Opimius won the election by an overwhelming majority, and he announced that as soon as he would be in office, he would nullify all Gaius' laws for the colony Iunonia because of the bad omens that had taken place at its inauguration. The victory of my son's enemies was now complete.

8.

Letters, sent by my friends, offer a detailed account of my son's final moments. After Opimius had submitted the annulment of Gaius' laws to the Tribal Assembly, my son's followers and his opponents flocked to the Capitoline where they arranged themselves opposite each other like hostile armies.

Opimius had organized the session to start with a sacrifice and Quintus Antyllius, one of his followers, who was carrying the innards, yelled at Gaius' supporters to get out of the way: "Make way for an honest citizen." As he shouted, he held up his bare arm, confronting his opponents with his extended finger. According to my friends, Gaius had stared at the man in anger, which one of his followers had taken as a signal. The idiot ran out and stabbed Antyllius with a stylus. My son was at his side in an instant and denounced the act in a loud voice, but he was too late. Just as what happened with Tiberius when a supporter gouged out the eyes of one of the Senators' slaves, this incident provided Opimius the argument that my son had started the violence.

Rain extended my son's life for another two days. A heavy downpour descended on the Forum, forcing Opimius to break off the meeting. The next day, he summoned the Senate to an emergency session. When the bier with the naked body of his murdered servant Antyllius reached the Forum, the clamor of the procession pierced into the Curia. As an accomplished actor in one of Accius' tragedies, Opimius looked up and asked who disturbed the meeting of the Senate. At his request, some Senators walked to the doorway where they witnessed the procession, raising their arms and lamenting the fate of our Republic. Followers of my son spotted the Senators and rushed forward, shouting they had murdered a Tribune, while Antyllius had been a mere servant. Others yelled the Senators had only gathered to plot the murder of their last champion.

Fighting broke out at the Forum with supporters and opponents hurling stones and chasing each other with clubs and sticks.

The Senators closed the doors of the Curia and authorized the Consul with a large majority to take any conceivable measure to defend the State. Opimius ordered all Senators to gather again the next day. They had to carry weapons and take their slaves along, allowing them to be armed.

In response, Fulvius brazenly issued the same orders and assembled in the course of that day thousands of supporters around him. According to my friends, my son took no part in these actions, which he regarded as senseless. After his visit to the Forum, he went home, followed at a distance by a large crowd of supporters. They remained that night in front of his house, just as they had done twelve years ago in front of the house of Tiberius. I am told that their behavior offered a stark contrast to Fulvius' supporters who indulged in heavy drinking and boasted throughout the night about the battle awaiting them in the morning. My son's followers were muted and quiet, full of anxiety about the fate of their champion and their motherland.

On the last day, shrouded in his toga as if he was on his way to the Forum, he left his home only armed with a small dagger. Licinia, with Sempronia next to her, threw herself in his way in a final attempt to stop him. "I knew when we married that his day would come, but it did not stop me. You are on your way to meet the murderers of Tiberius, unarmed as he was. If you both had fallen at Numantia, they would have returned the ashes, but now I shall have to search for you as Claudia searched in vain for your brother. Your death, like his, will do our State no good. I beg you not to go!" My son left his wife and child, unable to offer a word of comfort. After he was gone, slaves carried an inconsolable Licinia and my granddaughter to the house of her brother.

Just like in the days of old, my son and Fulvius occupied the Aventine. Fulvius had armed his followers with the war trophies he had collected from his campaign against the Gauls. At the urging of my son, Fulvius sent his son to the Senate, holding in his arms the mace of a herald. Fulvius' son was a young, adorable boy, and he acted with due respect. With tears in his eyes and trembling with fear, he offered a peace proposal on behalf of his father and my son. To the dismay of Opimius, a majority in the Senate seemed to be willing to find a compromise. He intervened and stated that the Senate could not negotiate with Gaius and Fulvius through an envoy. They were not above the law. They had to surrender and face trial like any other citizen. He told Fulvius' son not to come back at the risk of his life.

My son announced he was willing to go to the Senate and defend their case, but none of his followers supported him and they sent Fulvius' son again to the Senate. Opimius had the boy arrested and ordered the attack. Accompanied by four thousand Cretan archers and the supporting Senators, he stormed the slopes of the Aventine. A shower of arrows and stones rained down upon my son's followers, killing more than two thousand. Fulvius fled with his oldest son to a public bath where Senators killed them. Afterwards, Opimius offered Fulvius' youngest son his own choice of death.

Following the first wave of attack, Opimius interrupted the assault and ordered heralds to announce he would grant amnesty to all who would surrender. Many survivors heeded his call; others fled or made their last stand. My son had not taken part in the fighting. He first fled to the Temple of Diana, together with his slave Philocrates and two of his most faithful friends, Pomponius and Licinius. Here he attempted to deprive himself of his life, but his friends stopped him. They took his dagger away and urged him to flee. Enemies would later claim that my son begged Diana to make sure that the people, who had betrayed him, would forever be the slaves of his killers.

My son panicked. He ran to the Temple of the Moon, jumped from
the terrace, and managed, half limping, to reach the wooden bridge over
the Tiber. Pomponius and Licinius followed him to the middle of the
bridge, holding his pursuers off with their swords until slaves of the Senators killed them. By this time, my son had reached the other side of the
Tiber with only Philocrates. Spectators along the road urged him to escape, but despite his pleas, no one offered him a horse. Then he fled with
Philocrates into the cave where his enemies found him.

PART 7
HADES

The death of Gaius Gracchus
Painting by Francois Topino-Lebrun (1798)

1.

I believe in eternity. I share the view of Xenophanes that nothing can come out of nothing and that there was always something; otherwise, we simply would not exist. How violent and deadly a year may have been, its passing is still anchored in the eternal cycle of the seasons. What is born in the spring dies in the fall, but there will never be a last autumn. Our universe is like the sea and each wave that perishes on our shores is just like another year in the reckoning of time by the gods. If the end of all things would be desirable, then the gods would have been mortal and our universe finite.

Autumn is my most beloved season. In the fall, everything turns soft and round. The hysterical high-pitched trills, with which cicadas whip each other up in the scorching heat, die down. In the morning, patches of fog shroud the sunrise, coloring the oily surface of the sea pink rose. In the evening, twilight dyes my villa in blue tones and my household comes to a standstill. In the night, the moon takes over from the sun. Her pale light touches the moss, spawning strings of white spores, luminescent in the dark. The moldy fragrance of the mushrooms is melancholic but free of the smell of death. Only her ornament dies and underneath her soil, Mother Earth already nurtures the new season. When I walk in the morning through my little forest on the mainland, it smells like the library of my brother. The wind rustles through the golden crowns of the trees with the voice of a mountain stream. As a true descendant of King Midas, I wade with my feet through the amber foliage and when I pause, I hear the leaves whisper to one another about their growth, flourishing and fall.

Maybe it is my age, but my compassion and ability to love others only came to a full ripening after my heart was broken. I am now of the opinion that there is beauty in decay. The sight of a body in decline moves me, and my mother has become an almost permanent presence in my thoughts and inner dialogues. When she grew old, her world around her dissolved into small, pleasing details, which she observed with the eyes of a newborn child. Resting on her couch in the atrium, she praised in half-finished sentences the color of the hair of a young slave girl passing by, the flower arrangement in front of her, a vase in the hallway, a painting on the wall. She turned her praise to no one in particular, and it did not bother her that no one listened. Then her eyes got tired and she dozed off again. Old age leads to a golden acceptance of fate.

This is probably one of my last visits to the beach. My body is too old and stiff to be scrambling over the pebbles. I bring this visit as a tribute to my father. Last night he appeared in my dreams. He reminded me of his allegiance to Neptune. The dream carried an element of reconciliation, which I honored by offering some flowers to the sea.

I venture not deep, but allow the waves to spill over my feet. My body reacts immediately to their embracing movement. Familiar chills run over my limbs and back. My skin is still my memory. Seated on the pebbles and surrounded by flapping screens, I strike with my hands over the pebbles and listen to the sea. I am always surprised with how many different voices it can speak.

An old pastime comes to me. I stir up the sand with my hands, clouding my view. As the sand settles, the pebbles become visible again, but each time in a different configuration. We all receive the same images, but our thoughts and the meaning we assign to these images, vary for each one of us. What some may see as just a couple of stones, may hold for others a fateful warning about their future. As a child, I collected for years on the beach black and white pebbles. Depending on the events of that day, I threw a white or black stone into a chest, which I emptied out on the last day of the year. If the number of black stones exceeded the white, I knew the next year would be dark.

In my view, humans are unique and lonely. We are the only ones in this eternal universe on whom the gods have bestowed the gifts of reason as well as mortality. From childhood onward, we are aware of the fact that our life is only temporary and this knowledge beckons us to accomplish an exceptional feat, an act of statesmanship, a work of brilliance, a decisive victory. Only by leading an extraordinary life, memorized by many generations afterward, can man transcend his mortality and become the true master of his own destiny. Socrates already recognized it, 'there are those who live to eat and drink, and those who eat and drink to live.'

Priest, custodian, and warrior, all the men in my life have fulfilled these roles with varying degrees of success. My husband was the most successful in striking the right balance, but despite his achievements, I am not convinced he will be remembered by many future generations. I have no doubts about the fate of my father. As long as Rome exists, his name will be immortalized. His weak health undermined the life of my brother Publius, and I already encounter people who cannot recall his existence. The question is how will my sons fare. They were good warriors, but they lived in a time when the challenge was to protect our Republic against its own enemies and not war.

2.

It has been two weeks now since I returned from my visit to Rome and I have finally recovered. I was exhausted when I came back. I had forgotten that Rome is above all a city of freedmen, children, slaves, and retailers. The overriding presence of freedmen in the streets had startled me. Quite a few of my friends perceive them as a menace and they still praise my husband for having assigned them to only one city tribe. They contend he saved the voting in the Comitia Centuriata from their over-whelming presence.

I may have chosen for Miseno, so my house would not have the ap-pearance of a mausoleum, but I fear that the peace and quiet of my villa resembles my father's house more than I had imagined. The noise, the oppressive heat, and the intense traffic in Rome wore me down. At the end of each day, I suffered from a debilitating headache. Carts rattled off and on. Donkeys packed with vegetables, amphorae and building mate-rials brayed their way through the crowds. The alleys were teeming with children, street artists, fortunetellers, and beggars. Everyone was in a hurry. I am convinced that the people in Rome walk three times faster than in Miseno and in the background there was the constant reverbera-tion of the noise of the city.

The sight of the Forum came as a shock. The overwhelming scenery of white temples and marble buildings blended with images from the past. When I entered the Forum and gazed from the Basilica Sempronia to the Capitol, it looked as if the day had arrived in which the Gods had left our universe and our firmament no longer turned forward but back-ward. Scattered over the Forum and the Capitol, I saw little white clus-ters of Senators, strolling peacefully and gathering in small groups, de-bating the issues of the day. At the same time, images of a hill littered with bodies and red-stained, torn gowns hit me in my eyes. I felt as if half of my mind had already descended into Hades.

3.

At the urging of my friends, I had agreed to meet Gaius Marius. He had won election to the Praetorship and my friends advised me not to disregard his request, even though no one was able to explain why this man had wanted to see me. Five years ago, he was elected as Tribune, canvassing on promises that had been popular among the followers of Gaius. Some see in him a combination of Tiberius and Gaius, predicting tactfully that he would be more successful than my sons had been. Others accuse him of a boundless ambition, but everyone is full of praise for his military skills. When I thought about it, I remembered that Gaius had him mentioned in one of his letters from Spain.

He came in, accompanied by his lictors. I immediately noticed his energy. I had never seen a man so fidgety. He hands were constantly busy, picking things up only to put them down again. I found it both fascinating and unnerving. His gaze often slid away, making it impossible to see if we were still in conversation. He had the appearance of a muscular farmhand with a wrinkled forehead, sunken eyes and around his mouth deep, bitter lines. His movements were of a feline agility. If I had encountered him on the street, I would have taken him for a trainer of a gladiator school.

I did not know his family. From his sparse comments, I understood they belonged to the second or third class, with considerable possessions in Arpinum, not far from where Fregellae once had been. He spoke about them without any warmth and he clearly did not appreciate my probing. In response to my questions about his family, he changed the subject and recalled how my son-in-law, Aemilianus, had taken notice of him after he had watched him killing a Numantian. It did not surprise me. This man possessed all the qualities that my son-in-law would have liked. He told me that Aemilianus had invited him several times into his tent and he recounted how Aemilianus, after a Tribune had asked him if he knew someone who could succeed him, had turned his face to him and patted him on his shoulders, saying, "Here, maybe."

Despite his appearance, he was not discourteous. He asked me about my health and praised my sons. Oddly enough, he showed a keen interest in my villa. He asked all kinds of details that surprised me. I got the impression that he was trying to find out how long I wanted to remain there and whether I had arranged anything for when I was gone. I concluded that the real reason for his visit had been his interest in Miseno. I gathered that he did not like the presence of the Greek community and he admitted that he did not speak Greek. He contended that he found it useless to learn the language of a people who had been defeated, and the Greek theater meant nothing to him. I was stunned.

After he was gone, I felt sick; troubled by the disturbing thought I had spoken to a man without a soul. He had appeared to be just a body, a smart, slick, fast, energetic predator, craving for adoration and power. Does this man represent the outcome of all the struggles and sacrifices of my sons? A tyrant in the making whose sole purpose in life is to hold a triumph in our streets at all costs? If so, I am glad I only have a short span of life ahead of me.

4.

One morning, only accompanied by Simo and three bodyguards, we visited, armed with cypress branches, the cave where Gaius had met his death. As a gaping wound in the flank of the hill, I saw the opening already from afar. The cave was dedicated to the fates and in the chill of their presence, my breath became visible when I ventured closer to the opening.

Simo had brought a blanket to protect my old knees and with his help, I kneeled down. Facing the inside of the cave, I implored the Fates to grant my remaining family forgiveness, now that my sons and I have paid our price.

Their answer seemed to come after Simo had ignited a torch and moved inside the cave. I discerned in the light a stone plaque hidden in the back. It called on everyone not to befoul the space, not to leave waste, and not to perform ceremonies other than funeral rites. If someone had caused unintended damage, he should sacrifice an ox and offer it to Jupiter. Withered flowers on the floor underneath the plaque showed that people had come here to worship.

On my request, Simo spread the branches on the floor and removed all traces of our visit. The plaque had given me some consolation, but my supplications had not given me the peace of mind I had hoped to find. When I left the cave, the darkness closed in rapidly as if my presence had been an intrusion, which had angered the Furies. I made Simo and my bodyguards swear no to speak with anyone about our visit, leaving the cave with a heavy heart.

The messenger who had brought me the news of Gaius' death had told me that there were two different accounts of how Gaius had lost his life in the cave. In one version, his slave Philocrates had killed first my son and then himself. In the other, their pursuers found them both alive. According to this version, Philocrates shielded Gaius with his body, holding him so tightly that their pursuers had to shower him with blows until he succumbed and they could seize Gaius. The messenger believed the first story was closer to the truth, but I recognized in the second Philocrates' devotion for Gaius. I believe Philocrates killed Gaius at his request and then stayed alive to protect his master's body until they killed him too.

I did not yield at the time when the courier told me his repulsive story. They had set a price on Gaius's head – its weight in gold. A friend of the Consul Opimius – who else? – had stolen the head and put it on a spear. When it was weighed before Opimius, it came to seventeen and two-thirds of a pound. It immediately raised suspicion and soon it was revealed that the man had broken Gaius' skull open, removed his brains, and filled it with molten lead. There! This is how our Republic paid tribute to one of its best sons.

5.

A few days after my visit to the cave, a death notice reached me. Tiberius' son was killed in Sardinia; slain in action. The message made me immensely sad, especially since I had spent so little time with him. With his passing, my last hope for a continuation of the male line of my family had perished.

I suddenly longed to go back to Miseno. The message about my grandson overshadowed everything. I had intended to pay visits to the people who had remained loyal to Gaius in his last days, offering, if possible, help or consolation, but my willpower was gone. I had experienced Marius' questions about my villa as defilement and I needed to go home.

On my way back, I paid a visit to the tomb of my family just outside the city walls. It is one of the first family graves at the Via Appia. As soon as I stepped through the gate and walked over the pathway, paved with green marble and graced on both sides by lines of birches and cypresses, the hustle and bustle of the street traffic faded away. Birds sang in the trees, sometimes interrupted by excited twittering. Guards opened the doors and ringed by torchbearers, I stepped into the elongated space with niches on both sides. It was chilly and damp. Dewdrops flew together as I ran my hand over the names of the many Cornelii who have found their final resting place here.

My father is missing here. His body was cremated on the beach at Liternum and his ashes were scattered over the sea. To honor his memory, Aemilianus had placed in front of the tomb an image of my father, along with images of his brother Lucius and his favorite poet Ennius.[15] It had been against my father's wish, but when Aemilianus had asked for my consent, I had gratefully endorsed it. While I gazed at the works of Aemilianus with a saddened approval, I decided I would follow

---

[15] A writer and poet (c. 239–c. 169 BCE), considered the father of Roman poetry.

my father's example and have myself cremated near the sea. I also concluded that this had been my last visit to Rome. My hometown had nothing to offer me anymore.

However repulsive Marius may have been, the hard truth is that he had been right. The efforts of my sons to save the Republic as a union of free men had failed. Marius had called their struggles laudable but futile. We needed manpower, and if that required filling our ranks with proletarians or even mercenaries, so be it.

Maybe my despised brother-in-law Nasica Corculum had been right to object to Cato's endless rants about destroying Carthage. In Corculum's eyes, Roma needed the challenge of a rival power, if only to check the avarice and greed of its people. Ironically, the Carthaginian commander Hannibal had shared his opinion, contending a powerful state could never live in peace for very long. Once an enemy from without no longer challenges it, it creates an enemy within, like a healthy body, which for lack of infection is spoiled by its own strength. Call us naïve, simple-minded if you will, but neither my sons nor I had foreseen how much vitriol and hatred would burst to the surface if you try to stop the underbelly of a society to indulge in its greed.

I also see now how wrong I had been in assuming that the nameless hero I conjured to preserve my sanity after Tiberius' death would resemble in any way my father or my husband. When he arrives, he will be like a Marius.

This nameless champion will restore the Republic in name but, in fact, reign as tyrant. He will give the Latins and Italians our civil rights. His armies will consist of mercenaries and proletarians, and our provinces and allies will lionize him. He will give the Equestrians the law and order they yearn for. He will see a competitor in every competent Roman commander. He will distrust the army and surround himself with armed bodyguards within our city walls. He will have thousands of eyes and ears and sow the seeds of ruin under our old families. He will pack the

Senate and juries with his underlings. He will give the Roman plebs their bread and circuses. Our best Roman families will oppose him in the name of Libertas, which they have desecrated. They will appeal to age-old Republican values, which they have betrayed. When the great tyrant makes his appearance, the petty ones always clamor for freedom and justice. I can even foresee a situation when his bodyguards, who did all his killing, will take over the reign of our country. It will mark the end of Rome. Nothing will then remain of us other than our sewers, roads, bridges, and aqueducts.

I think it is fair to say that my son Gaius was more in love with ideas than humans, while Tiberius' love went in the first place to his loyal veterans who had served under him. Gaius died at least with the illusion that his laws would survive him, but his brother died without any hope. I have betrayed them both, but my pain is greatest when I think back to my eldest son. His program was a disaster, but he surpassed in his embracing love not only his enemies, but also his mother. The fact that I have never been able to tell him this has filled my heart with more grief than his death.

I crave for my upcoming departure with the prospect of reconciliation, and I long for the moment when the three of us will be united again in the Hades of our Republic.

POSTSCRIPT

Plinius the Elder described the statue of Cornelia. It displayed her while sitting and he comments on the fact that she wore strapless sandals. Excavations of the Porticus Octaviae in nineteenth century revealed a marble sculpture base that may have belonged to this statue.

In 109 BCE, former Consul Opimius was found guilty of corruption and exiled. He died in Dyrrachium (Greece).

The Roman historian and writer Valerius Maximus (working in the period of the Emperor Tiberius between 14 and 37 AD) mentions, in one of his little anecdotes, Sempronia, the elder sister of the Gracchi, calling her a token of courage and honesty. A certain L. Equitius claimed to be a son of Tiberius while running for the Tribunate in 102 or 101 BCE (the exact date is uncertain). He pressed Sempronia to recognize him as her relative in front of a riotous People's Assembly, but she declined. She must have been quite old at that time and maybe she had grown tired of people bullying her.

Her refusal led to a revolt. Equitius' supporters attacked his opposing candidate, Nunnius. They dragged him out of a house he had fled to and killed him. They also threatened to stone Censor Quintus Metellus after he refused to acknowledge Equitius' claim. The Consul Marius incarcerated Equitius, but the people stormed the prison and liberated him. He was elected as Tribune in 100 BCE.

In his testimony, Metellus stated that none of the sons of Tiberius was still alive. One was slain in Sardinia. The other two died prematurely; one in Rome, the other in Praeneste. The youngest one was born after the murder of his father.

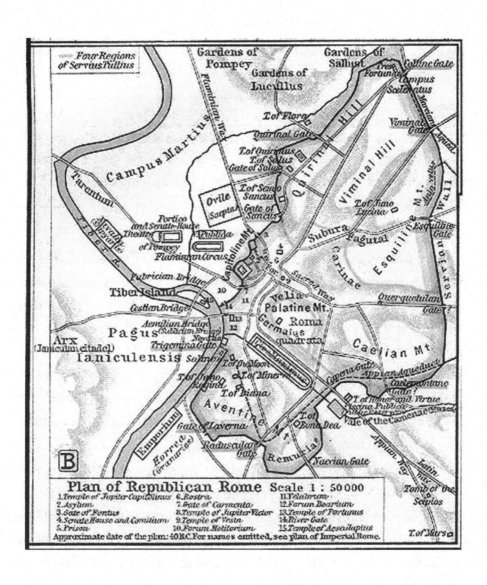

Plan of Republican Rome   Scale 1 : 50000

1. Temple of Jupiter Capitolinus   6. Rostra   11. Velabrum
2. Asylum   7. Gate of Carmenta   12. Forum Boarium
3. Gate of Fontus   8. Temple of Jupiter Victor   13. Temple of Fortunus
4. Senate House and Comitium   9. Temple of Vesta   14. River Gate
5. Prison   10. Forum Holitorium   15. Temple of Aesculapius

Approximate date of the plan: 40 B.C. For names omitted, see plan of Imperial Rome.

CHRONOLOGY

(SOME DATES ARE UNKNOWN {?} – ALL DATES ARE BCE)

237 Birth of Aemilia, mother of Cornelia

236 Birth of Scipio Africanus Maior, father of Cornelia

218-201 Second Punic War between Rome and Carthage

218 (?) Birth of Tiberius Sempronius Gracchus, father of the Gracchi

Hannibal, Carthaginian commander, crosses the Alps

217 Battle at Trasumennus, defeat of Rome

216 Battle at Cannae. Consul Lucius Aemilius Paullus, father of Aemilia, is killed.

215 Alliance between Carthage and Philip V of Macedonia; First Macedonian War.

211 Publius Cornelius Scipio, grandfather of Cornelia and his brother, Gnaeus Cornelius Scipio Calvus, are killed in Spain during two battles against Carthage

204 Publius Cornelius Scipio, father of Cornelia, invades Africa

202 Battle at Zama, Publius Cornelius Scipio defeats Hannibal

201 Annexation of Spain

200-196 Second Macedonian War

196 Flaminius declares Greece liberated

195 Rebellion of the women in Rome

194 (?) Birth of Cornelia, mother of the Gracchi

187 Trial against Scipio Africanus Maior and his brother Lucius Scipio

Tribunate of Tiberius Sempronius Gracchus Senior

186 Repression of the Bacchanalia sect

185 Birth of Scipio Aemilianus, natural son of Aemilius Paullus Macedonicus (brother of Aemilia, mother of Cornelia) and Papiria Masonis

183 Death of Scipio Africanus Maior, father of Cornelia (53 years old)

177 First Consulate of Tiberius Sempronius Gracchus Senior, together with Gaius Claudius Pulcher

176 (?) Marriage between Tiberius Sempronius Gracchus Senior and Cornelia (ca. 18 years old)

174 Birth of Sempronia, elder sister of the Gracchi Brothers

169 Censorship of Tiberius Sempronius Gracchus Senior, together with Gaius Claudius Pulcher

168 Battle at Pydna. The uncle of Cornelia, Lucius Aemilius Paullus Macedonicus defeats the Macedonian King Perseus

167 Campaign in Epirus by Lucius Aemilius Paullus Macedonicus and Cornelius Scipio Nasica Corculum. Abolishment of the Tributum tax

Death of Aemilia, mother of Cornelia (70 years old)

163 Birth of Tiberius Sempronius Gracchus Junior

Second Consulate of Tiberius Sempronius Gracchus Senior together with Manius Iuventius Thalna

162 Tiberius Sempronius Gracchus Senior visits as special envoy Greece, Pergamum and Syria

154 Birth of Gaius Sempronius Gracchus

151 (?) Death of Tiberius Sempronius Gracchus Senior (ca. 67 years old)

149-148 Fourth Macedonian War

149-146 Third Punic War

148   Annexation of Macedonia as a Roman Province

146   Destruction of Carthage

144   Construction of the Aqua Marcia, renovation of the Aqua Appia

143   Campaign of Appius Claudius against the Salassi

137   Quaestorship of Tiberius Sempronius Gracchus Junior in Spain

136-132 Slave rebellion in Sicily

135 (?)   Tiberius Sempronius Gracchus Junior marries Claudia, daughter of
      Appius Claudius

134   Censorship of Appius Claudius

134-133 Tribunate of Tiberius Sempronius Gracchus Junior

      Death of King Attalus III of Pergamum

      Death of Tiberius Sempronius Gracchus Junior (29 years old)

      Scipio Aemilianus destroys Numantia

132-129 Slave rebellion in Pergamum under Aristonicus

132   Death of Scipio Nasica Serapio

131   Consulate of Licinius Crassus. Killed in Pergamum

130 (?)   Death of Appius Claudius

129   Death of Scipio Aemilianus ; Blossius commits suicide

125   Construction of the Aqua Tepula

124-123 First Tribunate of Gaius Sempronius Gracchus (10 December – 10 De-
      cember)

123-122 Second Tribunate of Gaius Sempronius Gracchus (10 December – 10
      December)

121   Death of Gaius Sempronius Gracchus (32 years old)

115   Praetorship of Marius

115 (?)   Death of Cornelia Africana

Family Tree

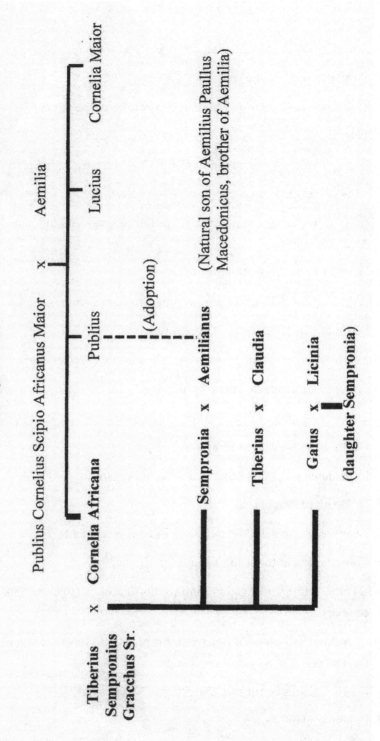

FULL NAMES OF MOST IMPORTANT PERSONS
(NOT MENTIONED IN THE FAMILY TREE)

Publius Licinius Crassus Dives Mucianus (180 BCE – 130 BCE)

Publius Mucius Scaevola (died ca. 115 BCE)

Publius Cornelius Scipio Nasica Serapio (ca. 183 BCE – 132 BCE)

Appius Claudius Pulcher (died in 130 BCE)

Gaius Claudius Pulcher (died 167 BCE)

Marcus Fulvius Flaccus (died in 121 BCE)

Lucius Opimius (Consul in 121 BCE)

Marcus Livius Drusus (died in 108 BCE)

Gaius Laelius Sapiens (born in 188 BCE)

Gaius Fannius Strabo (Consul in 122 BCE)

Gaius Marius (157 BCE– January 13, 86 BCE)

SOURCES

To construct, as much as possible, a true-life picture of ancient Rome, the author made use of numerous primary and secondary sources.

PRIMARY SOURCES

(*Loeb Classical Library*, London and Universal-Bibliothek, Stuttgart).

Latin: Plautus, Lucilius, Livius, Gellius, Accius, Cicero, Plinius, Cato, Martialis, Valerius Maximus, Cornelius Nepos, Frontinus, Fronto, Plotinus, Marcus Aurelius, Lucretius, Tacitus, and Varro.

Ancient Greek: Thales, Anaximander, Anaximnes, Pythagoras, Xenophanes, Heraclitus, Parmenides, Empedokles, Democritos, Leukippos, Zenon, Polybius, Plutarchos, Pindar, Thucydides, Callimachus, Theophrastus, Aristotle, Aristophanes, Plato, Isocrates, and Appian.

SECONDARY SOURCES

Barrington Atlas of the Greek and Roman World, Talbert, Richard J.A. (ed.), Bagnall, Roger S. (ed.). Princeton University Press, 2000.

Roma Antica, Il Centro Monumentale. Giuseppe Lugli; G. Bardi Editore, Roma 1946.

A New Topographical Dictionary of Ancient Rome, L. Richardson Jr. JHU Press 1992.

The Gracchi, Henry Charles Boren. Twayne Publishers, New York, 1969.

The Roman Republic, Henry Charles Boren. D. Van Nostrand. Reinhold, 1965, Anvil Original.

The Gracchi, David Stockton. Clarendon Press, New York: Oxford University Press 1979.

La vie quotidienne à Rome à l'apogée de l'empire, Jérôme Carcopino. Hachette, Paris, 1959.

Athenian democracy, A.H.M. Jones. Basil Blackwell & Mott Ltd, Oxford, 1957.

Griechische Geschichte, Herman Bengston. C.H. Beck, 1965.

Engineering in the ancient world, J.G. Landels. University of California Press, 1981.

"The Lex Repetundarum and the Political Ideas of Gaius Gracchus," A. N. Sherwin-White; *The Journal of Roman Studies*, Vol. 72 (1982), pp. 18-31, published by the Society for the Promotion of Roman Studies.

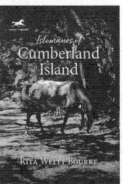